THE TRAP

Melanie Raabe grew up in Thuringia, Germany, and attended the Ruhr University Bochum, where she specialized in media studies and literature. After graduating, she moved to Cologne to work as a journalist by day and secretly write books by night. *The Trap* is her debut novel.

Imogen Taylor is a freelance translator and academic based in Berlin. She recently translated Sascha Arango's *The Truth and Other Lies*.

THE
TRAP

MELANIE RAABE

Translated by Imogen Taylor

First published in Australia 2016 by Text Publishing Company

First published in the UK 2016 by Mantle
an imprint of Pan Macmillan
20 New Wharf Road, London N1 9RR
Associated companies throughout the world
www.panmacmillan.com

ISBN 978-1-5098-1066-6

Copyright © Melanie Raabe 2015
Translation copyright © Imogen Taylor 2016

The right of Melanie Raabe to be identified as the
author of this work has been asserted by her in accordance
with the Copyright, Designs and Patents Act 1988.

Originally published in 2015 as *Die Falle* by Random House Germany

1 3 5 7 9 8 6 4 2

A CIP catalogue record for this book is available from the British Library.

Typeset by J&M Typesetting
Printed and bound by CPI Group (UK) Ltd, Croydon, CR0 4YY

Visit **www.panmacmillan.com** to read more about all our books
and to buy them. You will also find features, author interviews and
news of any author events, and you can sign up for e-newsletters
so that you're always first to hear about our new releases.

THE
TRAP

1

I am not of this world.

At least, that's what people say. As if there were only one world.

I am standing in the big, empty dining room I never eat in, looking out the large window. It's on the ground floor. You look onto the meadow behind the house, and the edge of the woods. Sometimes you see deer or foxes.

It is autumn, and as I stand here gazing out, I have the feeling I'm looking in a mirror. The colours are building to a crescendo; the autumn wind makes the trees sway, bending some branches and breaking others. It is a dramatic and beautiful day. Nature, too, seems to sense that something is coming to an end; it's summoning all its strength for one last surge. Soon it will be lying motionless outside my window. The sunshine will give way to wet grey and then crisp white. The people who come to visit me—my assistant, my publisher, my agent (there isn't really anyone else)—will complain about the damp and the cold. About having to scrape the windscreen with numb fingers before they could set off. About the fact that it's still dark when they leave the house in the morning and dark again by the time they get home in the evening. These things mean nothing to me. In my world, it is exactly 23.2°C, summer and winter. In my world, it is always day and never night. Here, there is no rain, no snow, no frozen fingers. In my world, there is only one season, and I haven't yet found a name for it.

This villa is my world. The sitting room with its open fire is my Asia, the library my Europe, the kitchen my Africa. North America is in my study. My bedroom is South America, and Australia and Oceania are out on the terrace. A few steps away, but completely unreachable.

I haven't left the house for eleven years.

You can read the reasons why in all the papers, although some of them do exaggerate. I am ill, yes. I can't leave the house, true. But I am not forced to live in complete darkness, nor do I sleep in an oxygen tent. It is tolerable. Everything is organised. Time is a current, powerful and gentle, in which I can drift. Only Bukowski introduces confusion into the order every now and then, when he brings in dirt on his paws and rain on his coat after a romp in the meadows. I love running my hand through his shaggy coat and feeling its dampness on my skin. I love the grubby traces of the outside world that Bukowski leaves on the tiles and on the parquet. In my world, there is no mud, no trees and no meadows, no rabbits and no sunshine. The twittering of birds comes from a tape, the sun comes from the solarium in the basement. It's not a wide world, my world, but it is safe. At least, that's what I thought.

2

The earthquake came on a Tuesday. There were no tremors beforehand—nothing that might have warned me.

I was in Italy when it happened. I travel frequently. I find it easiest to visit countries I know, and I used to go to Italy a lot. So I go back every now and then.

Italy is a beautiful and dangerous country because it reminds me of my sister.

Anna, who loved Italy even before she ever went there—Anna, who got herself Italian lessons on tape and listened to them so often that the tapes wore out. Anna, who saved assiduously for a Vespa and then careered around our home town, as if she were winding recklessly through the narrow alleyways of Rome.

Italy reminds me of my sister and of the way things used to be, before the darkness. I keep trying to drive away the thought of Anna, but it's sticky, like old-fashioned flypaper. Other dark thoughts get stuck to it; there's no stopping them.

So it was off to Italy, in spite of everything. For an entire week, I retreated to three spare rooms upstairs that I never use, and named them Italy. I put on Italian music, watched Italian films, immersed myself in documentaries about the culture and customs of the country, leafed through coffee-table books, and had delicacies from various regions of Italy delivered by caterers. And the wine. Oh, the wine. It almost made my Italy real.

And now I'm walking through the alleyways of Rome, in search of a particular restaurant. The city is muggy and hot, and I'm exhausted—exhausted from battling against the current of tourists, exhausted from warding off the advances of street hawkers, exhausted from drinking in all the beauty around me. The colours amaze me. The sky is hanging grey and low over the Eternal City but beneath it the Tiber flows a dull green.

I must have fallen asleep because, when I wake up, the documentary on ancient Rome is over. I'm confused when I come to. I can't remember dreaming, but I have trouble finding my way back to reality.

I seldom dream nowadays. In the first years of my retreat from the real world, I dreamed more vividly than ever before, as if my brain wanted to compensate for the lack of new impulses it was receiving during the day. It invented the most colourful adventures for me—tropical rainforests with talking animals, and cities of brightly coloured glass inhabited by people with magic powers. But, although my dreams always started off light and cheerful, they would sooner or later grow dark, like a sheet of blotting paper dipped in black ink. The leaves in the rainforest would fall, and the animals would stop talking. The glass became so sharp you could cut your fingers on it; the sky turned the colour of blackberries. And inevitably he would appear—the monster. Sometimes it was a vague sense of threat that I couldn't get a proper hold on, sometimes a shadowy figure lurking almost out of view. Occasionally he would pursue me and I would run, trying to avoid looking back because I couldn't endure the sight of his face, not even in a dream. Whenever I looked straight at the monster, I would die—die and wake up, every time, gasping for air

4

like a drowning woman. And in those first years, when the dreams were still coming, I had trouble driving away the thoughts that came at night and settled on my bed like crows. There was nothing I could do about them; no matter how painful the memories, I couldn't stop thinking of her in those moments—thinking of my sister.

No dream tonight, no monster, but I still feel uneasy. A sentence I can't quite make out is echoing in my head. There is a voice. I blink, my eyes gummed up. I notice that my right arm has gone to sleep, and I try to massage it back to life. The television's still on, and that's where the voice is coming from—the voice that had found its way into my dream and woken me up.

It's a man's voice, business-like and neutral, same as all the other voices on these news channels that broadcast the lovely documentaries I'm so fond of. I heave myself up and grope for the remote control, but I can't find it. My bed is vast, my bed is the sea, all these pillows and duvets, waves of coffee-table books and a whole armada of remote controls: for the television itself, for the receiver, for the DVD player, for my two Blu-ray players customised for different formats, for the sound system, for my old VHS recorder. I snort in frustration, and the news voice tells me about things in the Middle East I don't want to know—not now, not today. I'm on holiday, I'm in Italy, I've been looking forward to this trip!

It's too late. The real-world facts that the news voice is reporting on—all the wars and disasters and atrocities that I'd been hoping to block out for a few days—have forced their way into my head, chasing away my sunny mood in seconds. The Italy feeling has gone, the trip's off. Tomorrow morning I'll go back to my real bedroom and clear away all the Italy stuff.

I rub my eyes; the brightness of the screen makes them ache. The newsreader has left the Middle East and is now reporting on domestic affairs. I watch him with resignation, my tired eyes watering. Now the man's finished his spiel, and there's a live broadcast from Berlin. A reporter is saying something about the Chancellor's latest trip abroad, while behind him the Reichstag rises up out of the darkness, majestic and imposing.

My eyes sharpen their focus. I start, I blink. I can't believe it. But I see him! Right here in front of me! I shake my head, dazed. It's not possible. I can't believe my eyes. I blink again, blink frantically, as if I could get rid of the image that way, but it makes no difference. My heart contracts with a pang. My brain thinks: impossible. But my senses know it's true. Oh God.

My world is shaking. I don't understand what's going on around me, but my bed starts to tremble and the bookshelves sway and then crash to the floor. Pictures fall, glass shatters, cracks form on the ceiling—hairline cracks at first, and then rifts as thick as your finger. The walls collapse, the noise is indescribable, and yet it is silent— utterly silent.

My world lies in ruins. I sit on my bed among the debris and stare at the television. I am an open sore. I am the smell of raw flesh. There's a flash in my head, so dazzlingly bright that it hurts. My vision turns red, I clutch my heart, I am dizzy, my consciousness flickers. I know what it is, this keen, red feeling: I'm having a panic attack, I'm hyperventilating, any second now I'll faint, I hope I'll faint. This image—this face—I can't bear it. I want to avert my gaze but it's impossible; it's as if I've been turned to stone. I don't want to look anymore, but I have to. I can't help it; my eyes are fixed on the television. I can't look away—I can't; my eyes are wide open and I'm staring at it, staring at the monster from my dreams, and I'm trying to wake up at last, trying to die and then wake up, the way I always do when I see the monster up close in a dream.

But I'm already awake.

3

The next morning, I climb out from under the rubble and put myself back together again, piece by piece.

My name is Linda Conrads. I'm an author. Every year I discipline myself to write a novel. My novels are very successful. I am well off. That is, I have plenty of money.

I am thirty-eight years old. I am ill. The media speculate about a mysterious illness that prevents me from moving freely. I haven't left my house for over a decade.

I have a family. Or, rather, I have parents. I haven't seen my parents for a long time. They don't come to visit. I can't visit them. We seldom talk on the phone.

There is something I don't like to think about. But, at the same time, I can't not think about it. It has to do with my sister. It happened a long time ago. I loved my sister. My sister was called Anna. My sister is dead. My sister was three years younger than me. My sister died twelve years ago. My sister didn't just die; my sister was murdered. Twelve years ago my sister was murdered and I found her. I saw her murderer run away. I saw the murderer's face. The murderer was a man. The murderer turned his face towards me, then he ran away. I don't know why he ran away. I don't know why he didn't attack me. I only know that my sister is dead and I'm not.

My therapist describes me as highly traumatised.

This is my life. This is me. I don't really want to think about it.

I swing my legs over the edge of the bed and get up. That's what I mean to do, anyway, but in fact I don't budge an inch. I wonder whether I'm paralysed. I have no strength in my arms and legs. I try again, but it's as if the feeble commands from my brain aren't getting through to my limbs. Maybe it doesn't matter if I lie here for a moment. It's morning, but it's not as if I have anything other than an empty house waiting for me. I give up the struggle. My body feels strangely heavy. I stay in bed, but I don't go back to sleep. The next time I look at the clock on the wooden bedside table, six hours have passed. That surprises me; it's not good. The faster time passes, the faster night will come, and I'm afraid of the night, in spite of all the lamps in the house.

After several attempts, I do manage to get my body to go into the bathroom and then down the stairs to the ground floor—an expedition to the other end of the world. Bukowski comes rushing towards me, wagging his tail. I feed him, fill his bowl with water, and let him out for a run. Watching him through the window, I remember that it usually makes me happy to watch him run and play, but today I feel nothing; I want him to come back quickly so that I can get into bed again. I whistle for him. He's a tiny, bouncing speck at the edge of the wood. If he didn't come back of his own free will, there's nothing I could do. But he always comes back—back to me, back into my little world. Even today. He jumps up at me, begging me to play, but I can't. He gives up, disappointed.

I'm sorry, mate.

He curls up in his favourite spot in the kitchen and gives me a sad look. I turn around and go into the bedroom, where I get straight back into bed, feeling weak and vulnerable.

Before the darkness—before my retreat—when I was still strong and lived in the real world, I only ever felt like this when I was coming down with a bad bout of flu. But I'm not coming down with the flu; I'm coming down with depression, the way I always do when I think of Anna and all the things that happened back then that I usually block out so carefully. I managed to get on with my life undisturbed for a long time, suppressing all thought of my sister. But now it's back. And, however long ago it may be, the wound hasn't healed yet. Time's a quack.

I know I ought to do something before it's too late, before I get completely swallowed up in the maelstrom of depression that's sucking me into the blackness. I know I ought to talk to a doctor, maybe get him to prescribe me something, but I can't face it. The exertion seems insanely disproportionate. And, in the end, it doesn't matter. I'll get depressed, that's all. I could stay here in bed forever. What difference would it make? If I can't leave the house, why should I bother leaving the bedroom? Or my bed? Or the exact spot I'm lying now? Day passes and night takes its place.

It occurs to me that I could give someone a ring. Maybe Norbert. He'd come. He's not only my publisher; we're friends. If I could move the muscles in my face, I would smile to myself at the thought of Norbert.

I think of the last time I saw him. We sat in the kitchen, I cooked us spaghetti with homemade Bolognese sauce, and Norbert told me about his holiday in the south of France, about all the goings-on at the publishing house, and his wife's latest hang-ups. Norbert is wonderful—loud and funny and full of stories. He has the best laugh in the world. The best laugh in both worlds, to be precise.

Norbert calls me his extremophile. The first time he called me that, I had to Google it—and marvel at how right he was. Extremophiles are organisms that have adapted to extreme living conditions so that they can survive in habitats that are actually life-threatening: in great heat or freezing cold, in darkness, in radioactive environments, in acid—or simply, and this must be what Norbert was thinking of, in complete isolation. Extremophile. I like the word, and I like it when he calls me that. It sounds as if I'd chosen all this for myself. As if I loved living in this extraordinary way. As if I had a choice.

Right now, the only choice I have is whether to lie on my left side or my right, on my stomach or on my back. Hours pass. I make a huge effort not to think of anything. At some point I get up, go over to the bookshelves that line the expansive walls of my bedroom, take down a few books, fling them on the bed, put my favourite Billie Holiday album on endless loop and slip back under the duvet. I listen to the music, turning pages and reading, until my eyes ache and I'm soft and spongy from the music like after a hot bath. I don't want to read anymore. I'd like to watch a film, but I don't dare switch on the TV. I simply don't dare.

When I hear footsteps, I jump. Billie's stopped singing. At some point I must have silenced her sad voice with one of my many remote controls. Who's there? It's the middle of the night. Why doesn't the dog bark? I want to drag myself out of bed, grab something I can use to defend myself with, hide, do something, but I lie there, my breathing shallow, my eyes wide open. Somebody knocks. I say nothing.

'Hello!' a voice calls out. I don't recognise it.

And then again. 'Hello! Are you in there?'

The door opens. I whimper—my feeble version of a scream. It's Charlotte, my assistant. Of course I recognise her voice. It was my fear that made it sound so strangely distorted. Charlotte comes twice a week to do my shopping, take my letters to the post office, do anything that needs doing. My paid link to the outside world.

Now she's standing in the door, wavering. 'Is everything all right?'

My thoughts rearrange themselves. It can't be night if Charlotte's here. I must have been lying in bed for a very long time.

'Sorry to burst in like that, but when I rang the bell and you didn't answer I got worried and let myself in.'

The bell? I remember a ringing working its way into one of my dreams. I'm dreaming again after all these years!

'I feel a bit poorly,' I say. 'I was fast asleep and didn't hear you. I'm sorry.'

I'm ashamed of myself; I can't even manage to sit up. Charlotte seems worried, although she's not one to be easily flustered. That's precisely why I chose her. Charlotte is younger than me, late twenties maybe. She has a lot of jobs—waitressing in several cafés, selling tickets at a cinema in town. Things like that. And twice a week she comes to me. I like Charlotte—her short hair that she dyes a bluish black, her sturdy figure, her flamboyant tattoos, her dirty sense of humour, the stories about her little boy. The 'cheeky devil', she calls him.

If Charlotte seems nervous, I must look terrible.

'Do you need anything? From the chemist or anywhere?'

'No thanks, I've got everything I need in the house,' I say.

I sound funny—like a robot. I can hear it, but I can't do anything about it.

'I don't need you today, Charlotte. I should have let you know. I'm sorry.'

'Not to worry. The shopping's in the fridge. Shall I take the dog out, before I leave?'

Oh God, the dog. How long have I been lying here?

'That would be great,' I say. 'Give him something to eat too, would you?'

'Sure.'

I pull the duvet up to my nose to signal that the conversation is over.

Charlotte hovers a little longer in the doorway, presumably uncertain about whether she can leave me alone. Then she makes up her mind and goes. I hear the sounds she makes in the kitchen as she feeds Bukowski. I usually love it when there are sounds in the house, but today it means nothing to me. I let the pillows and duvet and darkness engulf me, but I can't get to sleep.

4

I lie in the dark, thinking about the blackest day of my life. I remember that I couldn't grieve when my sister was carried to her grave—not straight away. My head and body were bursting with one thought. *Why?* There was only room for one question: *Why did she have to die?*

I had the feeling that my parents were asking me this question— my parents, the other mourners, Anna's friends and colleagues, practically everyone—because, after all, I'd been there; I must have seen something. What, for heaven's sake, happened? Why did Anna have to die?

I remember the mourners crying, throwing flowers on the coffin, leaning on each other, blowing their noses. It all felt so unreal to me, so strangely warped—the sounds, the colours, even the feelings. A vicar who spoke in a strangely drawling voice. People moving in slow motion. Flower arrangements with roses and lilies—all monochrome.

Oh damn, the flowers! Thinking of the flowers catapults me back to the present. I sit up in bed. I forgot to ask Charlotte to water the flowers in the conservatory, and she'll have left by now. Charlotte knows how much I love my flowers and she knows I usually look after them myself, so it's unlikely she'll have given them water. There's nothing for it but to do it myself.

I get up, groaning. The floor is cool beneath my bare feet. I force myself to place one foot in front of the other, to walk along the hallway towards the stairs, go down to the ground floor, and cross the big sitting room and the dining room. I open the door to my conservatory and enter the jungle.

My house is dominated by empty spaces and dead objects—not counting Bukowski. But here in my conservatory, with its lush and rampant greenery, it's life that reigns. Palms, ferns, passionflowers, birds of paradise, flamingo flowers and, above all, orchids. I love exotic plants.

The steamy heat of the conservatory, which I think of as my own little hothouse, brings out the sweat on my forehead almost immediately, and the long baggy T-shirt I wear as a nightie clings to me. I love this green jungle. I don't want orderliness; I want chaos, life. I want the twigs and leaves to brush against me as if I were in a forest. I want to smell the scent of the flowers; I want to get drunk on it. I want to soak up the colours.

I look about me. I know that the sight of my plants should give me pleasure, but today I feel nothing. My conservatory is brightly lit, but outside it is night. Indifferent stars twinkle through the glass roof above my head. As if on autopilot, I carry out the tasks that usually give me so much satisfaction. I water the flowers. I touch the soil with my fingers, feeling if it's dry and crumbly and needs water, or clings to my hands.

I clear a path for myself to the back of the greenhouse. This is where I have my own private orchid garden. The plants with their extravagant blooms are crammed onto shelves, or hang in pots from the ceiling. My favourite is here—my favourite and my problem child. It's a small orchid, altogether unassuming alongside its lavishly flowering sisters, and almost ugly. It has only two or three dull, dark-green leaves and dry grey roots, no flowers, not for a long time now, not so much as a stalk. It's the only plant I didn't buy especially for the conservatory. I brought it with me from my old life, from the real world, many, many years ago. I know that it will never flower, but I can't bring myself to get rid of it. I give it some water. Then I turn my attention to a particularly beautiful orchid with heavy white flowers. I let my hand glide over the leaves, finger its velvety flowers. The buds are firm to the touch. They are bursting with life. Not long now until they come out. I think how nice it would be to cut a few of these flowering stems and put them in a vase in the house. And, while I'm thinking all this, I'm reminded of Anna again. Even in here, I can't get her out of my head.

When we were little, she didn't like picking flowers as much as I did, or as much as the other children. She thought it was mean to break off their beautiful heads. A smile steals over my lips as I think of it now. Anna's quirks. I see my sister before me quite clearly—her blonde hair, her cornflower-blue eyes, her tiny nose, her enormous mouth, the furrow between her pale eyebrows that would appear whenever she got cross. The small moles that formed a perfect triangle on her left cheek. The blonde down only visible if the summer sun lit up her face at the right angle. I see her quite plainly. And I hear her voice, clear as a bell, and her dirty, boyish laugh that contrasted so starkly with her feminine nature. I see her before me, laughing, and it's like being punched in the stomach.

I think back to one of the first sessions with my therapist, shortly after Anna's death. The police had no clues, and the identikit picture they'd assembled with my help was useless. Even I didn't think it looked much like the man I'd seen. But, no matter how hard I tried, I couldn't do any better. I remember saying to the therapist that I had to know why this had happened—that the uncertainty was a torment to me. I remember her telling me that it was normal, that not knowing was always the worst thing for the relatives. She recommended a self-help group to me. A self-help group—it was almost laughable. I remember that I said I'd do anything, if I could find out the reason. That much at least I owed to my sister. That much at least.

Why? Why? Why?

'You're obsessed with that question, Frau Conrads. It's no good. You have to let go, live your life.'

I try to shake off Anna's image and all thoughts of her. I don't want to think about her because I know where that leads me; back then I almost went mad, knowing that Anna was dead, and that her murderer was still somewhere out there.

Not being able to do anything was the worst. It was better to stop thinking about it altogether. Distract myself. Forget about Anna.

I try to do the same now, but it doesn't work this time. Why?

Then the news reporter's face flashes across my mind, and something in my head goes click. I realise that I've spent the past hours in shock.

And at last it's clear to me. The man on television I was so distressed by was real.

It wasn't a nightmare; it was reality.

I've seen my sister's murderer. It may be twelve years ago, but I remember every detail. It is compellingly clear to me what that means.

I drop the watering can. It lands with a clatter, and the water spills out over my bare feet. I turn around, leave the conservatory, stub my toe on the way into the house, ignore the pain, and hurry on.

Swiftly, I cross the ground floor, take the stairs to the first, skid along the hallway, and arrive in my bedroom out of breath. My laptop is lying on the bed, vaguely menacing. I hesitate, then sit down and pull it towards me, my fingers trembling. I'm almost afraid to open it, as if someone might be watching me through the screen.

I open Google and enter the name of the news channel where I saw the man. I'm nervous and keep hitting the wrong keys; it's not until the third try that I get it right. I bring up the homepage and click my way through to *Reporters*. I'm on the verge of thinking that the whole thing was just a figment of my imagination after all—that the man doesn't exist, that I dreamt him.

But then I find him; it only takes a few clicks. The monster. Instinctively, I hold my left hand in front of the screen to cover his photo. I can't look at him—not yet. The walls are starting to shake again, my heart is racing.

I concentrate on breathing, close my eyes. Nice and calm, that's the way. I open my eyes again and read his name, his profile. I see that he's won prizes—that he has a family and leads a successful, fulfilled life. Something inside me snaps. I feel something I haven't felt for years, and it's red hot. Slowly, I take down my hand from the screen.

I look at him.

I look into the face of the man who murdered my sister.

I am choked with fury, and I can think only one thing: *I'm going to get you.*

I clap my laptop shut, put it away, get up. My thoughts are racing. My heart is pounding.

The incredible thing is, he lives very close by! For any normal person, it would be no trouble to track him down.

But I'm trapped in my house. And the police—the police didn't even believe me at the time. Not really.

If I want to speak to him—if I want to confront him, to call him to account in some way—then I have to get him to come to me. How can I lure him here?

The conversation with my therapist flashes through my mind again.

'But why? Why did Anna have to die?'

'You have to accept the possibility that you're never going to get an answer to that question, Linda.'

'I can't accept that. Never.'

'You'll learn.'

16

Never.

I think it over, feverishly. He's a journalist. And I am a famous author, notoriously withdrawn, who's had all the big magazines and TV channels clamouring for an interview for years now. Especially when a new book's out.

I remember what my therapist said: 'You're only tormenting your-self, Linda.'

'I can't stop thinking about it.'

'If you need a reason, invent one. Or write a book. Flush it out of your system. And then you must let go. Live your life.'

Every hair on my neck is standing on end. My God, that's it!

Gooseflesh spreads over my body.

It's so obvious.

I'll write a new book. The events from back then in the form of a crime novel. Bait for the murderer and therapy for me.

All the heaviness has left my body. I leave my bedroom; my limbs are obeying me again. I go into the bathroom and have a shower. I dry and dress myself, go into my study, boot up my computer again and begin to write.

FROM *BLOOD SISTERS* BY LINDA CONRADS

1
_____

JONAS

He hit her with all his strength. The woman crashed to the floor. She managed to struggle halfway to her feet, and tried frantically to escape, but didn't have a chance in hell. The man was so much faster. He thrust her to the ground again, knelt on her back, grabbed her long hair and started to beat her head against the floor with full force, over and over again. The woman's screams turned to a whimper, and then she was silent. The man released his hold. Only a few moments before, his features had been contorted with blind hatred; now he was incredulous. Frowning, he considered his blood-smeared hands, while behind him the full moon rose, vast and silver. The fairies giggled and hurried up to the woman who was lying there as if dead. They dipped their slender fingers in her blood and began to smear it on their pale faces like war paint.

Jonas sighed. He hadn't been to the theatre for ages and he certainly wouldn't have come up with the idea himself. It was Mia who'd wanted to see a play again; it would make a change from the cinema. One of her girlfriends had recommended the new production of *A Midsummer Night's Dream*, and Mia had immediately booked tickets for them. Jonas had been looking forward to the evening. He had, however, been expecting a lighthearted comedy, and here he was instead watching nightmarish sprites, satanic fairies, and lovers, who—with intense physical effort and an inordinate quantity of fake blood—were tearing each other limb from limb in the dark woods. He glanced across at his wife, who was watching the action with shining eyes. The rest of the audience, too, was spellbound. Jonas felt shut out. He was evidently the only one in the theatre getting no pleasure out of the violent display.

Maybe he had once been like them. Maybe he had once found horror and violence fascinating and entertaining. He couldn't remember; it was probably too long ago.

His thoughts began to wander to the case he was working on. Mia would have given him a discreet nudge in the ribs if she had known that he was sitting in the darkness of the auditorium thinking about work again—but that's the way it was. He thought of the scene of the crime, and ran over in his mind the hundreds of different pieces of the puzzle, painstakingly gathered by him and his colleagues, which would most likely lead to the speedy arrest of the victim's husband...

Jonas gave a start as the theatre was plunged into darkness, and then flooded with light and filled with applause.

When the audience around him rose in ovation, as if by some secret agreement of which he alone had not been informed, Superintendent Jonas Weber felt like the loneliest person on the planet.

Mia didn't say a word as he drove home along the dark streets. She had got her enthusiasm for the performance off her chest in the cloak-room queue and on the way to the car park. Now she was listening to the music coming from the radio with a cheerful smile that wasn't meant for him.

Jonas flicked on the indicator and turned into the driveway. In the beam of the headlamps, their house emerged in grainy black and white. He cut the motor and was putting on the handbrake when his mobile began to vibrate.

He took the call, expecting Mia to react—to grumble or sigh, or at least roll her eyes. But she didn't. Her cherry-red lips formed a mute 'Good night' and she got out of the car. Jonas watched her go while his colleague's voice spilled out of the phone. He sat and watched as his wife moved away from him, her long, honey-blonde hair, tight jeans and dark-green top fading to monochrome as she was enveloped by the darkness.

In the past, he and Mia had fought for every last minute of shared time and were always sorry when a call to duty interrupted the hours they spent together. Nowadays they cared less and less.

Jonas forced himself to focus on the call. His colleague was reading out an address; he tapped it into his sat nav. He said, 'Yes, all right. I'm on my way.'

He hung up and breathed a sigh. It astonished him that he was already thinking of his barely four-year marriage in terms of 'then' and 'now'.

Jonas averted his gaze from the door that had closed behind Mia, and started up the car.

5

Things that don't exist in my world: conkers dropping from trees, children shuffling through autumn leaves, people in fancy dress on the tram, serendipitous meetings, short women being pulled along by enormous dogs as if they were on water skis. Shooting stars, duck-lings learning to swim, sand castles, rear-end collisions, surprises, lolly-pop ladies, roller-coasters, sunburn.

My world makes do with a meagre palette.

Films are my way of passing the time; books are my passion, my true love. But music is my refuge. Whenever I'm in high spirits, which isn't often, I put on a record—Ella Fitzgerald, maybe, or Sarah Vaughan—and it almost makes me feel as if someone else were happy with me. If, on the other hand, I'm feeling sad or low, then Billie Holiday or Nina Simone suffer alongside me, and sometimes even console me.

I'm standing in the kitchen, listening to Nina as I pour a handful of coffee beans into my old-fashioned grinder. I love the smell of coffee, that dark, powerful, comforting aroma. I turn the handle, taking pleasure in the crunch and crack of the beans as I grind them. Afterwards I pull out the wooden drawer where the ground coffee collects and put it in a filter. When I'm alone in the house and only making coffee for myself, which is to say most of the time, I always make it by hand. Filling the grinder, grinding the beans, boiling the kettle, watching the brewing coffee drip into my cup—it's a ritual. When you lead as quiet a life as I do, it's a good idea to take pleasure in small things.

I empty the filter and contemplate the coffee in my cup. I sit down at the kitchen table with it. The smell that pervades the room calms me.

From the kitchen window, I can see the drive that leads to my house. It lies there, quiet and peaceful, but it's not long now until the monster from my dreams will make his way up it. He'll ring at my door and I'll let him in. The thought frightens me.

I take a sip of coffee and pull a face. I usually like it black, but today I've made it too strong. I open the fridge, take out the cream that I keep for Charlotte and other visitors, and pour a good swig in. Then I watch in fascination as the little clouds of cream swirl around in my cup, contracting and expanding, their movements as unpredictable as those of children at play, and it dawns on me that I am putting myself in a situation that is as incalculable and uncontrollable as these swirling clouds. I can lure the man to my house, yes.

But what next?

The clouds stop their dance and settle. I stir the coffee and drink it in small sips. My gaze rests on the drive again. It is lined with old chestnut trees and will soon be covered in yellow, red and brown leaves. For the first time ever, it seems threatening to me; I suddenly find it hard to breathe.

I can't do this.

I tear my eyes from the drive and pick up my smartphone. I tap around on it for a minute or two until I find the setting that enables me to withhold my number. I get up and turn the music down. Then I enter the number of the police station that investigated Anna's murder. I know it off by heart, even now.

My heart begins to beat faster when I hear the ringing tone. I try to breathe steadily. I tell myself I'm doing the right thing, putting my trust in the police in spite of everything—leaving murder to the experts. I tell myself I'm going to stash the half-written manuscript in the bottom drawer of my desk, or, better still, throw it away and never give it another thought.

The ringing sounds a second time—agonisingly drawn out.

I'm as nervous as if I were about to sit an exam. It occurs to me that the police aren't going to believe me, just as they didn't believe me back then, and I begin to waver. I'm toying with the idea of hanging up, when someone picks up the phone and a woman's voice answers. I recognise it at once.

Andrea Brandt was on the murder squad all those years ago. I didn't like her and she didn't like me. My determination immediately falters.

'Hello?' Brandt drawls when I don't speak—impatient even before we've begun.

I pull myself together.

'Hello, could I speak to Superintendent Julian Schumer?' I ask.

'It's his day off today. Who's speaking, please?'

I swallow and don't know whether to confide in her (it had to be her, didn't it?) or whether I'm better off hanging up.

'I'm calling about an old case,' I say eventually, as if I hadn't heard her question. I can't bring myself to reveal my identity—not yet. 'About a murder that took place more than ten years ago,' I add.

'Yes?'

I can sense the policewoman pricking up her antennae and I could slap myself for not preparing for this conversation. My old impulsiveness is flaring up again when I least need it.

'What would you say,' I ask, 'if new evidence came to light so long after the event? From a witness who thought he knew the murderer?'

Andrea Brandt hesitates only briefly. 'Are you this witness?' she asks.

Damn it! Should I put my cards on the table? I struggle with my conscience.

'If you want to make a statement, you can call in at any time,' Brandt says.

'How often are these old cases solved?' I ask, ignoring her last remark.

I can almost hear her suppress a sigh, and I wonder how many of these calls she gets, yielding nothing tangible.

'I can't give you an exact number, I'm afraid, Frau…'

Nice try. I say nothing. The policewoman endures the awkward silence for a moment and then gives up trying to find out my name.

'What quite often happens is that cases known as "cold cases" are solved with the help of DNA data—the so-called "genetic fingerprint",' she says. 'This data is still totally reliable, even decades after a crime has been committed.'

Unlike witness statements, I think to myself.

'But, as I said, if you'd like to make a statement, we're always at your service,' says Brandt. 'Which case are we talking about?'

'I'll think about it,' I reply.

'Your voice sounds familiar. Have we met?'

I panic and break off the connection. Only now do I realise that at some point in the brief conversation I must have got up and started pacing around the room. An unpleasant feeling has settled in the pit of my stomach. I sit back down at the kitchen table, wait for my pulse to slow, and drink the remains of my coffee. It is cold.

I remember the head of investigations with warmth, but I would have preferred to forget the stand-offish young policewoman who was on the murder squad with him. Even as I made my witness statement, I had the feeling that Andrea Brandt didn't believe me. For a while, I even had the impression that she thought I was the murderer, in spite of all evidence to the contrary.

Now I have to explain to Andrea Brandt that I have recognised Anna's murderer in a respected reporter I've seen on a news broadcast twelve years after the event. And that I can't possibly go to the police station to make the statement because the very thought of setting foot outside makes me feel sick…

No. If I want the man to be called to account, I'll have to do it myself.

6

It sometimes happens that I look in the mirror and don't recognise myself. I'm standing in the bathroom, contemplating my reflection—something I haven't done for a long time. Of course, I look in the mirror every morning and evening when I clean my teeth and wash my face. But, on the whole, I don't *really* look. Today is different.

D-Day. The journalist I've invited to interview me in my house will be in his car, on his way. Any minute now, he'll come up the drive. He will get out, walk to the front door, and ring the bell.

I am prepared. I have been studying him. I know what I'll see when he's sitting opposite me. But what will *he* see? I stare at myself—at my eyes and nose, at my mouth, cheeks and ears, and then at my eyes again. I am surprised at my outward appearance: so that's what I look like—that's me, is it?

The sound of the doorbell makes me jump. I run through the plan in my head one last time, then I throw back my shoulders and head for the front door. My heartbeat is so loud that it reverberates all through the house, making the windowpanes rattle. I breathe in and out one last time. Then I open the door.

For years, the monster has pursued me even in my dreams. Now he's standing before me, holding out his hand. I suppress the impulse to run away screaming—to go berserk. I must not hesitate, I must not tremble. I will look him in the eye. I will speak loud and clear. That's what I've made up my mind to do; that's what I've prepared myself for. The moment has come, and now that it's here, it seems almost unreal. I press his hand. I smile and say, 'Please, come in.' I do not hesitate, I do not tremble. I look him in the eye and my voice is strong; it sounds loud and clear. I know the monster can't do me any harm. The whole world knows he's here—my publishing house, his editorial department... Even if we were alone, he couldn't do me any harm. He won't do me any harm. He's not stupid.

And yet... It's a tremendous effort for me to turn my back on him and lead the way into the house. I've decided the dining room is where the interview will take place. It wasn't a strategic decision but an intuitive one. Charlotte, my assistant, comes into the room, takes his coat, busies herself, bustles about, chatters, offers drinks, exudes charm—all the things I pay her for. None of this is any more than a job for her. She has no idea what's really going on, but her presence reassures me.

I try to appear relaxed and not to stare at him or size him up. He's tall, with a few streaks of grey running through his short, dark hair. But the most remarkable thing about him is his alert grey eyes, which take in the room with a single glance. He walks across to the dining table, so big it could be used for a conference. He puts his bag on the first chair he comes to, opens it up and glances inside. He's making sure he has everything with him.

Charlotte brings in bottles of water and glasses. I go over to the table where I've laid out a few copies of my latest novel, in which I describe the murder of my sister. He and I know it's not a work of fiction but an indictment. I take a bottle and pour myself a glass of water. My hands are steady.

The monster looks the same as on television. His name is Victor Lenzen.

'This is a beautiful house,' says Lenzen, wandering to the window. He glances at the edge of the woods.

'Thank you,' I say. 'I'm glad you like it.'

I'm cross with myself for adding this last remark; a simple 'thank you' would have been enough. Clear statements. Don't hesitate, don't tremble, look him in the eye, talk loud and clear.

'How long have you been living here?' he asks.

'Getting on for eleven years.'

I take a seat at the place already set with my cup of coffee. It's the place that gives me the strongest sense of security—my back to the wall and the door within eyeshot. If Lenzen wants to sit opposite me, he'll have to sit with his back to the door. That makes most people nervous and reduces their powers of concentration, but he accepts without protest. If he notices at all, he doesn't let it show. He takes notepad, pen and digital recorder from the bag beside his chair. I wonder what else he has in there.

Charlotte has politely withdrawn to the next room. The game can begin.

I know a great deal about Victor Lenzen; I've learnt a lot these past months. He may be the journalist here, but he's not the only one in the room who has done his homework.

'May I ask you a question?' he begins.

'That's what you're here for, isn't it?' I ask with a smile.

Victor Lenzen is fifty-three years old.

'Touché. But I wanted to ask you something before we got started on the official questions.'

Victor Lenzen is divorced and has a thirteen-year-old daughter.

'Well?' I ask.

'Well, I've been wondering—the thing is, it's common knowledge that you lead a secluded life and that it's more than ten years since you last gave an extensive interview...'

27

Victor Lenzen studied politics, history and journalism, then worked as a trainee reporter at a Frankfurt daily newspaper. He moved to Munich, rose through the ranks, and was made editor-in-chief at a Munich daily. Then he went abroad.

'I'm always giving interviews,' I say.

'You've given precisely four interviews in the last ten years. One over the phone and three via email, if I'm correctly informed.'

Victor Lenzen spent many years working as a foreign correspondent, reporting from the Middle East, Afghanistan, Washington, London and finally Asia.

'You've done your homework.'

'There are people who believe you don't exist,' he continues. 'They think Linda Conrads is a pseudonym.'

'As you can see, I do exist.'

'You do indeed. And now you've published a new book. The whole world's clamouring for an interview, and the only person who gets one is me. But I hadn't even asked for one.'

Six months ago, Victor Lenzen was offered a job at a German news station. He moved back to Germany permanently and since then he's been working in television and print media.

'What's your question?' I ask.

Victor Lenzen is reputed to be one of the country's most brilliant journalists. He has won three major national prizes.

'What made you choose me?'

Victor Lenzen has a girlfriend called Cora Lessing, who lives in Berlin.

'Maybe I admire your work.'

Victor Lenzen is faithful to Cora Lessing.

'Maybe you do,' he says. 'But I'm not an arts critic; I usually report on foreign affairs.'

Since moving back to Germany, Victor Lenzen visits his daughter Marie every week.

'Don't you want to be here, Herr Lenzen?' I ask.

'No, that's not what I meant! I feel honoured, of course. It was only a question.'

Victor Lenzen's mother died in the early nineties. His father is still living in the family home. Victor Lenzen visits him regularly.

'Do you have any more questions that aren't part of the official interview?' I try to sound amused. 'Or shall we begin?'

Victor Lenzen plays badminton with a colleague after work. Victor Lenzen supports Amnesty International.

'Let's begin,' he says.

Victor Lenzen's favourite band is U2. He likes going to the cinema and speaks four foreign languages fluently—English, French, Spanish and Arabic.

'All right then,' I say.

'No, wait, one more question,' says Lenzen. He hesitates—or pretends to.

Victor Lenzen is a murderer.

'It's just...' he says, and leaves the rest of the sentence hanging menacingly in the air.

Victor Lenzen is a murderer.

'Have we met before?' he asks at last.

I look Victor Lenzen in the eye and see someone quite different opposite me. I realise what a big mistake I've made. Victor Lenzen is not stupid: he is mad.

He hurls himself across the table at me. I tip backwards off my chair, my head hits the floor hard and I have no time to work out what's happening, or even make the slightest sound, because he's on top of me and his hands are on my windpipe.

I thrash about, trying to break free, but he's too heavy, and his hands have closed around my throat and he's squeezing hard. I can't breathe, and immediately the panic is there, rolling over me like a wave. I kick and struggle, nothing but the will to survive. I can feel the blood in my veins, heavy and hot and thick, and I hear a rushing in my ears as it swells and subsides. My head is bursting. I open my eyes wide.

He's staring at me, his eyes watering from exertion and hatred. He hates me—why? His face is the last thing I see. Then it's over.

29

I am not naïve. That's how it could happen, or something like that. I know all about Victor Lenzen, and yet at the same time I know nothing. But I'm going ahead with it. That much I owe Anna.

I pick up my phone, feel its weight in my hand. I take a deep breath. I enter the number of the Munich paper that Victor Lenzen writes for and ask to be put through to the editorial department.

7

Through my study window I look straight out onto Lake Starnberg. I am glad I was wise enough to make sure of a nice view when I bought the house. God knows there aren't many people as reliant on a view as I am. I only have the one—though that's not quite true because it changes every day. Sometimes the lake seems cold and unfriendly, sometimes enticing, and at other times it looks positively enchanted, so that I have no trouble at all imagining the water nymphs of local legend swimming with one another below the surface.

Today the lake is a mirror for a few coquettish clouds in an otherwise pure blue sky. I miss the swifts that in summer grace the sky with their giddy acrobatics. They're my favourite creatures. They live and mate and even sleep on the wing, never still in an unending sky—so wild, so free.

I'm sitting at my desk, thinking over the things that I have set in motion. In a few months, the journalist Victor Lenzen will interview mysterious bestselling author Linda Conrads. They'll talk about the new book—her first ever crime novel.

An interview with Linda Conrads is in itself a sensation. For years, the press has been asking for interviews and offering ridiculous sums of money, but the novelist has always declined. No wonder the media are so keen to talk to her; almost nothing is known about the writer concealed behind the name. She hasn't given readings for years, turns down interviews, lives cut off from society, doesn't have a Facebook or Instagram or Twitter account. If it weren't for the books that are published with such pleasing regularity, you might almost think Linda Conrads didn't exist. Even the author's photo and biography on her novels' jackets reveal nothing, unchanged for a good ten years. The black-and-white photo shows a woman who is maybe pretty, maybe ugly, who could be tall but then again could be short, a woman with either blonde or brown hair, and eyes that are green or perhaps blue. It shows her from a distance, in profile, and the brief biographical note states only my birth year and that I live near Munich with my dog.

That the former foreign correspondent Victor Lenzen is to have an exclusive interview with Linda Conrads is going to cause quite a stir.

I plan to challenge my sister's murderer with the only means at my disposal—literature. I am going to haul him over the coals with this book. And I want him to look me in the eye with the full knowledge that I have seen through him, even if no one else has. I am going to prove Victor Lenzen guilty and find out why Anna had to die. No matter what it takes.

That is the momentous task I have set myself. I am working on a crime novel in which I describe a murder that resembles the murder of my sister down to the last detail.

I have never had to write such a complex book: on the one hand, I want to stick as closely as possible to the truth; on the other, I must invent a story that leads to the murderer's arrest—an ending that has so far been denied to me in real life.

I've never tried to recreate reality in my books before. I would have considered it a waste. I have always had a prolific imagination, a head full of stories wanting to get out.

If my parents are to be believed, I was fond of making up tales even as a child. It was a catchphrase in our family: Linda and her stories. I remember once telling a primary-school friend that I had been for a walk in the woods with my mother and that, as we'd been picking wild strawberries, we'd caught sight of a small, spotted fawn in a clearing, asleep on the grass. I'd wanted to go up and stroke it, but my mother had held me back and told me that the fawn would smell of human afterwards and its mummy might reject it, so it was better to leave it to sleep in peace. She told me how lucky I was to have found a little fawn like that—it was very rare.

I remember how impressed my friend had been by the story. She went to the woods often and although she sometimes saw deer she'd never seen a fawn. I was so proud—I really had been tremendously lucky. I remember my mother taking me aside when my friend had gone home and asking why I told such stories. She said it wasn't nice to fib, and I told her indignantly that I hadn't been fibbing. Didn't she remember the fawn? I could, clearly. My mother shook her head—Linda and her stories—and told me we'd seen a fawn like that in a film the other day. And then it all came back to me. Of course, a film!

Imagination is a wonderful thing, so wonderful that I make a great deal of money out of it. Everything I've written so far has been as far removed as possible from myself and the reality I know. It is odd to let other people into my life now. I console myself with the thought that these aren't really scenes from my life but a displaced reality in which I immerse myself. A lot of the details are different, partly because I make a conscious decision to change them and partly because, after all this time, I can't be certain of every single detail. Only one chapter—the one everything revolves around—will be authentic: a night in high summer, Anna's flat, deafening music, blood and vacant eyes...

The book ought really to begin with that chapter, but I haven't yet been able to face going back to that place. Yesterday I promised myself I'd write the chapter today, and today I've put it off until tomorrow.

Writing is strenuous, but in a good way. It's my daily training. It does me good to have a real goal.

No one except me notices any difference. Everything's the same: Linda sits in her big, lonely house and tells her agent and her publisher that she's working on a new book. Linda does that once a year; it's nothing special. Business as usual for my agent, Pia, who's already been informed that a new manuscript is on its way and who is naturally delighted. (Although it does, of course, surprise her that I should suddenly want to change genre and write a thriller.) Business as usual for Charlotte, who at most notices how I'm spending less time reading and watching TV, and more time in my study. Business as usual for Ferdi, the man who tends my garden and may only notice that he's come across me in my pyjamas less in the middle of the day. Everything is the same. Only the observant Bukowski knows that I'm plotting something and gives me conspiratorial glances. Yesterday I caught him looking at me with concern in his big, knowing eyes, and I felt touched.

It'll all be fine, mate.

For a long time, I wondered whether to take anyone into my confidence. It would be wise. But I decided against it. What I'm planning to do is crazy. Any normal person would simply call the police. If I were to confide in Norbert, he'd tell me to do just that: *Call the police, Linda!*

But I can't. If the police believed me at all, they would probably question Victor Lenzen, and then he'd be forewarned and I'd never get a look-in. I might never find out what happened all those years ago. I can't bear that thought. No, I have to do it myself. For Anna.

There's no other way: I must look him in the eye and ask him questions. Not polite questions, such as a policeman might put to an influential journalist who seems unimpeachable. None of your 'Terribly sorry to bother you, but we have a witness here who thinks...'

None of your 'Where were you on the…?'

Proper questions, such as only I can ask and only if I'm alone. Besides, if I were to rope anyone else into this business, I am well aware that it would only be out of fear and selfishness. Victor Lenzen is dangerous. I don't want him coming into contact with people I love and cherish.

So I'm left to my own devices. In the end, there isn't anyone (not counting Norbert and Bukowski) whom I one hundred per cent trust, anyway. I don't even know if I can trust myself one hundred per cent.

So I haven't told anyone more than the bare essentials. I've spoken to my agent, to the head of publicity at the publishing house, and to my editor. They were all perplexed that I want to write a crime novel, and even more perplexed that I want to give an interview, but they swallowed it. I still have to talk with my publisher, but the most important things are already underway. I have a deadline for the manuscript and a publication date.

All of that is good. Having a deadline to work towards has given meaning to my existence over the years and has more than once saved my life. It's hard living all alone in this big house, and I have often thought about simply absconding—a handful of sleeping pills, or a razor blade in the bath…

In the end, it was always something as banal as a deadline that held me back. All that stuff was so real; I could always imagine what immense trouble I'd be causing my publishing house by failing to deliver. There were contracts and plans in place. So I carried on living and kept writing.

I try not to give too much thought to the fact that this book might be my last.

I have set a dangerous chain of events in motion by ringing up the newspaper's editorial department. It was a clever move on my part because now there's no turning back. It transpires that Lenzen works for a newspaper as well as in television, which is good because it would be counterproductive for him to turn up with a television crew. So I've arranged an interview with the newspaper—just the two of us.

I return to Jonas Weber, the young police officer with dark hair and grave eyes, one brown, one green. And to Sophie, for that's what I've decided to call my literary alter ego. Sophie reminds me of the way I used to be: playful, impulsive, incapable of sitting still for long. Early-morning walks in the woods, camping trips, sex in changing rooms, mountain-climbing, football matches.

I study the portrait of Sophie on the pages I've written. She looks like somebody who'd like to be challenged, who isn't yet broken. That's not me anymore. The eyes that discovered Anna's dead body twelve years ago are no longer mine. Bit by bit, they've been replaced. My lips are no longer the lips I pressed together when I watched my sister's coffin being lowered into her grave. My hands are no longer the hands that plaited her hair before her first job interview. I am someone else. That is not a metaphor; it's the truth.

Our body is constantly replacing cells—substituting, renewing. After seven years, we are, as it were, new. I know that kind of thing; I've had a hell of a lot of time to read over the years.

Now I'm sitting on a doorstep in the dark with Sophie, shivering, although it's a warm night. The sky is clear and starry. I watch Jonas and Sophie share a cigarette and I'm sucked into my own story; I lose myself in the characters. There's a kind of magic in sharing a cigarette with a stranger. I write and watch the two of them and almost feel the urge to take up smoking again.

The scene collapses when there's a ring at the front door. The shock goes right through me. My heart begins to thump like mad and I can feel how thin the membrane is that separates my newly won determination from my fear. I am frozen mid-movement—my hands poised above the keys of my laptop.

I wait apprehensively for a second ring but still jump when it comes. And at the third, and at the fourth. I'm scared. I'm not expecting anyone. It's late in the evening and I am alone with a small dog in a big house.

A few days ago I rang up the newspaper where my sister's murderer works and enquired after him. I have drawn his attention to me. I have done something stupid and now I'm scared. The doorbell keeps on ringing, and my thoughts begin to race. What should I do? I can't think straight. Should I ignore it? Play dead? Call the police? Creep into the kitchen and fetch a knife?

Bukowski begins to yap; he comes bounding up to me, wagging his tail—he loves visitors, after all. He streaks towards me and jumps up at me, and the angry ringing subsides for a moment. At the same time, my brain kicks back into action.

Keep calm, Linda.

There are a million explanations for why someone should ring my doorbell at half-past ten on a Thursday evening. Not one of them has anything to do with Victor Lenzen. Why would a murderer ring the doorbell? The whole thing is bound to be innocent. It's probably only Charlotte who's forgotten something, or my agent who lives round the corner and occasionally drops in, although rarely as late as this. Or perhaps something's happened nearby. Maybe someone even needs help!

I am functioning again. I rouse myself out of my paralysis and hurry down the stairs to the front door. Bukowski comes with me, still yapping and wagging his tail.

I'm glad I've got you, mate.

I open the door. Before me stands a man.

4
—

SOPHIE

The air was the consistency of jelly. It had engulfed Sophie the moment she stepped out of her air-conditioned car. She hated nights like this, when the heat was so intense she couldn't get to sleep because her skin felt sticky and she was bitten to death by mosquitoes.

She was standing at the door to her sister's flat, ringing the bell for the second time. She'd seen light on in Britta's flat when she'd parked the car, so she knew she was in. Britta probably wasn't opening on principle: she objected to surprise visits, considering it plain rude to breeze in unannounced when you could at least ring from your mobile on the way.

Sophie took her finger off the bell and put her ear to the door. She could hear music inside.

'Britta?' she called. But there was no reply.

Sophie was reminded of her mother, who worried at every little thing—organising a search party whenever either of her daughters was the least bit late, or envisaging lung cancer at the slightest cough. Sophie, on the other hand, was one of those people who believe that true misfortune only ever befalls others. So she shrugged her shoulders, rifled through her handbag for her bunch of keys that held the spare to Britta's flat, and opened the door.

'Britta?'

It was only a few steps down the hall to the room where the music was coming from. Sophie went in and stopped, rooted suddenly to the spot. What she saw on the floor was so overwhelming that she couldn't immediately take it in.

There was...Britta. She was lying on her back, her eyes wide open, an incredulous expression on her face. At first, Sophie thought her sister had had a bad fall and needed to be helped to her feet. She took a step towards her. Then she saw the blood and stopped again, her body rigid. The living room was a black-and-white stage set. No air, no sound, no colour. Only this horrific still life: Britta's fair hair, her dark dress, the pale carpet, shards of glass, an overturned tumbler, white flowers, a black high-heeled sandal slipped off a foot, and blood, also black, spreading out around Britta's torso.

Sophie gasped and at once the music was back. *All you need is love, la-da-da-da-da.* There was colour again, too, and all Sophie saw was deep, gleaming red.

While Sophie was trying to process this picture, she became aware of something moving in the corner of the room. She turned her head in panic and saw that it was only the curtains at the terrace door fluttering in the breeze. But then she saw the shadow. He stood quite still by the door, like an animal lying in wait, almost invisible. He looked at Sophie. Then he vanished.

8

I stare at Norbert, who still has his finger on the bell.

'About time,' he says and pushes past me without a word of greeting. A first breath of winter comes in at the door with him. I want to say something but don't get that far.

'Have you gone completely mad?' Norbert snarls at me.

Bukowski jumps up at him. He adores my publisher. That isn't saying a lot because Bukowski likes everyone. Norbert is fuming, but he softens for a moment to ruffle the dog's coat before turning to face me again, the furrow back between his eyebrows. If I'm honest, I'm bloody glad to see him, furious or not. Norbert may flare up easily, but he's also the kindest person I know. He simply gets hot under the collar about everything: politics, which is getting more and more stupid; publishing, which is getting more and more corrupt; and his authors, who are getting greedier and greedier. Everyone knows Norbert's outbursts and his heated tirades, which, when his blood is really boiling, he lards with juicy expressions from his beloved France: *putain!* or *merde!* or sometimes, if it's really bad, both at once.

'What's going on?' I ask, when I've begun to recover from the late-night intrusion. 'I thought you were in the south of France.'

He snorts.

'What's going *on*? That's what I'm here to ask you!'

I really and truly have no idea why Norbert is so furious. We've been working together for years. We're friends. What have I done? Or is there something I've forgotten to do? Has my work on the thriller made me overlook something important? My mind is blank.

'Come on in first,' I say. 'I mean, properly in.' I lead the way to the kitchen.

I switch on the coffee machine, pour Norbert a glass of water and put it down in front of him. He has taken a seat at the kitchen table, but he gets up again when I turn to face him, too cross to keep still.

'Well?' I ask.

'Well?' Norbert echoes, in a tone that makes Bukowski back away in confusion. 'My author, Linda Conrads, who's had my support as a publisher for over a decade, has taken it upon herself to abandon the marvellous literary novels she's been writing with pleasing regularity for years, and to piss off her readers and critics (not to mention me) by making her next book a blood-and-guts thriller. No consultation, no nothing. As if that weren't enough, Her Ladyship has to rush off and tell the press, without once talking it over with her publisher. Because she is obviously of the opinion that I am not just the head of a pretty big, pretty lucrative business with a pretty large number of employees, who works his balls off day after day, not least for her and her books, but that I am, above all else, one thing: her very own printing press. *Putain bordel de merde!*'

Norbert's face has assumed a deep-red hue. He picks up the glass and takes a sip. He's about to say something else, but changes his mind and drains his glass instead, making angry glugging noises.

I don't know what to say. I hadn't for a moment thought Norbert might cause me any trouble, but I realise he's capable of causing me immense trouble if he wants to. Getting my book published and seeing that it receives the usual press is a fundamental part of my plan.

40

No book, no interview. Damn it, I don't have the time or energy to quarrel with Norbert, or go looking for a new publisher. I have other problems. Of course, any publisher would give his right arm to have me: I'm successful and I'm sure the new genre isn't going to scare off my fans. A few of them, maybe, but for those who give up on me, there'll be others. Anyway, that's not the point; I don't care in the slightest how many books I sell, as long as Lenzen takes the bait. But I can't say that to Norbert—that it's not merely a book at stake here.

I don't want a row, least of all with one of my only friends. My brain is working overtime as I consider whether to let Norbert in on my secret. It would be wonderful to have his support.

'All right, I'll repeat my first question,' Norbert says, putting his glass down on the table and jolting me out of my thoughts. 'Have you gone completely mad?'

I think to myself how much I'd like an accomplice, someone I can trust. I think to myself that in a crisis, a genuine, full-blown crisis, there's no one I'd rather have at my side than Norbert.

'Well?' he asks impatiently.

Fuck it, I'm going to tell him. I pull myself together and take a deep breath.

'Norbert…'

'Don't say anything yet,' he hisses, raising a hand to silence me. 'I've forgotten something.'

He dashes out of the room. Bewildered, I hear him open the front door and vanish into the night. A few seconds later, he reappears with a bottle of wine.

'For you,' he says, putting the bottle on the kitchen table. He still looks grumpy.

Norbert almost always brings me wine from the south of France when he comes to visit—the best rosé I know. But, then, he's not usually cross with me.

Norbert notices my confused expression.

'Just because you behave like a silly cow doesn't mean I'm going to let you go thirsty,' he says, giving me a see-how-nice-I-am-to-you look. I suppress a smile, but at the same time I feel like crying. I think how incredible it would be to have Norbert on board—he'd believe me; he might even understand me. But it's too dangerous; I can't drag him into all this. Damn it. What am I to do?

The coffee machine interrupts my thoughts with its gurgling, and I pour us both a cup.

'Don't think you're let off the hook,' Norbert says. 'You owe me an explanation.'

I sit down. Norbert settles opposite and I grope around for a plausible story.

'How is it you've already spoken to the others in-house and not to me?'

'Because I wanted to talk to you in person when you got back from your holiday instead of writing you a silly email,' I say. 'Only you spoilt my plans. I didn't even know you were back!'

It's the truth. Norbert gives me a piercing look.

'And why a thriller?' he asks. 'Seriously!'

I hesitate, then decide to stick as close as possible to the truth—but without giving too much away.

'Do you have brothers and sisters, Norbert?'

'No,' he says. 'I'm an only child. My wife says it shows.'

I almost laugh. Then I grow serious again.

'I had a sister. Her name was Anna.'

Norbert frowns.

'Had?' he asks.

'Anna is dead. She was murdered.'

'Oh God,' says Norbert. 'When did that happen?'

'A long time ago now—twelve years last summer.'

'*Merde!*' says Norbert.

'Yes.'

'Did they catch the culprit?'

'No,' I say and swallow hard. 'Never.'

'*Putain,*' says Norbert softly. 'That's awful.'

We're both silent for a moment.

'Why have you never told me this before?'

'I don't like talking about it,' I say. 'I'm not very good at pouring my heart out. Maybe that's why I've never really got over it. I have a different way of dealing with things, you know; I get over what's happened by writing about it. And that's exactly what I'm doing now.'

Norbert is silent for a long time. Then he nods.

'I see,' he says.

As far as he's concerned, that's the end of the matter. He gets up, searches in the kitchen drawer for a corkscrew, finds one, uncorks the bottle of wine he's brought me and pours us each a glass. A ton is lifted off my mind.

One hour, a great deal of talking, three espressi, a bottle of excellent French rosé and three quarters of a bottle of whisky later, we're sitting at the kitchen table doubled up with laughter. For what must be the tenth time, Norbert is telling me the story of how he once got so smashed in a bar with a certain politician (who in those days was still fat and endearingly slobbish) that afterwards he was caught by two policemen trying to fit his car key into the door of someone else's Porsche.

Every time he tells me this story, I laugh. I even smile for Norbert when he gets onto the subject of his fiftieth birthday party and the way I freaked out because the band had the nerve to play *All You Need is Love* by the Beatles.

I remember that evening as if through a veil. It was one of the better evenings not long after Anna's death, in that strange in-between time, after the shock and before the breakdown, when I was by no means myself anymore but still functioning.

Norbert and I didn't yet know each other well; I had only recently switched publishers and he had no idea what I'd gone through. Didn't even know I'd had a sister. I remember drinking Prosecco despite the antidepressants and dancing with Marc, my fiancé, even though I no longer felt anything for him. I remember that I stuck to the dress code and wore white, although I had been going around in black up until then. I remember thinking that this could be my life—going to

43

parties, and drinking Prosecco and dancing, and granting eccentric friends their innocuous wishes. And I remember that I was on the dance floor when the earthquake started—dancing with Marc as the first bars struck up *love, love, love*—and reality was swallowed up in an insatiable vortex, leaving me behind, leaving me with the blood— with Anna and the blood. I gasped for air and struggled to surface from the blackness, but the song had me in its grasp. I opened my eyes wide. The people around me were singing along. I was gasping for air. Stop! Stop! I cried, inaudibly, and they carried on singing; they didn't hear me. *All you need is love, la-da-da-da-da.* Then I really screamed, as loud as I could: *Stop! Stop! Stop!* I screamed until my throat was sore, and the people around me stopped singing and dancing and turned to look at me, and the band stopped, nonplussed, and I stood there on the dance floor, shrieking: *Stop! Stop! Stop!* I was still caught in the vortex, still in Anna's flat, still helpless, still alone, and Marc's arms were round me and his voice was whispering: *Shh, calm down, it's all okay*, and out loud it was saying: *Sorry, my fiancée's had too much to drink. Could you let us through, please?*

Norbert doubles up with laughter as he recalls it. He has no idea what really happened that night—thinks I'd simply had one too many, and suffered from a deep-seated and unaccountable aversion to the Beatles.

I don't talk about what happened to Anna now and I never have done. The fact is, there is no longer a single person left in my life who knows that I once had a sister and what happened to her—not counting my parents, that is. No old friends, no classmates, no mutual acquaintances. For the people around me, Anna has never existed.

So how could Norbert associate my freaking out with the murder? That's why it's okay for him to laugh. He has no idea about that moment when I entered Anna's flat and found her lying on the floor, dead or dying, and then spotted her murderer lurking, his eyes cold and pale. For a few horrific seconds I was turned to stone, while Anna had turned to stone forever. I was a statue and Anna was ghastly, rigid and unmoving. The whole room seemed to freeze, except for a single ghostly movement at the edge of my vision. The record player, so cruel and false, with the record—an old record of mine that I'd given to Anna—spinning.

All you need is love, la-da-da-da-da.

The song that is the reason I never listen to the radio, out of sheer terror it might be played.

I swallow the lump in my throat and push the thought far away. It's good that Norbert's laughing. Doesn't matter what he's laughing at.

I enjoy having him here. I love his sense of humour and his arch cynicism, the kind only those well treated by life can afford. I wish he'd spend the night; there is certainly no shortage of spare rooms. I want to call him a cab, but Norbert insists on driving home, saying something about a meeting the next morning. Damn it! Just when it's all so nice and normal—a friend here with me who is as close as a big brother, and my dog asleep at his feet, his eyebrows twitching in a dream, as if he's encountered something quite astonishing. It's only the three of us, but at this moment my house is full of life.

I suppress a sigh. Of course, it can't stay this way. I shouldn't even hope to hold onto such a lovely moment. Any minute now, something will happen to destroy it. What will it be?

It's Norbert. He gets up. I suppress the impulse to cling to him.

'Please stay,' I murmur. 'I'm scared.'

He doesn't hear me; maybe I didn't even say it. Norbert takes his coat, glares at me, says that if I absolutely have to write a bloody thriller, the manuscript had jolly well better be good, and staggers off towards the front door. I shouldn't let him drive in that state. I follow him. My limbs feel like lead.

He turns to face me, grabs me by the shoulders and looks me in the face. I can smell the whisky on his breath.

'A book must be an axe for the frozen sea within us,' he says in an almost accusatory tone.

'Kafka,' I say. Norbert nods.

'You were always quoting that. A book must be an axe, Linda.

45

Don't forget it. Thriller or not, I need something real from you—something about life and emotions and…'

He mumbles something incomprehensible, lets go of my shoulders and begins to button up his coat. Starts all wrong, gets in a muddle, begins over again, gets it wrong again, nearly blows his top, gives up, leaves his coat undone.

'This book is an axe, Norbert.'

He looks at me, suspicious, then shrugs his shoulders. With a single look, I try to say all the things I can't put into words. I scream: I'm terribly frightened, I don't want to die, I need someone to talk to, I'll drop down dead if he leaves now, I feel like the loneliest person on the planet. I don't scream loud enough.

My publisher says goodbye with a smack on each cheek. I watch him disappear into the night. I don't want him to go. I want to tell him everything—about the earthquake, about Anna. I want to tell him my plans. He's my last chance—the safety of the shore, my anchor. I open my mouth to call out to him, but I can no longer see him. It's too late; he's disappeared, cast off.

I'm on my own.

6

JONAS

He clutched the gun with both hands, steadied himself, took aim and shot.

Jonas Weber hated the idea of ever having to point his gun at a real person. Once, he'd needed to fire a warning shot, and he hoped it would stay that way. But he loved target practice at the range; he'd always liked shooting. As a child he'd shot at tin cans with his father's air gun; as a teenager he'd taken idiotic pot shots at sparrows and pigeons with his mates. Now he shot at targets with his service gun. He liked the caution required when handling firearms—the care, the rituals involved. Usually it didn't leave much room for other thoughts, but today his brain wouldn't settle.

He remembered the scene of the crime that he'd been called to the previous night—all that blood. He remembered the corpse, and the witness who had found the dead woman and surprised the murderer. A peculiar story. So much to get straight, and so many questions.

The night had been long and strenuous. No chance of going home before dawn and crawling into bed with Mia. Then he'd made a stupid mistake. Even now, he didn't know how he could have let it happen. He was usually so unfazed when dealing with victims' relatives. No idea why the whole thing had got under his skin like that. The victim *had* looked pretty awful—seven stab wounds. But it wasn't the first time he'd seen such a thing. True, he'd been exhausted. But he was used to that.

It must have been the woman, maybe a few years younger than himself—the witness who'd found her sister stabbed to death and seen the murderer escape. Jonas had caught himself watching her as he talked to his colleagues. A paramedic draped a blanket round her shoulders—an odd gesture given the heat that night. The woman was sitting there, deep in thought. She hadn't trembled or cried. Perhaps the shock, Jonas thought, until she turned her head and looked straight at him with a strange intensity. Not tearful or confused or dazed or in shock in any way, but utterly lucid.

Since then, the scene had kept coming back to him; he couldn't get it out of his head. The woman had shaken off the blanket, come towards him, and looked him in the eye. As if full sentences required too much energy, she spoke only a single word.

'Why?'

Jonas had to swallow.

'I don't know.'

But he had the feeling that wasn't enough—that he must give her something more—and before he had time to think, added, 'I don't know what happened here, but I promise you I'll find out.'

He could have hit himself. How could he make promises to a relative? They might never find the culprit. He didn't know anything about the crime. He had behaved with a complete lack of professionalism! Like an idiot policeman in some stupid film.

He recalled the reproachful look his new colleague Antonia Bug had given him: wasn't he supposed to be more experienced and less easily fazed than her? He'd expected her to mention it as soon as they were alone together, and how grateful he'd been when she hadn't.

Jonas reloaded his gun. He tried to concentrate, to shake off the scene. He had enough problems as it was; he couldn't go wallowing in self-reproach for some small blunder. He hadn't really promised the woman anything. He couldn't make promises—everyone must know that. It was something you said sometimes: 'promise'. Just a word. Anyway, the statement had been taken now; he'd probably never see the woman again. He raised his gun, tried not to think of anything, and shot.

9

I fight my impulse to flee. It is difficult for me. I feel my pulse racing and notice that my breathing is frantic. I try to apply what I have learnt—to work with my physical reactions instead of ignoring them. I concentrate on my pulse and count my breaths—twenty-one, twenty-two, twenty-three. I focus my attention on my revulsion instead of making a pointless effort to suppress it. My revulsion is in my chest, beneath my fear. It is thick and sticky like mucus. I examine it carefully; it swells and subsides, like toothache. I want to dodge it; I want to get away. It's a normal desire—that's something else I have learnt.

The instinct to flee is normal. But there's no point in evasion, in trying to avoid pain and fear. I grope for the mantra I've formulated with the therapist and cling to it: *The way out of fear leads through fear. The way out of fear leads through fear. The way out of fear leads through fear.*

The man looks at me enquiringly. With a mute nod, I signal to him that I am ready, although the exact opposite is the case. But I have been looking at the bird-eating spider for ages now. It is sitting in its jar, quite still most of the time, only stirring now and then, making my hair stand on end. Everything about it looks wrong: its peculiar movements, its body, its black and tan leg joints.

The therapist is patient. We've come a long way today. At first I couldn't even be in the same room as that creature.

It was Charlotte who opened the door to the man with the bird-eating spider and cajoled me into greeting him. Charlotte thinks I'm researching for a book; she thinks the goings-on today are research for a novel, just like all the other crazy things that I've got up to here in the house these past weeks.

It's a good thing she thinks that; it means that she doesn't bat an eyelid when I shut myself away with a retired policeman to study interrogation techniques, or have ex-army trainers explain to me how elite soldiers are made mentally fit enough to withstand torture without disclosing information. These experts, who come to my house day after day, are received by Charlotte discreetly, and she passes no comment on the arrival of the therapist specialising in treating people with phobias using 'confrontational therapy'. Charlotte has no idea that I'm trying to find out how much fear I am capable of withstanding before I collapse.

I am soft and I know it. The life I've led over the past years has been free of discomfort. I've been mollycoddled so much that it's an incredible act of willpower for me to have a single cold shower instead of a warm one. I have to learn to be tough on myself if I want to take on my sister's murderer.

Hence the bird-eating spider. Can't get more discomforting than that. As long as I can remember, there's been nothing I loathe more than spiders.

The therapist takes the lid off the jar where he'd temporarily stowed the spider while I got used to the sight of it.

'Wait,' I say. 'Wait.'

He pauses. 'Don't think about it too much,' he says. 'It doesn't get any easier, no matter how long you wait.'

He looks at me, waiting for a sign. He won't do a thing until I've given him the go-ahead. That's the deal.

I recall our conversation at the beginning of the session. 'What are you frightened of, Frau Conrads?' he'd asked.

'The spider, of course,' I replied, annoyed at the question. 'I'm frightened of the spider.'

'The bird-eating spider that's in a container in my bag?'

'Yes!'

'Are you frightened right now?'

'Of course I'm frightened.'

'What if there was no container in my bag with a bird-eating spider inside?'

'I don't understand.'

'Let's assume, for a moment, that there's no spider because I forgot to pack the container. What would you be frightened of then? You couldn't be scared of the spider, if there wasn't an actual spider.'

'But I thought there was.'

'Exactly. You thought. That's where fear begins. In your head. In your thoughts. The spider has absolutely nothing to do with it.'

I pull myself together.

'Okay,' I say. 'We'll do it now.'

Once again, the therapist removes the lid and places the jar on its side. The spider begins to move at a speed that terrifies me. I force myself to keep looking at it, even when the therapist lets it crawl onto his hand. I suppress the urge to jump up and run away, and I feel a drop or two of cold sweat running down my spine. I force myself to remain seated and watch. The spider comes to rest on the man's hand—a nightmare of legs and fuzz and repulsiveness.

Once again, I try to apply what I have learnt over the past weeks. I focus my attention on my body and realise what an unnatural posture I have adopted. My torso is inclined as far to the left as it can go, and I'm cowering in the far corner of the sofa. I ask myself whether this is the way I want to be: like a rabbit in front of a snake. Whether I can afford to act like this, either now or in future.

I sit up straight, throw back my shoulders, lift up my chin. I reach out my hand and give the man with the spider a nod. My fingers are trembling, but I do not withdraw them.

'Are you okay?' the therapist asks.

I nod, letting all my energy flow into my hand, which I hold still.

'All right then,' says the therapist and brings his hand nearer to mine. For a moment, the creature squats there, motionless. I watch it, with its thick, hairy legs and its round body—that, too, is hairy but with a small bald spot. The legs are striped: black and tan, black and tan—each with an orange dot in the middle. I only notice that now. The spider sits there, quite still on the man's hand, and I tell myself I can do it.

Then it starts to move. Everything about it looks wrong. My stomach rebels. Specks of light dance before my eyes, but I keep still, and the creature crawls onto my hand. The first tentative movement of its legs on my palm throws me into panic, but I remain motionless. The bird-eating spider crawls onto my hand. I feel its weight, the touch of its legs, its body brushing my skin. For a terrible moment I think it's going to crawl up my arm and across my shoulder to my neck and face, but it stops on my hand. It squats there, shifting its legs. I stare at it. This isn't a nightmare, I think; this is real life, it's happening right now and you can take it. This is your fear; this is what your fear feels like, and you can take it. I feel dizzy; I'd like to faint, but I don't. Instead I sit there with a bird-eating spider on my hand. It has stopped moving. My fear is a dark well that I have fallen into. I'm suspended vertically in the water. I try to touch the bottom with my toes, but I can't.

'Shall I take it off you?' the therapist asks, startling me out of my trance.

I can only nod again. Carefully, he picks up the creature in the hollow of his hand and stows it back in the container that he carries in a kind of sports bag.

I stare at my hand. I feel the throb of my pulse, the furry feeling on my tongue, my tense muscles. My T-shirt is clinging to me, drenched in sweat. My face contracts as if I were about to cry, but as so often in the past years, no tears come and I cry in dry, painful sobs.

I've made it.

10

I'm sitting in my favourite armchair, looking out into the darkness and waiting for the sun to rise. The edge of the woods lies before me. I would love to see an animal in the cool light of the stars, but nothing stirs. Only an indefatigable owl gives a hoot every now and then.

A clear sky arches over the treetops. Who knows how many stars are really up there. Stars only have one means of telling us that they no longer exist: they stop shining. But if a star is a thousand light years away and stopped shining yesterday, then it would, in theory, be a thousand years before we found out on Earth.

Nothing is certain.

I curl up in my armchair and try to nap. An interesting day lies behind me, and a hardworking night. Tomorrow I have an important talk with an expert and want to be prepared.

It's soon clear to me that I'm not going to sleep. I try to relax in my armchair, to build up a bit of energy even without sleeping. My gaze rests on the meadow behind the house, and the glistening shore of the lake. I sit there like that for a long time. At first I think I'm imagining things when the stars seem to shine paler and the sky begins to change colour. But then I hear the birds twittering through the window; they start up as if an invisible conductor had signalled to them with raised baton. Then I know the sun is rising. To begin with, it is a mere gleaming streak behind the trees, but soon it starts to climb, vast and blazing.

It is a miracle. I remind myself that I am on a tiny planet that is moving at an insane speed through a boundless universe, never tiring of its flight around the sun, and I think to myself: it's crazy. That we exist at all, that the Earth exists and the sun and the stars, and that I can sit here and see and feel all this. It's incredible; it's a miracle. If this is possible, anything's possible.

The moment passes. A clear morning lies before me. I glance at the time. It will be another few hours before the man arrives to teach me about interrogation techniques.

I get up, make myself tea, fetch my laptop and sit down at the kitchen table. I have another quick look at the article I'd studied the night before. When Bukowski comes lumbering up to me, I let him out and watch him go to meet the day.

When the time comes, the sun has long since passed its zenith. I'm sitting in the kitchen with Charlotte, who's brought around the week's shopping.

'Would you mind taking the dog out again before you knock off?' I ask.

'Sure, no problem.'

Charlotte knows I like to be left alone with my experts; she knows that's the only reason I'm sending her out again with Bukowski. I look out of the window and watch the gardener cutting the grass. He raises a hand in greeting when he sees me. I wave back and close the window in the room where I plan to receive Dr Christensen.

Less than half an hour later, I'm sitting across from him. The blond German-American has icy blue eyes. His handshake is firm and I can only withstand his gaze because I've put in a substantial amount of practice over the past weeks. Charlotte has been gone a while; dusk is falling. I arranged this private consultation some weeks ago and had to cough up a great deal of money to get Christensen to come to my house. He is an expert in wringing confessions from criminals. His speciality is the notorious Reid technique, a questioning method not officially permitted in Germany, which employs a range of psychological tools and tricks to make the suspect break down.

Maybe it's naïve to hope that Lenzen will confess.

But having got so far, I want to be as well prepared as possible. I must somehow get him to talk to me beyond the framework of the interview—ask him questions, get him to tie himself up in contradictions, provoke him if necessary, and somehow pin him down. If there's anyone who can help me find out how to impose my will on a criminal and talk him into confessing, it's Dr Arthur Christensen.

And in case Lenzen is a tough nut to crack, I always have something else up my sleeve…

When Christensen realised that I wasn't interested in his theoretical explanations (which you can easily mug up on in the specialist literature on the subject) but in quite concrete information on how to break a culprit and force him to confess—that is to say, how it works in practice and what it feels like—he seemed peeved. But the large sum of money I was prepared to spend, combined with his realisation that I am not a criminal mastermind but merely a sick, weak woman novelist, persuaded him to demonstrate his skills to me.

So now we're sitting face-to-face. I've done my homework. Christensen has suggested demonstrating his method of interrogation on me: that seemed the most straightforward way of showing me what it feels like to be put through the Reid technique. He began the consultation by asking me to think of something I was particularly ashamed of—something that I never wanted to reveal. Of course, I came up with something, just as anybody would have done, and now Christensen is trying to wheedle the information out of me.

He's getting closer. Over an hour ago he understood that it's something to do with my family. His questions are getting more penetrating and I am getting thinner-skinned. To begin with, I felt indifference towards Christensen, maybe even sympathy. I have come to detest him: for his questions, for his persistence, for the fact that he won't leave me in peace. He instructs me to sit down again when I want to go to the loo. Reprimands me every time I want to drink anything. I'm not allowed to drink until I've confessed. When he saw me wrap my arms around myself because I was shivering, he opened all the windows in the room.

Christensen has the habit of constantly clearing his throat. I didn't notice at first, but when I did I dismissed it as an endearing mannerism. Now it's driving me crazy, and every time he does it I want to jump up and yell at him to bloody well stop it. Stress brings out the worst in me—my irritability, my quick temper. Everyone has triggers. Mine are mainly acoustic: throat-clearing, sniffing, or that noise when someone chews gum and keeps popping the bubbles. Anna was always doing that, often only because she knew it annoyed me—I could have killed her!

The thought has hardly taken shape in my mind before I'm ashamed of myself. How could I think such a thing? Christensen is tenderising me; I'm starting to yield. I'm tired, I'm cold, I'm hungry, I'm thirsty. Following Christensen's instructions, I didn't sleep last night and have hardly eaten all day. If I were in custody under his supervision, says Christensen, he'd have made damn sure that I went hungry and got as little sleep as possible.

'It's astonishing how quickly we start to crack up when we're deprived of the mainstays of our physical wellbeing,' Christensen had explained to me on the phone.

I am not, it is true, going to be in a position to deprive my sister's murderer of food or sleep, but I am at least learning to cope better in situations of tremendous stress. Who knows whether I'll sleep at all in the nights before the interview with Lenzen—or manage to eat.

Christensen's questions go on and on. I'm sick of them. I'm tired.

Above all, I'm emotionally exhausted. I'd really like to tell him every-thing, to get it over and done with. And why not—it's only an exercise, after all.

But I realise this is a dangerous way of thinking. Just the kind of self-justification that might trigger my capitulation. I notice that I'm sweating, in spite of the cold.

When Christensen finally leaves, I feel as if I've been through a mincer. Physically and mentally drained. Burnt out. Empty.

'Everyone has a breaking point,' he'd said to me towards the end of the consultation. 'Some people reach theirs sooner, others later. It all depends on how much a secret is worth protecting, or what far-reach-ing consequences a confession might have.'

I open the front door to see him out. It's late. He lays a genial hand on my shoulder and I try my hardest not to flinch at the contact.

'You've done a good job today,' he says. 'You're a tough nut.'

I wonder whether I'd feel better if I'd given in—more relieved. Part of me wanted to share my secret. I wonder whether people like Victor Lenzen feel the same. I wanted to confess.

But I didn't reveal my secret. I didn't reach my breaking point.

I try to recover my equilibrium. I close the windows and warm myself. I eat and drink. I have a shower and wash away the cold sweat. Only sleep will have to wait. I divide my day up strictly. I write early in the morning, then I do research and work out, and after that I return to my desk, often working far on into the night. I'm so exhausted I'd love to take tonight off, but there's still so much to be done if I'm to meet the deadline—and I have to meet the deadline.

I sit down at my desk and open my laptop. If I'm going to proceed in sequence, I must now write something difficult about grief and feelings of guilt. I stare at the empty screen. I can't, not now. I want to write something nice today, after such a strenuous day—one nice chapter in this horrific story.

I sit and think. I remember what I was like twelve years ago—what

I felt, what it felt like to be me. Another life. I think back to a particular night in my old flat and notice a wry smile creep across my face. I had forgotten what it's like to have a happy memory. I take a deep breath and begin to write, immersing myself in my old life. I see everything in all its colours, hear a familiar voice, breathe in the smell of my old home—relive everything. It feels lovely—almost real. I don't want to return to the present when I get to the end of the chapter, but I have no choice. It is deep into the night when I look up from the laptop. I am hungry and thirsty. I press save and close the file. But I can't resist opening it again, rereading and warming myself at the memory of life as it once was.

After I've read it through, I tell myself that it's too private, that this book isn't about me. I'm writing it for Anna, not for myself, and nice chapters have no business to be there. I close the file, about to drag it to Trash, when I change my mind; I create a new folder called 'Nina Simone' and put it in there. I open a new Word document and psych myself up to write what has to be written next.

Not tomorrow, but now.

9
—

JONAS

On the short flight of steps up to his house, someone was sitting, smoking. It had been dark for some time but, as Jonas rounded the corner, he could see the figure from a distance. As he got nearer, he realised that it was a woman. She took a drag on her cigarette and her face lit up in the glow. It was the witness he'd met the other day. Jonas's heart began to beat faster. What was she doing here?

He felt uneasy about encountering her like this. He was drenched in sweat from head to foot. Mia was out with her girlfriends, so he'd finally taken the time to go for a long jog in the nearby woods and mull things over. He'd pondered on how swiftly things had changed between him and Mia—and unprovoked. No lies, no affairs, not even the usual rows about having children or buying a house. No major scenes of any kind. They still liked one another a lot. But they no longer loved one another.

The realisation had hit him harder than the disclosure of an affair. Presumably he was to blame because, even leaving aside what had been going on in their relationship, he'd been feeling odd lately, kind of cut off from life, as if in a diving bell. It wasn't Mia's fault; the feeling had been dogging him for ages, a vague phantom pain that made him afraid he'd never be able to understand anyone, or be understood. He felt it at work. He felt it when he was talking to his friends. He'd felt it at the theatre.

Sometimes he wondered whether this diving-bell feeling was normal, whether this was what it felt like to enter a midlife crisis. But, then, it was a bit early for that. He'd only recently turned thirty.

Jonas brushed the thought away, took a deep breath and approached the woman with the cigarette.

'Good evening,' she said.

'Good evening,' Jonas replied. 'What are you doing here, Frau…'

'Please, call me Sophie.'

Jonas knew that he should send her away; it was impertinent of her to come and waylay him in private like this. He should send her away, go inside, have a shower and forget all about this curious encounter.

Instead he sat down.

'All right then: Sophie. What are you doing here?'

She seemed to reflect for a moment.

'I'd like to know what happens next,' she said.

'I'm sorry?'

'You asked me what I'm doing here. I'm here to ask you what happens next. In the…' She faltered. 'In the case.'

Jonas contemplated the young woman beside him, shrouded in cigarette smoke, her long legs bent like a wounded grasshopper's, one arm flung around her body, as if she felt cold in spite of the summer heat.

'Shouldn't we discuss this in my office tomorrow?' he asked, knowing he was going to have to take a firmer line if he really wanted to get rid of her.

Then why don't I? he wondered.

'Now that I'm here, we might as well talk.'

'I don't know what to say.' Jonas said with a sigh. 'We'll continue to gather all the evidence we can. We'll take a very close look at what forensics say. We'll talk to a great many people—we'll do what we can. That's our job.'

'You'll find the murderer,' Sophie said. It was not a question.

Jonas grimaced. What had he gone and promised her? He should have got a grip on himself. The scene of the crime was a forensic nightmare. Only a few nights before her death, Britta Peters, the murder victim, had hosted a birthday party in her flat for a friend—a party that had been attended by almost sixty people. Almost sixty people who'd left enormous quantities of fingerprints and traces of DNA all over the flat. If the identikit picture didn't yield anything and the victim's acquaintances couldn't come up with any relevant evidence, it was going to be tricky.

'We'll do our best,' said Jonas.

Sophie nodded. She took a drag on her cigarette.

'Something wasn't right in Britta's flat,' she said. 'I can't work out what it was.'

Jonas knew that feeling—like a low note that you hear not with your ears but with your belly.

'Can I have one too?' he asked. 'A cigarette, I mean.'

'This is my last. But you can have a drag.'

Jonas took the lit cigarette that Sophie held out to him. Her fingertips brushed his. He took a deep drag and returned the cigarette. Sophie raised it to her mouth.

'I think Britta was an accidental victim,' she said.

'May I ask why you think that?'

'No one who knew her could have done a thing like that,' Sophie said. 'No one.'

Jonas was silent. Again he accepted the cigarette that Sophie held out to him, took a drag, gave it back. Sophie stubbed it out in silence. She sat there beside him, staring into the darkness.

'Can I tell you about Britta?' she asked eventually.

Jonas didn't have the heart to say no. He nodded. Sophie was silent again, for a while, as if wondering where to begin.

'Once, when Britta was five or six, we went up to town with our parents,' she began at length. 'We were walking along the street with ice-cream cones in our hands—it was summer; I remember it like yesterday. Sitting on the pavement was this homeless man, dressed in rags caked with dirt, a mangy dog beside him, and bottles in a shopping trolley. We'd never seen a homeless person. I was appalled, because he smelt so bad and looked so ill and because I was scared of his dog. But Britta was curious; she said something to him—"Hello, mister" or something—the kind of thing children say to strangers sometimes. The man grinned at her and said, "Hello, young lady." My parents hurried us past him, but somehow Britta couldn't get the man out of her head. She went on pestering my parents with her questions for hours afterwards. What was the matter with the man and why did he look so funny and why had he talked so funny and smelt so funny? My parents told her that the man was probably ill and didn't have a home. From then on, whenever we went up to town with my parents, Britta would pack some food to take with her, and always looked out for him.'

'Did she find him?'

'No. But it wasn't just that man, you know. I can't begin to tell you how many injured animals Britta brought home for our parents to help nurse back to health. When Britta was twelve she started work as a volunteer in an animal refuge. Since moving into town she's worked in a soup kitchen for the homeless. She never forgot that man, you see?'

Jonas nodded. He tried to imagine her alive, the delicate blonde woman now lying in forensics, tried to imagine her running around, going about her everyday life, talking to her sister, laughing. But he couldn't. He'd always found it impossible to imagine murder victims alive. He never got to know them in life, only ever in death, and with his weak powers of imagination he was unable to envisage anything else.

'It's so easy to ridicule,' Sophie said. 'It's so easy to belittle people like Britta—to call them do-gooders. But Britta really was that way: not a do-gooder, but someone who actually *did* good.'

Jonas looked at her, trying to picture her together with her sister. The two women were so unalike—the delicate, elfin Britta, with her long hair and who, in all the photos he'd seen of her, emanated shyness and fragility; and Sophie, with her short hair and boyish appearance, who seemed so tough in spite of all she was going through.

'Stabbed seven times,' Sophie said, and Jonas started. 'I saw it in the paper. Can you imagine what it did to my parents, reading that?' she asked.

Jonas nodded his head automatically—and then shook it. He couldn't, not really.

'You have to find him,' Sophie said.

Jonas looked at her. The light, which had been triggered by the motion detector when he'd approached the house, went out. Sophie's eyes gleamed in the dark. For a second, Jonas felt himself sinking into them. Sophie returned his gaze. Then the moment passed.

'I'd better be going,' she said abruptly, and stood up.

Jonas stood too. He picked up her leather bag from the steps and handed it to her.

'God, it's heavy. What have you got in there? Weights?'

'Books,' Sophie replied, swinging the bag over her shoulder. 'I find it comforting always having something to read with me.'

'I can understand that,'

'Really? Do you like reading too?'

'Well, to be honest, I don't know when I last picked up a book,' Jonas said. 'I don't have the patience for novels. I used to be obsessed with poetry. Verlaine, Rimbaud, Keats—anything in that line.'

'Oh God,' Sophie groaned. 'Right from being at school I couldn't stand poetry. If I'd had to recite Rilke's "The Panther" one more time in Year Nine, I think I'd have gone crazy. "Its gaze, from pacing by the passing bars / Is so worn out that it can hold no more..."'

She shuddered in mock horror.

Jonas had to grin.

'You're unfair to good old Rilke,' he said. 'Who knows, maybe one day I'll try to convince you to give poetry another chance. You might like Whitman, or Thoreau.' Even as he said the words, he cursed himself. What was he doing?

'I'd like that,' said Sophie.

She turned to leave.

'Thank you for your time. And sorry for bothering you.'

She disappeared into the night. Jonas watched her go for a moment. Then he turned back and climbed the steps to the front door.

He paused in amazement.

The diving-bell feeling had vanished.

11

My muscles are on fire. I'm determined to prepare myself as well as I can for D-Day. Apart from anything else, that means physical training. If I'm to stand a chance of holding out in a situation of extreme stress, I must prepare myself physically as well as mentally. A well-trained body can cope better, so I'm working out. For years there's been a fitness studio in my basement that I hardly ever use. I was plagued with backache for a time, and got the better of it with the help of a personal trainer and disciplined weight training. Apart from that, I have never had much reason to bother about my body. I'm pretty slim and relatively fit and I couldn't care less about my bikini figure. In my world, there are no beaches.

It feels good working out. It's only now that I'm beginning to reinhabit my body that I realise how much I've neglected it over the past years. I have been living in my head, forgetting that I also have arms, legs, shoulders, back, hands and feet.

I work out hard. I enjoy the pain during the last round of weight-lifting—that burning, screeching feeling that tells me that I am still alive, after all. It does something to me. My body remembers different things from my brain: walks in woods and aching calves; nights of dancing and sore feet; jumping in a pool on a hot day and the way your heart seizes up before it decides to carry on beating. My body reminds me what pain feels like. And it reminds me what love feels like—dark and crimson and confusing. I realise what a long time it is since I last touched anyone, or since anyone touched me.

I wish I could run away from this raw, yearning feeling I've come up against. But I'm jogging on a treadmill and I can't run away, no matter how fast I am. I shake off the thought and ratchet up the speed a notch or two.

My pulse quickens; I gasp for air. All of a sudden I remember last night and the horrific nightmare from which I had such trouble extricating myself, and from which I finally awoke thrashing about and breathless. It wasn't my first nightmare about the meeting with Lenzen, but it was by far the worst. Everything had gone so terribly wrong. It all felt so real—my fear, Lenzen's grin, Charlotte's blood on his hands.

But at least the nightmare was good for something. I now know that I have to keep Charlotte out of everything. I don't want to, but I must. Subconsciously, I've known that for a long time, but my fears had made me selfish. Because I hadn't wanted to face Lenzen without someone familiar at my side, I ignored the fact that I would be exposing Charlotte to incalculable danger by bringing her into contact with a murderer.

I don't know why Lenzen murdered Anna. I don't know whether he is calculating or impulsive. I don't know whether he killed anyone before or has done so since. I know nothing. I'll make sure Charlotte doesn't meet him. A physical attack may be unlikely, but I'm not taking any risks.

First thing this morning, I took my telephone off charge and rang Charlotte to tell her to take the day of the interview off. So I'll be alone with Lenzen.

I finish my work out and stop the treadmill, drenched in sweat.

My body is exhausted and I relish the feeling. On the way to the bathroom I pass my old, wilting orchid on the hall windowsill, shy and unprepossessing. I don't know why, but I feel the need to take it into the house and coddle it up—maybe because I've started to coddle myself up. I reach the bathroom and can hardly get my T-shirt over my head, it's clinging to my body. I get under the shower, turn on the warm water and enjoy the feel of it running down my shoulders, back and thighs. My body is waking up after years of numbness.

I have the urge to feel more: for loud rock music and the buzz in my ears afterwards, for alcohol-induced dizziness, painfully spicy food. For love.

My body makes a list of the things that don't exist in my world: other people's cats that take a sudden liking to you, coins you find on the street, awkward silences in lifts, messages on lampposts—'I saw you at the Coldplay concert last Thursday and lost you in the crowd. You're called Myriam with a Y and have brown hair and green eyes. Please contact me on 0176...' The smell of hot tar in the summer, wasp stings, train strikes, emergency stops, open-air theatres, spontaneous concerts, and love.

I turn off the water and brush these thoughts aside. There's so much to do.

Less than ten minutes later, I'm sitting in my study, writing, while on my window the first ice flowers blossom.

10

SOPHIE

The perfect moment came between waking and dreaming.

As soon as Sophie fell asleep, the same unvarying nightmare would fall upon her, and as she woke, the painful reality would break over her. But the brief instant in between was perfect.

Today, like every day, it passed in the wink of an eye, and everything came flooding back. Britta was dead. That was the reason for the despair in her heart. Britta was dead, Britta was dead. Nothing would ever be right again.

Sophie had lain awake in bed for hours until the previous sleepless nights had caught up with her and she had at last dropped off. Now she lay there blinking, trying to make out the digits displayed in luminous red on the radio alarm clock. A little before four. She had slept barely two hours, but she knew there was no point staying in bed a moment longer.

She swung her legs over the edge of the bed, then stopped mid-movement. A snapshot image of Britta's flat flashed through her head. There was something wrong; something had been bugging her ever since that evening. For nights on end she had lain awake trying to work it out, but the thought had been slippery, impossible to get a hold on. Now it seemed to her that the crucial detail had come to her in a dream.

Sophie closed her eyes and held her breath, but it was gone. She got up, noiselessly, so as not to wake Paul, and closed the door behind her. She heaved a sigh of relief at having left the room without rousing him. Nothing would be worse right now than her fiancé smothering her with his gooey care and concern. The last thing she needed was for Paul to ask her how she was again.

Sophie went into the bathroom, undressed and stood under the shower. She could feel her legs trembling as if she'd run a marathon; it was ages since she'd last eaten. She turned on the water. It oozed out of the showerhead, viscous, like jelly that hasn't quite set. Sophie closed her eyes and held her face under the jet. The water bubbled over her slowly, sticky as honey. No, not quite like honey, Sophie thought—more like blood. She opened her eyes and saw that she was right. Blood, everywhere. It ran down her body, forming a small pool in her belly button and dripping onto her toes. Sophie gasped, closed her eyes again, and counted. Twenty-one, twenty-two, twenty-three, twenty-four, twenty-five. Forced herself to open her eyes again. The water was its usual consistency; the red had vanished.

Less than five minutes later, Sophie was in her studio, dried and dressed. The room was full of painted canvases and the smell of dried oils and acrylics. She'd been prolific lately; her studio was getting too small; the whole flat was. They'd been able to afford more space for quite some time—a lot more space, if they wanted. Sophie's new gallerist was selling her pictures like hot cakes and at prices Sophie had never imagined in her wildest dreams. Paul's solicitor's office was doing well too. If Sophie hung onto the flat, it was only out of laziness, because she didn't feel like getting involved with estate agents. But it was time she did.

She went over to the easel, mixed colours, dipped in the brush and began to paint, quickly and unthinkingly, going for it with big brushstrokes. When she'd finished, and stood back from the canvas out of breath, Britta stared out from behind dead eyes. Sophie backed away a step, and then another. Then she turned and staggered from the studio.

Painting had always been her refuge, a place of relief, but in the past weeks it had given her nothing but blood and pain.

Sophie went into the kitchen and tried to open the fridge, but the handle wobbled like custard. Stars danced before her eyes. She drew up a chair and sat down, struggling to remain on the surface of her consciousness.

She couldn't eat. She couldn't sleep. She couldn't paint. She couldn't talk to anyone. Somewhere out there was Britta's murderer. As long as that was the case, there was only one good reason to get out of bed in the morning: to find him.

Sophie struggled to her feet. She went into her study, dug out a blank notebook, booted up her laptop and began her investigations.

12

There is something in the corner of my room, in the dark. A shadow. I know what it is, but I don't look. I can't sleep; I'm afraid. I lie in bed, the blankets pulled up to my chin. It's the middle of the night and tomorrow—no, today, to be precise—is the day of the interview. I would normally watch TV on long, pale nights like this when sleep shuns me. But I can't go drifting on an ungovernable tide of information; I want to be able to control the thoughts and images that enter my head.

When I woke up, and before I opened my eyes and looked at the clock, I had hoped that it wasn't the witching hour—that terrible time between three and four in the morning. Dark thoughts cling to me like leeches whenever I wake then. It's the same with everyone. It's natural to feel awful in the witching hour, when night is at its coldest and the human body is at its lowest ebb. Blood pressure, metabolism, body temperature—everything drops. No wonder more people are said to die at that time than at any other.

After I had pondered all this, I opened my eyes and tried to make out the digits on my clock. I swallowed hard; it had just gone three, of course.

Now I'm lying here, letting the words melt on my tongue: *witching hour*. I'm familiar with it; I know it well. But today is different, even darker, even deeper, than usual. The shadow in the corner stirs. I only glimpse it from the corner of my eye. It smells of bewilderment and fear and blood. A few hours now before the interview begins.

I try to compose myself. I tell myself I can make it, that Victor Lenzen will be under as much pressure as me, if not more. He has a great deal to lose—his career, his family, his freedom. That is my advantage: that I have nothing to lose. But it makes no difference to my fear.

There are people who would think me crazy if they knew what I was planning to do. I am aware of how inconsistently I am acting. I'm terrified, and yet I summon a murderer to my house. I feel vulnerable, but even so I believe I am going to win the day. Things can't get any worse in my life. And yet I'm afraid of losing it.

I switch on the bedside light, as if by doing so I could dispel my gloomy thoughts. I snuggle up under the duvet, but shiver at the same time. I reach out for the battered old book of poems on my bedside table, sent to me years ago by some fan. I run my fingers over the binding, exploring the tears and creases in the thick paper. I was always a woman of prose rather than poetry, but this book has more than once brought me succour. It falls open at the passage in Whitman's 'Song of Myself', which I have read so often that the book has taken note of it.

Do I contradict myself?
Very well then I contradict myself,
(I am large, I contain multitudes.)

It is good to read about somebody who feels the way I do. Once again, my thoughts stray to Lenzen. I can't begin to imagine how the day ahead will turn out. Much as I'm dreading it, I can't wait for it to dawn at last. The waiting around and the uncertainty are gnawing away at me. Daybreak seems so distant. I long for the sun, for its light.

I sit up cross-legged and drape the duvet over my shoulders like a cloak. I leaf through the book and find the passage I was looking for.

To behold the day-break!
The little light fades the immense and diaphanous shadows,
The air tastes good to my palate.

In the darkest hour of the night, I warm myself at a sunrise described by an American poet well over a hundred years ago, and I feel better, and less cold.

Then I see it again, on the edge of my vision. The shadow in the dark corner of my bedroom is moving.

I summon up all my courage and walk unsteadily towards it with outstretched hand. My fingers meet only with whitewashed wall. The corner of my bedroom is empty—only a faint smell of caged predator hangs in the air.

13

The day that I have longed for and dreaded in equal measure has arrived.

After warm weather these last few days, this morning is cool and clear. Thick frost covers the meadow and sparkles seductively in the sun. Children will find frozen puddles on their way to school and skid around on them, maybe poking them with the tips of their boots until they crack.

I have no time to take pleasure in the view. I have a lot to do before Lenzen arrives at midday.

I will be prepared.

A trap is a device to catch or kill.

A good trap should be two things: foolproof and simple.

I'm in the dining room, looking at the caterers' food I've had delivered. There's enough to feed an army, but there will only be three of us: Lenzen, the photographer he's bringing with him, and me. I am, however, confident that the photographer won't need more than an hour to shoot his pictures and will then leave us alone.

The light lunch consists of salads and other titbits prettily served in little jars, and wraps filled with vegetables and chicken. There are small pieces of cake set out on elegant porcelain and a nicely arranged fruit basket. I didn't choose any of this food on grounds of taste; my sole criterion was whether the person eating it was likely to leave a decent sample of DNA behind. The salad and cake are ideal. You can't eat them without using a fork and leaving traces of saliva behind. The basket of fruit is likewise promising. If Lenzen should bite into an apple, I could gather up the remains as soon as he'd gone, and have them analysed. As for the wraps: you can hardly eat them without making quite a mess with the sauce, which comes oozing out when you bite into them, so it's likely anyone having one will wipe his fingers and mouth on a napkin afterwards. In that eventuality, I can expect usable traces of DNA on the napkin.

I remove the cutlery and napkins provided by the caterers. Then I pull on disposable latex gloves, take my own salad forks and cake spoons that I sterilised yesterday evening and arrange them on the serving trolley. Finally I open a new packet of paper napkins. I step back and survey my work. The food looks incredibly appetising. Perfect.

I pull off the gloves, throw them in the kitchen bin, put on new ones and take the only ashtray I have in the house out of the cupboard. I place it on the dining table where Lenzen and I are to sit. I have already laid out a few advance copies of my book, a thermal coffeepot, cream, sugar, cups and spoons, as well as bottles of mineral water and glasses.

The ashtray is by far the most important object on the table. I have discovered that Lenzen smokes. If he leaves a cigarette butt it will be like winning the lottery, so he shouldn't have to ask my permission to smoke—he should find an ashtray ready and waiting on the table.

I glance at my phone. I still have loads of time before Lenzen arrives. I breathe in and out, pull off the second pair of gloves and throw them away too. Then I collapse onto the sofa in the living room and go through my mental to-do list. I soon come to the conclusion

74

that I've taken care of everything that needed doing.

I look about me. The cameras and microphones that were installed for me a few days ago by two discreet members of a security company really are invisible. Good. If I can't see them, even though I know they are there, then Lenzen certainly won't be able to. My entire ground floor is bugged. It may seem naïve to presume that Lenzen is going to incriminate himself, but if psychologists—and other experts like Dr Christensen—are to be believed, some murderers are secretly longing to do just that: to confess.

I am prepared. I spent half an hour on the treadmill when I got up this morning—long enough to flood my brain with oxygen but not so long as to wear myself out. I had a shower. I dressed with care. I'm wearing black. Not blue, which conveys trust, or red, which emanates aggression and passion, or white, which stands for innocence, but black. Black means seriousness, gravity—and, yes, mourning.

I've had a good breakfast. There was salmon and spinach: pure brain food, according to a nutritional expert I once spoke to. After breakfast, I fed Bukowski and put him in one of the upstairs bed-rooms with a bowl of water, something to eat for later and some of his favourite toys.

Now here I am on the sofa.

I think back to the telephone call I made some weeks ago to an expert from the regional criminal investigation department, and recall Professor Kerner's cheerful manner, which stood in such stark contrast to the topic of our conversation.

I had decided to ask him for his discretion, and then to lay all my cards on the table and tell him everything. I told him about my sister Anna. I told him about the unsolved murder case. And I wound up by asking him my most important question: whether the traces of DNA that were gathered at the scene of the crime all those years ago had been kept.

'But of course!' he replied.

I am glad I talked to Kerner. Because, of course, if there's one thing I want more than anything else, it's for my sister's murderer to break down in front of me. I have to find out what happened on that goddamn night, and I have to hear it from his own mouth. The thought of Kerner and his DNA samples reassures me. He is my safety net. I'm going to get Lenzen. One way or another.

I glance at the clock. It's a little after eleven. I still have almost an hour to relax and go over everything in my head one last—

There's a ring at the door. I start up in alarm. Adrenalin fills my belly and rushes to my head like a surge of cold water. My composure has vanished. I steady myself on the arm of the sofa, take three deep breaths, and then head for the door. Maybe the postman. Or a travelling salesman—do such people still exist?

I open the door.

For years, the monster has pursued me even in my dreams. Now he's standing before me.

'Good morning,' says Victor Lenzen with an apologetic smile, and holds out his hand to me. 'I'm Victor Lenzen. We're a bit early. We left Munich in good time to make sure we weren't late, but the traffic was much better than we expected.'

I suppress the impulse to run away screaming. I feel caught out, but I don't show it.

'No trouble at all,' I say. 'I'm Linda Conrads.'

I shake his hand. I smile. *The way out of fear leads through fear.*

'Please come in.'

I do not hesitate. I do not tremble. I look him in the eye and my voice sounds strong and clear. It is only now that my tunnel vision opens out a little and I notice the photographer. He is young (mid-twenties, at most), and when I give him my hand he looks a bit nervous—nervous, but keen. He says something about being a fan of mine, but I have trouble focusing on him.

I let the two men into my house. They both wipe their feet politely. Lenzen is wearing a dark coat, which he takes off to reveal immaculate clothes: dark trousers, a white shirt, a black jacket, no tie. He is

76

greying stylishly, and has just the right kind of wrinkles.

I take his coat and the photographer's parka and hang them on the hooks in the hall, casting stolen glances at the two men as I do so. Victor Lenzen is one of those people whose charisma cannot be reproduced on a photo, whose presence transforms the atmosphere of a room. Lenzen is surprisingly attractive, in an unusual and dangerous way.

I'm annoyed at my flitting thoughts, and try to concentrate.

The men seem apprehensive in the large, elegant hallway of the house of this egocentric novelist who never sets foot outside. They feel like intruders. That's good; uneasiness is good. I lead the way to the dining room, taking the moment to collect myself. Here goes. Their early arrival was, of course, intentional on Lenzen's part, calculated to put me off my stride and allow him to take the helm, to dictate the course of action, to show me right from the start that I was not in control of the situation. It did, it is true, throw me briefly, but I have recovered my composure. I am surprised at how little I actually feel, now that everything's under way. I'm in a kind of daze; I feel like an actor when the curtain goes up, an actor who's playing the part of Linda Conrads. All this is a kind of act, really—a show put on for the cameras and microphones in my house, to which Lenzen and I are performing.

My decision to conduct the interview in the dining room was not a strategic one; it was purely intuitive. The living room seemed wrong to me. We'd have had to sit on the sofa, close up to one another— the soft, comfy sofa; it wouldn't have been right. My study is up the stairs, along the corridor, at the end of the passage; it's too far away. The dining room, on the other hand, is ideal. It is close to the front door; it has a large table that creates a certain distance. And it has one further advantage: apart from the times I stand here looking out the window, contemplating the edge of the woods, I hardly ever use it. When I'm alone, I eat in the kitchen. I'm alone a lot. I'd rather sit face-to-face with Lenzen in a room that doesn't mean as much to me as, for instance, the kitchen, where I'm used to chatting to Norbert while we drink rosé and I stir the saucepans. Or the library upstairs, where I travel and dream and love. Where I live.

I try to appear relaxed and not to stare at Lenzen. Out of the corner of my eye I can see him taking in the room in a few sweeping glances. He walks across to the dining table. He puts his bag down on the first chair he comes to, opens it up and glances inside. He's making sure he has everything with him. He seems a tad awkward, almost nervous, but then so does the photographer. If I didn't know any better, I would presume they were simply intent on making a good job of the interview, and put their jumpiness down to that. As far as the photographer is concerned, this may well be the case.

I glance at the large, empty dining table where I've laid out the copies of my new novel. It was not, of course, necessary to display the book; I am sure that everybody here is acquainted with the contents. But from a psychological point of view, it can't be a bad idea to have the indictment to hand. The photographer will think the books are supposed to feature in the pictures. He's fiddling about with his equipment while the monster takes a look around the room.

I sit down, take a water bottle, open it, pour myself a glass. My hands do not tremble. My hands—I ask myself whether it's the first time I've shaken hands with a murderer. After all, you never know. I ask myself how many people I've shaken hands with altogether in my life and how long I've been alive. I do a quick sum in my head. Thirty-eight years: that's about 13,870 days. If I'd shaken hands with one person every day of my life, that would make almost fourteen thousand people. I wonder how many had committed murder, and arrive at the conclusion that this is probably not the first murderer I've shaken hands with—just the only one I know about.

Lenzen glances at me. I force my thoughts to settle down; they're flapping about like startled chickens, but eventually do as I tell them. I'm annoyed. And I'm annoyed that I'm annoyed. This is precisely the kind of carelessness that could prove fatal. I must concentrate from now on—that much I owe Anna.

I look at the monster. I look at Victor Lenzen. I hate his name.

Not only because it's the monster's name, but also because I know that Victor means 'conqueror' and I believe in the magic of names. But this time the story is going to end differently.

'Beautiful house you have here,' says Lenzen, going over to the window. He looks across at the edge of the woods.

'Thank you,' I say, getting up to join him.

When I opened the door to him, the sun had been shining through the clouds. Now there's a light drizzle falling.

'April weather in March,' says Lenzen.

I don't reply.

'How long have you been living here?' he asks.

'More than ten years.'

I jump when I hear the landline ringing in the living room. No one ever rings me on the landline. Anyone who wants to get hold of me calls my mobile. I see Lenzen give me a sidelong glance. The telephone is still ringing.

'Don't you want to answer it?' he asks. 'I don't mind waiting.'

I shake my head, and the ringing stops.

'I'm sure it wasn't important,' I say and hope I'm right.

I take my eyes off the edge of the woods and sit back at the table. It's the place that gives me the strongest sense of security—my back to the wall and the door within eyeshot.

If Lenzen wants to sit opposite me, he'll have to sit with his back to the door. That makes most people nervous and reduces their powers of concentration, but he accepts without protest. If he notices at all, he doesn't let it show.

'Shall we?' I ask.

Lenzen nods and takes a seat opposite me.

He takes out notepad, pen and digital recorder from the bag that he has placed on the floor beside his chair. I wonder what else he has in there. He's focusing his mind. I sit up straight. I feel the urge to cross my legs and fold my arms, but I resist. No protective gestures. I place both feet firmly on the ground. I rest my lower arm on the table and lean forwards, taking up space, asserting myself—what Dr

79

Christensen calls 'power poses'. I watch Lenzen straighten his papers and square up the recorder with the corner of the table.

'Well,' he begins. 'First of all I'd like to thank you for your time. I know that you rarely give interviews and I feel honoured that you've invited me to your house.'

'I'm a great admirer of your work,' I say, hoping to sound noncommittal.

'Really?' He puts on a face, as if he were genuinely flattered. There is a pause and I realise that he's expecting me to elaborate.

'Oh yes,' I say. 'Your reports from Afghanistan, Iran, Syria—you do some important work.'

He lowers his eyes and smiles modestly, as if embarrassed by the praise that he has elicited from me.

What are you playing at, Herr Lenzen?

With my upright posture and my controlled, steady breathing, I am sending my body all the signals it needs to be focused yet relaxed, but still my nerves are tense, almost snapping. I can't wait to find out what questions Lenzen has prepared and how he intends to conduct the interview. He must be just as tense, wondering what I'm hoping to achieve, what kind of a hand I've dealt myself, what trumps I have up my sleeve. He clears his throat and glances at his notes. The photographer is busy with his camera; he takes a trial shot, then goes back to looking at his light meter.

'All right,' says Lenzen. 'My first question is the one all your readers must be asking. You're famous for your literary, almost poetic novels. Now, with *Blood Sisters*, you've written your first thriller. Why the switch in genre?'

That is the question I'd expected him to start with and I relax a little. I do not, however, get round to answering, because at that moment I hear noises coming from the hall—a key turning in the lock, then footsteps.

I catch my breath.

'Excuse me,' I say, and get up.

I have to leave Lenzen alone for a minute. But the photographer is there with him, and the idea that *he* might be in cahoots with Lenzen doesn't make any sense at all.

I go out into the hall and my heart sinks.

'Charlotte!' I cry, unable to conceal my dismay. 'What are you doing here?'

She frowns at me, her coat dripping.

'Isn't it the interview today?'

She hears the murmurs of the two men coming from the dining room and looks at her watch in bewilderment.

'Oh God, I'm not late, am I? I thought the whole thing didn't start until twelve!'

'I wasn't actually expecting you at all,' I whisper, because I don't want Lenzen to hear. 'I left a message on your voicemail. Didn't you get it?'

'Oh, I lost my mobile the other day,' Charlotte says casually. 'But now that I'm here…'

She leaves me standing there, puts her bunch of keys down on the sideboard next to the door and hangs up her flimsy Little Red Riding Hood coat.

'What can I do for you?'

I have to restrain myself from slapping her and pushing her back out with force. The murmuring in the dining room has stopped—the men must be eavesdropping.

I need to get a grip on myself. Charlotte is looking at me expectantly. In this brief moment of silence, the telephone starts to ring again. I do my best to ignore it.

'I've finished getting everything ready,' I say. 'But you could make some coffee—that would be great.'

I have already made coffee; it's in the thermal pot on the table. But no matter—I don't know whether I can avoid an encounter between Charlotte and Lenzen, though I'll try to at all costs.

'Sure,' says Charlotte. She glances in the direction of the living room, where the insistent ringing continues, but she passes no comment.

'I'll come and collect the pot in a minute,' I call after her. 'I'd like to be left undisturbed until then.'

Charlotte frowns again, because I'm not normally like that, but presumably puts it down to the unusual situation: I never have strangers to the house and certainly never give interviews. The telephone goes quiet. I toy with the idea of looking to see who the persistent caller was, but think better of it. Nothing can be as important as this.

I return to the dining room.

12

SOPHIE

From her car, Sophie watched a ginger and white cat lying on the lawn in front of the house giving itself a thorough wash. For a good ten minutes now, she'd been trying to psych herself up to enter the building where Britta had lived.

The day had got off to a bad start. When she had finally dropped off after a sleepless night, Sophie had been woken by a journalist wanting to speak about her sister. She had hung up, furious. Then she had rung Britta's landlord to find out when she could collect Britta's belongings from the flat, but couldn't get hold of him. Instead, she had talked to his son, who had offered her his condolences and then plunged into a story about his brother, who had died in a car crash as a schoolboy—so, of course, he knew exactly what Sophie was going through.

Now she was sitting here, in the car. It was a hot day; the sun was beating down on the black roof. Sophie didn't want to get out; she wanted to sit and watch the cat for a little while longer. But, as if the creature had guessed her thoughts and didn't fancy being watched, it rose elegantly, casting a disdainful look in her direction, and marched off.

Sophie sighed, summoned all her energy and got out.

From somewhere nearby, maybe from behind the house, came the sound of children playing. There was no sign that anything terrible had ever happened here. All the same, Sophie had to force herself to take every step that brought her nearer the front door. When she finally stood at the door of the block of flats, she swallowed, scanning the names on the doorbell panel. Britta's makeshift label was still there, written in her schoolgirl handwriting and stuck on with sticky tape. Sophie averted her eyes and, pressing her lips together, rang the bell of the elderly lady on the second floor. A crackle indicated that someone had activated the intercom.

'Yes?' came a faint voice. 'Who is it?'

'Hello, it's Sophie Peters—Britta Peters' sister.'

'Oh. Ah ha. Come on up, Frau Peters.'

The door buzzed. Sophie gritted her teeth and found herself in the hallway. She hurried as quickly as she could past the door to Britta's ground-floor flat and on towards the stairs. On the second floor she was met by an old lady with smartly cut short hair and a pearl necklace.

Sophie held out her hand.

'Come on in,' the woman said.

Sophie followed her along a passage into an old-fashioned living room. The pastel colours, the lace doilies, the antiquated wall unit and the lingering smell of boiled potatoes were improbably soothing.

'Nice of you to come so quickly,' the old lady said, after offering Sophie a seat on the sofa and a cup of tea.

'But of course,' Sophie replied. 'I came as soon as I got your message.'

She blew on her tea and took a small sip.

'The neighbours said you'd been asking whether anyone had seen anything.'

'I thought people might tell me more than they'd told the police,' Sophie replied. 'You never know. To be honest with you, I go mad at the moment if I don't get out of the house a bit.'

The old lady nodded.

'I know what it's like,' she said. 'I was the same when I was a girl—always up and doing.' She took a sip of her own tea.

'I was at the doctor's when you were asking around,' she said. 'That's why you didn't find me in.'

'I see. Have you told the police what you saw?' Sophie asked.

'Oh, them...' said the old lady with a dismissive gesture.

Sophie frowned. 'But you did see somebody?'

The old lady began to rub away at an invisible stain on her dress. Sophie put her tea down and leant forward. She could barely control her trembling hands.

'You said you'd seen the man who killed my sister,' she prompted her, when the woman showed no sign of volunteering any information.

The old lady stared at her for a moment, then gave a loud sob and slumped down in her chair.

'I still can't believe it,' she said. 'Such a lovely girl. She always did my shopping for me, you know. I'm not as steady on my feet as I used to be.'

Sophie watched the woman cry for a few moments. She wasn't capable of feeling anything much at the moment. She rummaged in her bag for a tissue and handed it to the woman, who took it and dabbed at her eyes.

'You said you'd seen somebody,' Sophie repeated, when the old lady had calmed down a little. Every muscle in her body seized up as she waited for the reply.

Going over the conversation in her head as she drove along the motorway, Sophie could hardly contain her anger. The whole thing had turned out to be a huge disappointment. The woman was lonely and had fancied a chat with someone about Britta, who had visited her regularly. On top of everything else, she had cataracts and was nearly blind. Sophie had listened to her for a little while longer and then made a dash for it.

She thought of Britta as she overtook a car—Britta, who had helped old ladies with their shopping and must have listened to their stories with the patience of a saint.

Sophie drove as if in a trance. Eventually, she slowed the car and flicked on the indicator. She had reached her destination.

The young woman who opened the door flung her arms around Sophie's neck.

'Sophie!'

'Hello, Rike.'

'How lovely to see you. Come in. We'll sit in the kitchen.'

Sophie followed Friederike into the house.

'How are you? And your parents? How are they bearing up?'

Sophie was used to these questions by now and was ready with a stock phrase. 'We do our best,' she said.

'You were all so brave at the funeral.'

Friederike's lower lip trembled. Sophie opened her handbag and, for the second time that afternoon, took out a tissue.

'I'm so sorry,' Friederike said tearfully. 'I should be the one comforting you!'

'Britta was your best friend,' Sophie replied. 'You have as much right to be sad as I do.'

Friederike took the tissue and blew her nose.

'It was so odd at the funeral,' she said. 'Throwing flowers on the coffin, when Britta hated cut flowers.'

'I know,' Sophie said and almost had to smile. 'It was the same when my parents and I were planning the funeral. The undertaker looked at us as if we were mad when we said that Britta didn't like them. "What do you mean? All women love flowers!"'

Friederike gave a sniffly laugh.

'Not Britta,' she said. 'The poor flowers. Imagine, you're standing there in a meadow, minding your own business, and somebody comes along and snaps off your head.'

The two women had to laugh.

'Sometimes Britta could be a real fruitcake,' Sophie said.

Friederike smiled, but the moment passed as quickly as it had come. Tears welled up in her eyes again.

'It's so unbelievably awful. I can't get my head round it.' She wiped her tears away. 'Did you really see him?'

Sophie winced.

'Yes,' she said simply.

'My God. I'm so glad *you're* all right, at least.'

She cried for a while, sobbing loudly, then made an effort to pull herself together.

'Do you know what I miss most?' she asked.

'What?'

'Ringing Britta when I need advice,' Friederike said. 'It's weird. I'm three years older than her, but she was definitely the more grown-up of the two of us. I don't know what I'll do without her.'

'I know what you mean,' Sophie said. 'Britta always said out loud the things everyone else was only thinking: "You've put on an awful lot of weight, my dear sister. Maybe you should be a bit more careful what you eat!" "Sophie, are you sure Paul's the right man for you? I don't like the way he looks at other women." "That bag's real leather, isn't it, sis? Are you all right with that?"'

Friederike gave a quick burst of laughter.

'That really does sound like Britta,' she said. 'It's funny. It used to annoy me sometimes. Now there's nothing I'd like more than to hear one of Britta's lectures on our plastic-polluted oceans, or the atrocities of factory farming.'

Friederike sniffed, then blew her nose.

'What did you want to talk to me about, Sophie?'

'I wanted to ask you something.'

'Go on.'

'Do you know if Britta had been seeing anyone lately?'

'A man, you mean?'

'Exactly.'

'No. Not since Leo left her.'

Sophie sighed. The crime of passion theory favoured by the police (that much she had managed to glean from the interviews) was seeming less and less likely. Britta had not been in a relationship at the time of her murder.

'Why did they split up?' Sophie asked. 'Britta never talked about it.'

'Because he's a complete prick, that's why. He even accused her of cheating on him.'

'Excuse me?'

'Yeah,' Friederike snorted. 'Britta—unfaithful! Can you believe it? If you ask me, there'd been something going on for a while between him and that Vanessa he's going out with now, and he wanted to blame the break-up on Britta.'

'Why would he have done that?'

Friederike shrugged.

'It doesn't matter now anyway,' she said at length.

Sophie nodded. Her heart sank. She hadn't really believed the police would be proved right about the *crime passionnel*, but that didn't stop her from hoping that Britta had been seeing someone in secret. Crimes committed within a relationship were almost always solved. But when there was no obvious connection between perpetrator and victim, it became tricky for the investigators, and the chances of solving the crime plummeted.

'Anyway,' Friederike said, jolting Sophie out of her thoughts, 'it wouldn't have made sense for Britta to go on dates. Why would she have carried on dating?'

'What do you mean?' Sophie asked.

'Oh my God,' said Friederike. 'Didn't you know?'

14

I am having trouble getting used to the idea that Charlotte's in the kitchen making coffee, when I wanted to avoid having her here at any price. Nothing I can do about it now.

Victor Lenzen looks at me with raised eyebrows when I enter the dining room.

'Everything all right?' he asks, and I have to admire his cold-bloodedness, because of course he knows I'm not remotely all right.

He's still sitting in the same place, digital recorder in front of him, while the photographer has spread out his equipment on the floor and is eating cake.

'Everything's great,' I reply, taking care not to let my body language say the opposite. I look at the glass of water at my place at the table, and make a mental note not to drink another drop from it now it's been unsupervised for a few minutes.

I wonder whether Lenzen has had the same thought and thinks that *I* might try to poison *him*. Is that the reason he's not eating anything?

I'm about to sit down when the photographer stops me.

'Frau Conrads, could we get the photos out of the way first? Then I won't have to interrupt the interview later.'

I hate having my photograph taken, but of course I don't say so. Fear of cameras is a weakness. A minor one, perhaps, but a weakness nevertheless.

'Of course. Where would you like me?'

He considers for a moment.

'Which is your favourite room?'

The library, no doubt about it, but it's upstairs and I'm damned if I'm going to let these men traipse all through the house to my inner sanctum.

'The kitchen,' I reply.

'The kitchen it is, then,' says the photographer. 'Great!'

'See you in a second,' says Lenzen.

I register the look that the photographer gives him. It's only a brief glance, but I realise that the two men don't like each other. This makes the photographer immediately sympathetic to me.

I lead the way. Lenzen is left alone in the dining room. I can see him out of the corner of my eye, playing with his phone. I hadn't intended to let him out of my sight for an instant, but I have no choice. This has all got off to a bad start.

We enter the kitchen, where Charlotte has put the coffee on. The gurgle of the machine, the smell—it's familiar and comforting.

'We're just going to take a few photos,' I say.

'I'm on my way out,' Charlotte replies.

'You're welcome to stay and watch if you like,' I say, to prevent her from going into the dining room. Even as I say it, I realise it might sound strange. Why would I want her to watch me having my photo taken?

'I'll go and see what Bukowski's up to,' Charlotte says. 'Where is he?'

'In my bedroom. Make sure he doesn't get out—we need peace and quiet down here,' I say, and ignore her disapproving look.

She slips out. The photographer positions me at the kitchen table, arranges the newspaper and coffee cups in front of me, takes aim and shoots.

I'm having trouble focusing. My thoughts are on Lenzen in the dining room. I wonder what he's doing, what he's thinking, what his plan of action is.

I ask myself what he knows about me. He's read the book: that much is clear. He will have recognised the murder he committed. I can only speculate on what he felt as he read it. And what about his feelings in the hours, days and weeks that followed? Anger? Fear of discovery? Uncertainty? He had two possibilities: to turn the interview down and keep out of my way, or to come here and face me. He's gone for the second option. He's taken the bait. Now he'll want to find out my plans, and what I have that can be used against him. Over the years, he's bound to have given a fair amount of thought to the witness to his crime—to that moment when, for an awful instant, we looked each other in the eye in an apartment laid waste by death. Has his crime haunted him? Was he afraid of being discovered? Did he make any attempt to find out who the witness was? Did he find out? Did he think of getting rid of her? Her—me?

'You're completely different from what I'd imagined,' the photographer says, startling me out of my thoughts.

Concentrate, Linda.

'Really? In what way?'

'I don't know. I thought you'd be older, crazier. Not as pretty.'

That is blunt, but it's clear that he means it, and I give him a smile.

'You thought I was an old lady?' I say, feigning the amazement that befits a reclusive but by no means crazy author. Then I add coyly, 'Didn't you say you were a fan?'

'Oh, yes, I think your books are terrific,' he says, as he focuses the camera. 'But I somehow imagined the author to be old.'

'I see.'

I really do. Norbert once told me I have the mind of an

eighty-five-year-old man, and I know what he meant. I'm stuck in my head. I have nothing in common with other women my age. The reality of my life is far removed from that of a normal thirty-eight-year-old. I lead the life of an old lady, with children grown up and gone, husband dead a long time, most friends likewise dead. A frail, housebound old lady. Bodiless. Asexual. Stuck in her head, as I said. That's the way I live, the way I am, the way I feel—and presumably also the way I sound when I write.

'Apart from anything else,' the photographer continues, 'when you hear about a woman who never leaves the house, the first thing you think of is some dotty old thing who lives with twenty cats. Or else a wacko eccentric—Michael Jackson style.'

'I'm sorry I don't live up to your expectations.'

I say that more brusquely than I'd intended and he falls silent. He goes back to fiddling around with his camera, takes aim once more and shoots. I look at him. He is the picture of health. He is tanned and athletic. He's wearing a T-shirt, even though it's winter. He has a small graze on his left hand—I bet he goes skateboarding or something.

The photographer pours a cup of steaming coffee and hands it to me.

'This will look great—with the steam from the coffee in front of your face. I'll see if I can capture it.'

I take the cup, drink. He shoots.

I look at him and try to guess his age. He seems so young. He's probably in his late twenties. We're only separated by a decade, but I feel a hundred years older than him.

My stomach seizes up as if I had a cramp. Charlotte is sitting opposite Lenzen. There's something the matter with her face; it looks... different. Wrong. There's something not quite right about her eyes, her mouth, her hands, her whole body; her entire manner is somehow *wrong*. She looks up when I enter the room and leaps to her feet. I've interrupted a conversation—damn it, they've been talking to each other for goodness knows how long; the photo shoot has taken a while. Think of all the things that could have happened in that time! I recall my nightmare—Lenzen's bloody hands, Charlotte with her throat slit, her little boy, the 'cheeky devil', sitting in a pool of blood, and Lenzen looking at his hands and grinning.

I run through all the things Charlotte knows about me and wonder whether she could have said anything that might get me into trouble. But she knows nothing. She knows nothing, thank God, about the microphones in the house, or the cameras, or any of that. But here she is, face-to-face with my sister's murderer; she exchanges another glance with him, brushes a strand of hair behind her ear, touches her throat with the tips of her fingers, and Lenzen notices—his laughter lines deepen (he has laughter lines and I hate him for his laughter lines; he doesn't deserve them) and, for a second, I see him through Charlotte's eyes—an attractive middle-aged man, educated and sophisticated—and at last I know why she looks so wrong to me. She's flirting. I realise that I have a very one-sided idea of Charlotte. I've never seen her with other people, and I realise how out of touch I am with real life, and how little I know about people and relationships. Everything I do know is informed by distant memories and books. Charlotte is flirting quite openly with Lenzen!

When Lenzen notices me, he turns and gives me a friendly smile.

'Should I go back out?' I ask. I try to sound lighthearted, but I can hear that I've failed.

'I'm sorry,' Charlotte says guiltily. 'I didn't mean to disturb you.'

'Don't worry, it's all right,' I reply. 'But I don't think I'll be needing you anymore today, Charlotte. How about taking the rest of the day off?'

If Charlotte is aware that I'm trying to get rid of her, she ignores it.

'Shouldn't I go and check on Bukowski first?' she asks.

'Who's Bukowski?' Lenzen intervenes.

My heart seizes up.

'He's Frau Conrads' dog,' Charlotte blurts out before I can reply. 'Such a cutie, you wouldn't believe it.'

Lenzen purses his lips with interest. I could cry. Lenzen shouldn't be in the same room as Charlotte and he shouldn't know anything about Bukowski. In this appalling moment, I know I was wrong to think I had nothing to lose. There are still things that I am fond of. I have a great deal to protect, and therefore to lose. The monster knows that.

Lenzen smiles. The menace in his smile is meant only for me.

I suddenly feel dizzy. I focus on getting back to my chair without tripping or falling. Luckily, Lenzen isn't paying attention to me at this moment.

'Are you done?' he asks the photographer, who appears in the doorway just as Charlotte is leaving. She manoeuvres her way past him, laughing.

'Nearly. I'd like to shoot another couple of photos during the interview itself, if that's all right with you, Frau Conrads.'

'No problem.'

I grip the edge of the table. I must calm down. Maybe I should eat something. I let go, satisfy myself that my legs will bear my weight again, and stagger over to the serving trolley. I help myself to a wrap and bite into it.

'Please, have something to eat too,' I say, turning to Lenzen and the photographer. 'Otherwise I'll be left with all this.'

'I won't wait to be asked twice,' the photographer replies, taking a jar filled with lentil salad.

To my immense relief, Lenzen also gets up and heads to the serving trolley. I hold my breath as he takes a chicken wrap and begins to eat. I do my best not to stare at him, but I can see a smidgen of coronation sauce clinging to his upper lip. I see him lick it off; I see him finish the wrap. I watch in suspense while Lenzen wipes his fingers on a napkin and then finally, as he's sauntering coolly back to the table, passes the napkin over his mouth.

I can't believe it. Is it really that easy? I sit down. Lenzen looks at me. We're sitting face-to-face like finalists at a chess tournament. Lenzen's smile has vanished.

JONAS

Sophie was calm and collected; a less astute observer would hardly have noticed the strain she was under. But Jonas saw her jaw clench whenever Antonia Bug asked her a question.

He looked away. He felt sorry for her. He always tried to see the events through the eyes of the witnesses and the images were often harder to shake off than he would have liked. Without shedding a tear, Sophie had once again given a precise and detailed account of how she had found her sister murdered in her flat. Only the way her knuckles had stood out white under the skin of her clenched fists had betrayed how tense she really was. Jonas was struggling to see her as merely another witness called back for questioning—as a murder witness, not the woman who'd sat on his front steps and, with a few phrases, a few glances, a smile and half a cigarette, dispelled the feeling of alienation that had been plaguing him for so long. A witness, he told himself. Nothing more.

Antonia Bug had been about to ask another question, but Sophie got in first.

'There's one more thing,' she said. 'Of course, I don't know whether it's important.'

'Everything is important,' said Jonas.

'I went to see Friederike Kamps yesterday—my sister's best friend. She told me that Britta had been planning to leave Munich.'

'So?' asked Bug.

'I don't know,' Sophie said. 'It seems odd to me. Britta loved Munich. She didn't want to leave. When she graduated a year ago, she was offered a great job in Paris, but turned it down because she didn't want to move to another city.'

Sophie hesitated.

'As I said, I don't know whether it's important. But maybe there's a connection. Maybe Britta wanted to leave Munich because she felt threatened.'

'Did your sister ever mention feeling threatened?' Jonas asked.

'No! Never! I've told you that a thousand times,' Sophie snapped.

'And yet you believe...' Bug said. Sophie interrupted her.

'Listen! I'm clutching at straws here. As far as I know, everything was fine with Britta.'

'And you were very close to each other, you said?' Bug asked.

Sophie suppressed a sigh. Jonas sensed that her patience was wearing thin.

'Yes,' was all she said.

'What were you doing at your sister's at that time of night?' Bug asked.

'Nothing in particular. I'd had a stupid row with my fiancé and wanted to talk to Britta.'

'What was the row about?' Bug asked.

Jonas saw Sophie shift on her chair—a preliminary to that uneasy wriggling which he had so often observed when the awkward questions went on too long. He cast a glance at his colleague. Bug was like a pit bull when it came to interrogations.

'I don't see what that has to do with my sister's murder,' Sophie replied.

'Please answer my question,' Antonia Bug said calmly.

'Listen, I've given you a description of the man who ran out of my sister's flat. Shouldn't that be of more interest to you than the ups and downs of my relationship?'

'Of course,' said Bug, noncommittal. 'Just a few more questions. What time did you arrive at your sister's?'

'I've already been through all this,' Sophie said and got up. 'I'm going to my parents' now. There's a lot to do—clear out Britta's flat and...'

She left the sentence hanging.

'We're not finished yet,' Bug protested, but Sophie ignored her and picked up the bunch of keys from the chair beside her.

'Please let me know if you hear anything,' she said to Jonas. 'Please.'

She looked him in the eye one last time, then she was gone.

Antonia Bug stared at Jonas.

'If you hear anything?' she echoed. 'What's that supposed to mean? Since when have we been service providers for witnesses?'

Jonas shrugged. His young colleague didn't know that the witness had only recently been standing at his front door—or rather, sitting on his front steps. Thank goodness she didn't. If anyone suspected that he'd been talking to a witness about the investigation, he'd be in serious trouble.

'You don't believe her, do you?' Bug asked.

'Of course I believe her,' Jonas replied. 'And so do you, even if you don't like her.'

Bug snorted. 'You're right, Herr Weber,' she said. 'I don't like her.'

Jonas looked at her and smiled. Sometimes she really got on his nerves, but he liked her bluntness. Bug had only been on the team for a few months, but her drive and gutsiness had almost immediately made her irreplaceable.

'Isn't it time we were on first-name terms?' he asked.

Antonia Bug's face lit up.

'Toni,' she said.

'Jonas.'

She made a big deal of shaking hands with him, as if to clinch the matter.

'Well,' she said, looking at the clock, 'we need to be going next door. Team meeting.'

'All right,' said Jonas. 'You go on ahead; I'll join you in a second. I'm just going out to have a smoke.'

'Okay.'

Jonas watched Bug disappear in the direction of the conference room, her ponytail bouncing behind her. His thoughts strayed to Sophie Peters. All through the questioning she'd held up bloody well—no outbursts, no tears. Jonas put a cigarette between his lips as he headed outside; he felt for his lighter and was about to snap it open when he saw her, sitting on the low wall that edged the patch of lawn in front of the building.

She was slumped over, her face buried in her hands. Her heaving shoulders told him how hard she was crying. Jonas froze. Sophie hadn't seen him. He wondered whether he should go to her, then thought better of it.

Back in the conference room, he couldn't get Sophie out of his head. He watched the last of his colleagues trickle in for the meeting and felt a loathing for this room, with its strip lighting and its smell of PVC and coffee, where he had already spent so many hours.

Silence fell. Jonas realised that everyone was looking at him expectantly, and forced himself to concentrate.

'Well,' he said, addressing no one in particular. 'Who would like to begin?'

Antonia Bug plunged in.

'First of all,' she began in her staccato-like way, 'there's the ex-boyfriend, who probably wasn't even in the country at the time of the murder. That's something we're looking into.'

Jonas had a very clear image of what Bug must have been like as a child—precocious, overeager, a swot. But popular all the same— blonde ponytail, glasses, her cutesy exercise books filled with neat, joined-up handwriting.

He let his thoughts wander. He'd long since read all the information that the team had put together about the victim and her social milieu: Britta Peters, twenty-four years old, graphic designer for an internet start-up, single, in good health. Killed with seven knife wounds. No sexual assault. The murder weapon, probably a kitchen knife, missing. It all pointed to a row with someone she knew—an outburst of rage, an act of panic, a sudden fit of anger. The partner. Whenever anything like that happened, it was always the victim's partner; the mystery murderer only exists in films. Yet the victim's sister claimed to have seen the murderer, and not only she but all the victim's acquaintances swore that Britta Peters had been single, that she had lost interest in dating after a painful separation, nothing in her head but work, work, work.

The voice of Volker Zimmer, a colleague known for his ped- antry, brought Jonas back to earth. Bug had come to the end of her monologue.

'I've been asking around in the block of flats where the victim lived and in the neighbourhood,' Zimmer said. 'It didn't yield much to begin with. But then I talked to a woman who lives in the flat above the victim and is about the same age.'

Jonas waited for Zimmer to get to the point. He was familiar with

Zimmer's wordiness, but he also knew that he only ever spoke if he really had something to say.

'She claims that Britta Peters was furious because her landlord had several times taken the liberty of going into her flat while she was out. It seems that she was more than a little upset by this; she'd even thought of moving out.'

'Understandable,' Bug threw in.

'Does the landlord live in the same block?' Jonas asked.

'Yes,' Zimmer replied, 'he has the big penthouse flat at the top.'

'Have you spoken to him?'

'He wasn't in. But I'll drive round again later.'

Jonas nodded pensively and his thoughts began to drift again, as Michael Dzierzewski, a dependably cheerful elderly colleague with whom Jonas went to the occasional football match, began to report on details concerning the victim's place of work.

When the meeting came to a close, the team dispersed to check up on ex-boyfriends, landlords and male colleagues. Jonas watched his own colleagues go about their work with professional zeal. He thought of Sophie and the promise he had made her, and wondered whether he would be able to keep it.

Back in his office, he sat down at his desk. He glanced at the framed photograph of him and Mia in happier times. He contemplated it for a moment, then decided that now was not the time to be dwelling on his marriage, and set to work.

15

Victor Lenzen has amazing eyes—so clear and cold. They stand in contrast to the wrinkles in his weather-beaten face. Victor Lenzen resembles a beautiful ageing wolf. He looks at me and I still haven't got used to his look. In my absence, he has taken off his jacket and hung it over the back of the chair. He has also rolled up the sleeves of his white shirt a little.

My gaze comes to rest on his lower arm, on the texture of his skin. I can see the individual cells that make it up. I imagine running a finger along a protruding vein, feeling the warmth emanating from him, and I am choked by an emotion that I could really do without right now. I have been alone for a very long time. A handshake or a fleeting hug are all the physical contact I've tolerated over the past years. Why do I have to think these thoughts now?

'Can we?' Lenzen asks.

Here we go. I must concentrate. I've survived the photo shoot and now we're off—the interview can begin.

'I'm ready,' I say.

I sit up straight, aware of my rigid body.

Lenzen gives a quick nod. He has his papers in front of him but doesn't refer to them.

'Frau Conrads, once again thank you very much for inviting us to your beautiful house.'

'Not at all.'

'First question then—how are you?'

'I'm sorry?' I say, surprised at the question, and realise from the soft click on my left that the photographer has recorded the moment. I am still struggling with dizziness and surges of nausea, but I don't let it show.

'I mean, you live a very secluded life—that's common knowledge. So it's only natural that your many readers should wonder how you are.'

'I'm well,' I say.

Lenzen's nod is barely perceptible. He looks me in the face, not taking his eyes off me. Is he trying to read me?

'You've had great success with your novels. Why have you switched genre and written a thriller?'

Back to the opening question, which I didn't get round to answering earlier because Charlotte interrupted us. Good. I am prepared for this question—which cannot be said of Lenzen's bizarre preamble. I give him the spiel I've rehearsed.

'As you mentioned before, my life is far from normal. I don't leave the house, don't go to work, don't go to the baker's or the supermarket. I don't travel, I don't meet friends in cafés or clubs. I live a life that is very secluded, which means it is not always easy to avoid boredom. Writing is my way of allowing myself to escape a bit, and I wanted to try out something different. Of course I understand if some of the people who liked my previous books are surprised by the new direction, but I needed a kind of literary change of scene.'

While I'm talking, Lenzen takes a sip of water—very good. The more traces he leaves behind, the better.

'And why, of all the genres available to an author, did you choose the thriller?' Lenzen persists.

'Maybe because it offers the greatest possible contrast to my previous work.'

Sounds plausible enough. It is important to get the interview off to a normal start. Let Lenzen wonder what I'm hatching—I don't care. I'll strike when he's least expecting it.

He has a quick look through his notes now, and my gaze falls on the ashtray on the table

'You don't happen to have a cigarette for me, do you?' I ask.

Lenzen looks at me in surprise. 'Yes, I do,' he says.

My heart gives a leap when Lenzen digs a blue packet of Gauloises out of his pocket and holds it out to me. I take one.

'Do you have a light?' Lenzen asks.

I shake my head. Hope I'm not going to have a coughing fit; I haven't smoked for ages. Hope to goodness it's not all for nothing, and that Lenzen's going to take one too. He feels in the breast pocket of his jacket for his lighter and finds it. He gives me a light across the table. I get up and lean towards him. His face comes closer; my pulse quickens, and I can see that he has freckles—how amazing, he has a few freckles in among his wrinkles. Our eyes meet, I lower my gaze, my cigarette catches. A click tells me that the photographer has pressed the shutter release button.

I suppress a cough, my lungs are on fire.

Lenzen turns the cigarette packet over in his hands—once, twice—then puts it away.

'I smoke too much,' he says and returns to his notes.

What a shame!

Bravely, I smoke the cigarette in long, slow drags. It tastes revolting. I am dizzy. My body isn't used to the nicotine; it rebels against it. I feel weak.

'Where were we?' Lenzen asks. 'Ah yes, the switch in genre. Do you read thrillers yourself?'

'I read everything,' I reply.

I had hoped that, as time went on, I would get used to his wolfish eyes, but it's not happening. For some minutes, I've been trying not to run my hand through my hair, because I know it's a gesture of insecurity, but now I can't hold it back any longer. Once again, the photographer releases the shutter.

'What thrillers have impressed you recently?' Lenzen asks.

I list a handful of authors I rate highly—a few Americans, some Scandinavians, the odd German.

'You live an extremely secluded life. Where do you find your inspiration?'

'There are good stories on every street corner,' I say, stubbing out the cigarette.

'Only you never go out on the street,' Lenzen replies smugly.

I choose to ignore him.

'I am very interested in what goes on in the world,' I say. 'I read the papers, watch the news, spend a lot of time on the internet, gathering information. The world is full of stories; you have to keep your eyes open. And, of course, I'm extremely grateful to modern means of communication and to the media for making it possible for me to bring the world into my house.'

'How do you research? Also on the internet?'

I am about to reply when I hear it. My breathing and heartbeat suddenly quicken.

It's not possible. You're imagining things.

My jaws tightens.

'I do most of my research by…' I say, trying to concentrate. 'For this book, I read, I read…'

I'm not imagining things; it really is there. I hear music. Everything's spinning.

'I read a lot about the psyche of… I…'

Love, love, love. The music swells. I blink, my breathing is galloping, I'm close to hyperventilating. Lenzen is right in front of me, his cold, pale eyes turned on me, cruel and patient.

I gasp, disguise it as a cough, break off. For a moment, everything

102

goes black. Keep breathing! Nice and calm! I grope for an anchor, find my water glass, feel it in my hand, smooth and cool. Up, help me up, I have to surface! Here, this smooth, cool feeling in my hand, this is reality—not the music. But it's still playing; I hear it quite clearly, that awful tune.

All you need is love, la-da-da-da-da...

My throat is so dry. I pick up the glass, try to guide it to my lips, spill a little. I'm trembling. I struggle to drink, and then remember that I'm not supposed to drink out of the glass, and put it back down.

'Sorry,' I manage to croak.

Lenzen says something. I hear him as if from under water. The photographer comes into view, a blur. I try to put him in focus. I get hold of the edge of the pool and although the music is still playing—*la-da-da-da-da*—I surface. I look at the photographer. I look at Lenzen. They don't react. I can still hear the music, but they can't. I don't dare ask them. I mustn't seem mad.

'I'm sorry, what was the question again?' I say, and clear my throat.

'How did you go about the research for your latest book?' Lenzen asks.

I get a grip on myself and reel off the answer I've prepared. The photographer circles us and snaps, and I'm back on track, talking on autopilot. Inside, though, I'm in shock. My nerves are playing a trick on me; I'm hearing things, terrible things, and just when I need to be mentally tough.

Bloody hell, Linda, bloody hell.

Lenzen asks another trivial question and I reply. The music goes quiet. The world is turning again. The photographer is staring at his camera. Lenzen looks at him expectantly.

'Are you done?' he asks.

'Yep,' the photographer replies, without looking at Lenzen. 'Thank you, Frau Conrads,' he says. 'It was a pleasure to meet you.'

'Nice to meet you too,' I reply and get up, weak-kneed as a newborn calf. 'I'll see you to the door.'

It does me good to walk a few metres and get my circulation going again. I had almost fainted. It was a near thing. It mustn't happen again—not as long as that man's in my house.

The photographer packs up and shoulders the bag with his equipment. He gives Lenzen a nod, then follows me to the front door. The dizziness is only gradually subsiding; it's still coming at me in brief bursts.

'See you,' the photographer says, taking his parka down from the coat hook. He gives me a warm handshake and looks me in the eye for a moment. 'Take care of yourself,' he says, then he's gone.

16

For a few seconds I watch him go, then I throw back my shoulders and head back to the dining room. I come to an abrupt halt when my eye falls on Lenzen's coat. I'd better give it a quick frisk—you never know. I glance at the dining-room door. I can't hear anything. Quickly, I search the coat pockets, but they are empty. My heart skips a beat when a sound comes from behind me. I spin round.

Victor Lenzen is standing in front of me. He looks at me searchingly.

'Everything all right?' he asks.

His gaze is inscrutable.

'Everything's great. I'm looking for a tissue,' I say, pointing at my cardigan, which is hanging on the hook next to the coat.

For a moment we stand there, neither of us saying a word. The moment drags on. Then Lenzen's face brightens and he smiles at me. What an actor.

'I'll wait for you in the dining room.'

And he turns around and is gone.

I take a deep breath and count to fifty. Then I, too, return to the dining room. Lenzen is sitting at the table; he gives me a friendly look as I go in. I'm on the point of telling him we can continue when the landline starts up again. Who can it be?

'Maybe you should answer it,' says Lenzen. 'It seems to be important.'

'Yes,' I reply. 'Maybe I should. Please excuse me.'

I walk into the living room and approach the mad ringing. I give a baffled frown when I see the Munich number on the display. I know the number; I dialled it just the other day. With trembling fingers, I pick up the receiver, well aware that, in the next room, Lenzen can hear every word I say.

'Linda Conrads.'

'Frau Conrads,' says Professor Kerner. 'I'm glad I've got hold of you.'

He sounds strange.

'What is it?' I ask, instantly alarmed.

'I'm afraid I have rather bad news for you,' he replies.

I hold my breath.

'You enquired about the traces of DNA at the scene of your sister's murder,' Kerner continues. 'Well, I was curious and looked into the matter.'

He hesitates. A dark foreboding creeps over me. If he's going to say what I think he's going to say, I don't want to hear it. Least of all now.

'I'm afraid that the DNA traces from the murder are unusable,' says Kerner.

Everything goes black. I sit down on the bare floorboards, gasping for breath.

As if through cotton wool, I hear Kerner telling me that, unfortunately, it does occasionally happen that samples of DNA get contaminated or go missing. He's very sorry. It was before his time, otherwise it certainly wouldn't have happened. He had deliberated for a long time whether or not to inform me but, in the end, he had said to himself that everybody deserves the truth, even if it's not pretty.

I try to breathe normally again. In the next room, the monster

106

is waiting. Apart from Charlotte, who is still upstairs playing with Bukowski, we are quite alone in this big house, and my plan has come to nothing; all the DNA samples in the world can't help me now. No more safety net. Just Lenzen and me.

'I'm sorry, Frau Conrads,' says Kerner. 'But I thought you ought to know.'

'Thank you,' I say lamely. 'Goodbye.'

I glance out of the window. The cold, sunny dawn that greeted me this morning has turned into a grey day with low-hanging clouds. Somehow I find the strength to get up and return to the dining room. Lenzen turns to look at me as I enter the room. That dangerous man is so cool and collected that it's hard to believe. He watches my every move, like a snake lying in wait, and I think to myself:

I need a confession.

17

SOPHIE

Thick, matronly clouds were hanging low over the houses opposite. Sophie looked out of the window at the sky where a few swifts were darting about. Out there, somewhere under that sky, Britta's murderer lived and breathed. The thought had a cold, metallic taste. Sophie shuddered.

She wondered what it would be like never to leave the flat again. To never again have to set foot in that terrifying world. She brushed the thought aside and looked at her watch. If she wanted to get to the party anywhere near on time, she was going to have to get a move on. She used to love parties and had enjoyed giving her own. Since Britta's death, however, she was glad not to have to laugh and make conversation.

That was exactly what was expected of her today. Her new gallerist, Alfred, with whom she hadn't been working for long, was throwing a lavish garden party to celebrate his fiftieth birthday. The upside was that most of the guests would be from the city's art scene—eccentric artists, wealthy art lovers—people, in a word, with whom Sophie had nothing in common other than her love of painting, and who, for the most part, she didn't know. Nobody, not even her host, knew that her sister had died recently, so no one would embroil her in one of those embarrassed conversations of condolence. At least she was safe from that.

All the same, she had come close to not going. It had been Paul who had thought cancelling would be rude, and that it would also do her good to take her mind off things.

Now Sophie was standing in front of her wardrobe faced with the difficult task of choosing something to wear. The dress code on the invitation demanded summery white; Sophie had worn nothing but black over the past weeks, and going in white felt like fancy dress. She sighed and took out a pair of white linen trousers and a white top with spaghetti straps.

It was a humid evening. The clouds had passed without fulfilling their promise of rain and cooler temperatures. When Sophie and Paul arrived at Alfred's villa, the party was already in full swing. The garden was large and surrounded by dense trees and shrubs like a natural clearing somewhere in the woods. A myriad of lights twinkled in the bushes and trees, giving the garden and the thronging people an unreal quality.

There was nowhere to sit apart from a small swing seat in a remote corner of the garden, where two men were snogging, lost to the world. Beneath an enormous chestnut bearing innumerable lanterns like ripe fruit, a dance floor had been improvised, and next to it a small stage had been put up for the live band, which was nowhere to be seen. Piped music from the speakers was drowned out by the hum of voices that hung over the scene like the soft drone of bumblebees. Now and then the crowd parted to let through the waiters with trays of drinks and canapés. They, too, were dressed in white, in keeping with the dress code, and would hardly have been distinguishable from the guests if not for the dainty antlers they all wore on their heads.

Sophie decided to give in to Paul's pleas and switch off as best she could. She drank a cocktail—then another and another. She ate a few canapés. She wished her gallerist a happy birthday. She helped herself to another drink.

Eventually Alfred stepped onto the small stage. He made a speech, thanked his guests, opened the dance floor, asked the band onto the stage and dedicated the first song of the evening to his wife. Sophie had to smile when Alfred and his wife—the only one dressed not in white but in bright red—blew each other kisses. Her smile died on her lips, however, when the four-man band struck up the first bars of the Beatles' *All You Need is Love*. The world disappeared, a chasm gaped, and Sophie was swallowed up.

17

The tune is still ringing in my ears when I return to the dining room. I sit down, determined to keep my cool from now on.

Lenzen still has on his friendliest face.

'You look pale,' he says. 'If you need a little break, it's no trouble at all. I have plenty of time—I can fit in around you.'

If I didn't know he was a wolf, I would have no trouble believing his concern to be genuine.

'No need,' I say coldly. 'Feel free to continue.'

Inside, however, I am in turmoil. I try to remember all the things Dr Christensen taught me. But the shock is deep; it's as if my head has been swept clean.

'All right then,' says Lenzen. 'What about writing? Do you enjoy writing?'

I look him in the eye. 'Very much,' I reply mechanically.

My sister was called Anna.

'So you're not one of those authors who wrestle with every sentence?'

When I was little, I envied Anna her name that you could read back-wards as well as forwards. She was very proud of that.

'Not at all. Writing for me is like having a shower or cleaning my teeth. In fact, you could almost say it's part of my daily hygiene. If I don't write, I feel as if all my pores are blocked.'

Blood gave Anna the creeps.

'When do you write?'

When I grazed my knee as a child, I would ignore it, and when I cut my finger, I would pop it in my mouth and marvel at the taste of iron, and that I knew what iron tasted like. When Anna grazed her knee as a child, or cut her finger, she would scream and cry and I would say, 'Don't be such a girl!'

'I prefer to start early in the morning, when my thoughts are still fresh and I'm not yet saturated with phone calls and news and every-thing that I see and read and hear in the course of the day.'

'Tell me about your working methods.'

My sister Anna was stabbed seven times.

'I'm disciplined. I sit down at my desk, spread out my notes, open my laptop and write.'

'You make it sound so easy.'

'Sometimes it is.'

'And when isn't it?'

The human body contains four-and-a-half to six litres of blood.

I shrug my shoulders.

'Do you write every day?'

The body of a woman my sister's size contains roughly five litres of blood. After thirty per cent blood loss, the body enters a state of shock. This serves to slow down the rate at which the blood is pumped out of the wound and to reduce the energy and oxygen requirement of the body.

'Nearly every day, yes. Of course, when I've finished a book, there's a phase when I'm looking for new ideas and researching—when I'm still preparing for the next project.'

'On what basis do you decide what your next project will be?'

The last thing Anna saw was her murderer.

'Gut instinct.'

'Your publisher gives you a free hand?'

Before I got my driving licence, I did a first-aid course.

'He does now, yes.'

'How much of yourself do you put in your characters?'

Most of the time, however, I spent flirting with the instructor.

'That's never really a conscious decision. I don't sit down and decide: this character should have thirty per cent of my feelings and that one should have the same childhood memories. But, of course, there's a bit of Linda in all my characters.'

'How long did you take to write your last novel?'

The paramedics and the police all told me that Anna was already dead when I entered the flat.

'Six months.'

'That's not long.'

'No, it's not.'

But I'm not so sure.

'What made you write this book?'

Perhaps the last thing Anna saw was her useless sister.

I don't reply. I reach for a new bottle of water and open it. My hands tremble. I take a sip. Lenzen's eyes track my every move.

'What illness do you have again?' he asks casually, pouring himself a glass too.

Clever wolf. He says it as if it were common knowledge. But we both know that I have never talked publicly about my illness.

'I'd prefer not to talk about it,' I say.

'When did you last leave the house?' Lenzen continues.

'About eleven years ago.'

Lenzen nods.

'What happened eleven years ago?'

I have no answer.

'I'd prefer not to speak about it,' I say.

Lenzen accepts that, only raising his eyebrows slightly.

'How do you cope with being housebound?' he asks.

I sigh. 'What can I say to that?' I reply. 'I don't know how to describe it to somebody who has never experienced it. The world is suddenly very small. And, at some point, you have the feeling that your own head is the world and that beyond your head there is nothing. Everything you see through the windows, everything you hear—pelting rain, deer at the edge of the woods, electric storms over the lake—it all seems so far away.'

'Is that painful?'

'At first it was very painful, yes,' I say. 'But it's amazing how quickly something that begins as unbearable becomes normal. We can resign ourselves to anything, I suppose. Maybe not get to like anything, but resign ourselves. Pain, despair, servitude...'

I make an effort to provide detailed answers, to keep the conversation flowing. A standard interview. Let him stay on his guard. So what if he's left guessing, kept on tenterhooks?

'What do you miss most?'

I consider for a moment. There are so many things that don't exist in my world: other people's brightly lit living rooms for peeking into during the evenings, tourists asking the way, clothes wet from the rain, stolen bikes.

Dropped ice-cream cones melting on hot asphalt, maypoles.

Disputes over parking spaces, meadows of flowers, children's chalk drawings on the pavement, church bells.

'Everything,' I say at length. 'Not necessarily the big things—safaris in Kenya or parachuting over New Zealand or lavish weddings, although of course all that would be nice too. More the little, everyday things.'

'Such as?'

'Walking along a street, seeing someone you like the look of, smiling at him and watching him smile back. The moment when you find out that a new, promising-looking restaurant has opened on the premises that have been empty for so long.'

Lenzen smiles.

'The way little children sometimes stare at you.'

He nods.

'Or the smell in a florist's… Things like that. Having the same human experiences as everyone else and feeling…how can I put it?… connected to everyone else as a result, in life and death and work and pleasure and youth and old age and laughter and anger and everything.'

I pause and realise that, although this isn't really about the interview, I'm making an effort to answer the questions honestly. I don't know why. It feels good to talk. Maybe because I so seldom have anyone I can talk to, or anyone asking me questions.

Bloody hell, Linda.

'And I miss nature,' I say. 'A lot.'

I suppress a sigh because I can feel desire rising in my throat like heartburn.

Maybe all this would be easier if Lenzen were repulsive.

Lenzen is silent, as if to let my words resonate. He seems to be reflecting on them for a moment longer.

But he is not repulsive.

'Are you lonely?' he asks.

'I wouldn't really describe myself as lonely. I have a great many friends and acquaintances, and even if they can't visit me all the time, there are plenty of ways and means to keep in touch nowadays without constant personal contact.'

It is hard to be immune to Lenzen's presence. He is an excellent listener. He looks at me and, without meaning to, I wonder what he sees. His gaze rests on my eyes, strays to my lips, my neck. My heart beats faster with fear and I-don't-know-what.

But when he asks, 'Who are the most important people in your life?' alarm bells are set off in my head.

I'm damned if I'm going to reveal my vulnerabilities to a murderer. I could lie, but decide it would be better to play the cagey celebrity.

'Listen,' I say, 'this is starting to get a bit too personal. I'd prefer to concentrate on questions about my book, as we agreed beforehand.'

Everything is churning away inside me. Somehow I have to get Lenzen to answer my questions.

'Sorry,' says Lenzen, 'I didn't want to intrude.'

'Good,' I reply.

'Are you in a relationship?' Lenzen asks, and I can't help frowning.

He immediately backs off and follows up with another question.

'Why exactly are you giving an interview again after such a long time?'

As if he's not quite sure why he's here.

'I'm doing it at the request of my publishers,' I lie, without batting an eyelid.

A smile plays on Lenzen's lips.

'Back to my last question,' he says, parrying my move. 'Are you in a relationship?'

'Didn't you say you didn't want to intrude?' I ask.

'Oh, sorry. I didn't know that asking about a partner was too private,' Lenzen says. He's put on a remorseful expression, but his eyes are smiling. 'All right then, back to the book. Your main character, Sophie, goes to pieces when her sister dies. I very much like the passages where we are plunged into Sophie's thoughts. How did you manage to work your way into the mind of such a broken and ultimately self-destructive character?'

The hit below the belt is unexpected. After all, Sophie—the broken woman—is me. I swallow hard; my throat is dry. I tell myself that this is the beginning of a conversation that I have to put myself through. I am here as prosecutor, jury and judge. Trial, presentation of evidence, verdict.

Here goes then.

'I would consider it one of my personal strengths that I am extremely good at empathising with all my characters,' I say. 'But, as I see it, Sophie is by no means broken. She almost breaks down at the death of her sister—that's true, I suppose. But in the end she musters all her strength to prove her sister's murderer guilty and eventually succeeds.'

Just as I will succeed. That is the subtext of what I've just said, and Victor Lenzen knows it. He seems to swallow it.

115

'Another interesting character for me is the police officer. Is he based on a real person?'

'No,' I lie. 'I have to disappoint you there.'

'Didn't you consult real policemen when you were working on the book?'

'No,' I say. 'I do admire fellow authors who go to such lengths and carry out meticulous research. But I was more interested in the dynamics between the characters. Psychology is more important to me than technical niceties.'

'As I was reading, I had the feeling that the main character and the married police officer had got quite close to one another—that there were the beginnings of a romance there,' says Lenzen.

'Really?'

'Yes! Reading between the lines, I felt that something could have happened.'

'In that case, you know more than the author,' I say. 'The two characters like each other; that was important to the story. But that's as far as it goes—a few moments of complicity, nothing more.'

'Did you specifically avoid incorporating a love story?' Lenzen asks.

I don't know what he's driving at.

'To be honest with you, it didn't occur to me for a second.'

'Do you think you'd write different books if you led a normal life?'

'I believe that everything we do and experience has an influence on the art we produce, yes,' I say.

'If you were in a relationship, then maybe boy would have got girl at the end of the novel?'

I try not to snort. How stupid does he think I am? But it's a good thing he's getting personal again, because I've had an idea.

'I don't quite follow your line of reasoning,' I say. 'And I've already told you that I don't want to talk about personal matters.'

I hope he won't leave it at that, and my prospects are good, because he's bound to be under orders to wheedle as much personal information out of me as possible. My new book may be of some interest, but

116

there is no doubt that a glimpse into the psyche of the famous and mysterious Linda Conrads is worth so much more.

'It's hard to separate the artist from her work,' says Lenzen.

I nod. 'But you must also understand that I feel uncomfortable talking about personal matters to a stranger,' I reply.

'Okay,' he says, hesitantly. He seems to be wondering how to continue.

'Do you know what,' I say, then pause, pretending I've only recently hit upon the idea, 'I'll answer your questions if, for every question you ask, I can ask one of my own.'

He looks at me in bewilderment, but recovers, conjuring an amused expression.

'You'd like to ask me something too?'

I nod. Lenzen's eyes blaze. He senses that the preliminary skirmish is now over. He imagines I'm going to open the game at last.

'That sounds fair,' he says.

'Then ask away,' I say.

'Who are the most important people in your life?' asks Lenzen without a moment's hesitation.

My thoughts stray to Charlotte, who's still wandering around somewhere in the house, unaware that she met a murderer a moment ago, and maybe a psychopath. To Norbert, who is goodness knows where, but probably fuming. To my parents. To my sister, who has been dead a long time now, but who has also become the most important person in my life since her death. Like a tune you can't get out of your head.

Love, love, love, la-da-da-da-da.

'Nowadays, it's mainly people connected with work,' I say. 'My publisher, my agent, the other people in the company, a handful of friends.'

That is vague and it's best that way. Now it's my turn. I'll begin with innocuous questions to find out how Lenzen replies and reacts when he's relaxed, and then proceed to more provocative questions. Like a lie-detector test.

'How old are you?' I ask.

'What would you guess?'

'I'm asking the questions here.'

Lenzen grins. 'I'm fifty-three,' he replies.

His eyes narrow.

'Are you in a relationship?' he asks again.

'No.'

'Wow,' he says.

That puzzles me.

'Wow?'

'You know what I mean,' says Lenzen. 'You're young, beautiful, incredibly successful. And yet so alone. How on earth do you manage to write about relationships when you're not in one yourself?'

I do my best to forget everything he's said and not to wonder if it's true—that he thinks I'm beautiful, for example.

'It's my turn,' is all I say.

Lenzen shrugs.

'Where did you grow up?' I ask.

'In Munich.'

He's leaning back in his chair and seems on the defensive. Maybe my question-and-answer game is more upsetting to him than he's prepared to admit, even though we've only just begun. But it's his move.

'How do you manage to write about relationships when you're not in one yourself?'

'I'm a writer,' I say. 'I can. Besides, I haven't always lived the way I live now.'

My move.

'Do you have brothers and sisters?' I ask.

A strike below the belt—hard not to think of my own, dead sister. Lenzen must realise that I'm homing in on the real issue. But he doesn't bat an eyelid.

'Yes, an older brother. Do you have brothers and sisters?' he asks, returning the question.

Cold-blooded. I control my emotions and simply say, 'Yes.'

'Brother or sister?'

'It's not your turn, Herr Lenzen,' I say.

'You're very strict, Frau Conrads,' he counters, grinning.

'A sister,' I reply, looking at him steadily.

He withstands my gaze.

'Do you have a good relationship with your parents?' I ask.

'Yes,' says Lenzen. 'That is to say—my mother is no longer alive. But with my father, yes. And with my mother, too, when she was still around.'

Lenzen's hand goes to his temple; I'm watching him closely. It's not what is called a 'tell' in poker—a minute gesture that would reveal that he was lying—because he hasn't lied yet. I know a great deal about Victor Lenzen. I hope he doesn't return my last question; I'd prefer not to think about my parents right now.

'Do you miss being in a relationship?' he asks.

'Sometimes,' I say, and go straight to my next question. 'Do you have children?'

'A daughter.'

Lenzen takes a sip of water.

'Would you have liked a family?' he asks. 'A husband, children?'

'No,' I say.

'No?' he asks.

'No,' I say. 'Are you married?'

'Divorced.'

'Why did your marriage fail?'

'My turn,' Lenzen says. 'Do you miss sex?'

He leans forward again.

'Excuse me?'

'Do you miss sex?' he repeats.

I am scared, but I don't show it.

'Not much,' I say. Keep going. 'Why did your marriage fail?'

'Because I work too much, I suppose, but you'd have to ask my ex-wife.'

Once again, his hand strays to his temple. The question upsets him—all mention of his family upsets him; I must remember that. But I need a lie from him. I want to know what he looks like when he tells a lie. It is, however, his move.

'Do you have a good relationship with your parents?'

'Yes.'

That's the third lie I've told.

'Have you ever had an affair?'

'No,' he replies and ploughs straight on. 'What were you like as a child?'

'Wild,' I say. 'More the way you'd imagine a little boy.'

He nods, as if he has no trouble picturing me.

'Have you ever been to a prostitute?' I ask.

'No.'

Impossible to tell whether or not he's lying.

'Do you have a good relationship with your sister?' he asks.

Alarm bells.

'Why do you ask that?'

'Because I'm fascinated by the dynamics between the sisters in your book. You told me earlier that you had a sister, and I wonder whether that's the reason you describe the love between the sisters with such sensitivity. Well?'

'Yes,' I say, 'a very good relationship.'

I swallow. No emotion now—no pain. Keep going.

'Do you consider yourself to be a good father?' I ask.

His hand goes to his temple; it's definitely a pattern.

'Um…yes,' says Lenzen.

A weak point. Good. I hope he's wondering what I'm driving at with all these questions. I hope it's making him nervous. Nervousness is good. He needn't know that I'm not driving at anything; that my only aim is to disconcert him.

'Do you draw inspiration from real-life events?' he asks.

'Sometimes I do, sometimes I don't.'

'And in your latest book?'

As if he didn't know.

'Yes.'

Time to hit below the belt.

'Have you ever raped a woman?' I ask.

Lenzen frowns and gives me a shocked look.

'What's all this about?' he asks. 'I don't know if I like your mind games, Frau Conrads.'

He looks genuinely aghast. I feel tempted to applaud.

'Just say no,' I say.

'No,' he says.

The angry furrow between his eyebrows is still there. Silence.

'What's your dog called again?' Lenzen asks at last.

'That's your question?' I ask in surprise.

'No, it slipped my mind, that's all,' he says.

Is it supposed to be a threat? Has he started talking about my dog because he can imagine how much I love the creature and how unbearable it would be to me if anything were to happen to it?

'Bukowski,' I say and am about to start on my next question when Charlotte appears in the door.

I jump because I had quite forgotten she was still here.

'Sorry to bother you again,' she says, 'but if there's nothing else I can do for you, I think I will be getting on my way now.'

'That's fine, Charlotte,' I say. 'You go home.'

'By the way, there's supposed to be a storm this evening. Remember to close all the windows before you go to bed.'

'All right,' I say. 'Thanks.'

The thought that I am about to be left alone in the house with Lenzen is not an agreeable one. But even less agreeable is the way his dangerous eyes are turned on Charlotte. She goes up to Lenzen, her hand held out. He rises politely.

'It was a real pleasure to meet you,' says Charlotte, brushing a non-existent strand of hair behind her ear. She blushes.

Lenzen smiles noncommittally, sits down and turns to me again. Once more I see him through Charlotte's eyes: his composure, his charisma. People like that have a talent for getting away with almost anything.

'Maybe see you around,' Charlotte says.

Lenzen only smiles. I realise that he's not flirting with her—she's the only one flirting. He's barely taking any notice of her; all his attention is on me. Charlotte hangs around a moment longer in the dining room, like a woman who's been stood up, while Lenzen's eyes are on me again. She gives me a quick nod, then she's gone.

I draw a deep breath.

'Your assistant and I had a little chat earlier on, and found out by chance that we live only a few streets away from one another,' Lenzen explains casually. 'Funny that we've never met in Munich before. But you know how it is—once you know someone, you're always bumping into them.' He grins at me, gets up, grabs a wrap from the caterers' serving trolley, bites into it, chews. Advantage.

His threat is clear to me. He has realised that I am fond of Charlotte. And he has told me that it is not remotely in my power to keep him away from her.

19

JONAS

He could feel himself losing control, growing irrational, but couldn't do anything about it. He had no business being here. What was he doing, calling in on the witness?

During the night, something had shifted in the atmosphere over the city. The light was different. The leaves on the trees had not yet started to change colour, but he had sensed, as he walked through the streets, that summer was coming to an end, autumn on its way.

Jonas parked the car, got out, rang the bell. The buzzer sounded. He stepped into the hall and began to walk up to the fourth floor. Sophie was waiting for him at the door.

'It's you!' was all she said when she recognised him. 'Please tell me they've caught him!'

Jonas swallowed. It hadn't occurred to him that Sophie would assume there had been developments in the investigations.

'No,' he said. 'I'm sorry, but that's not why I'm here.'

'Then why? More questions?'

'Not really,' Jonas replied. 'May I come in?'

Sophie ran her hand through her hair, hesitating for a moment.

'Of course,' she said. 'Please. I've made coffee.'

Jonas followed her along a hallway cluttered with cardboard boxes.

'Are you moving?'

'No,' Sophie said tersely, 'my fiancé's moving out.'

Then she snorted and corrected herself.

'My ex-fiancé.'

Jonas didn't know what to say, so said nothing.

'Would you like to sit down?' Sophie indicated one of her kitchen chairs.

'I'd rather stand,' Jonas said. 'Thanks.'

He looked about him at the big, light, high-ceilinged room: white-washed walls, a few framed reproductions—Egon Schiele, he thought but wasn't sure. A solitary orchid stood on the windowsill, an empty coffee cup beside it. The dishwasher was on; there was something comforting about its gentle drone.

'Milk and sugar?' Sophie asked.

'Just milk, please.'

Sophie opened a carton of milk and pulled a face.

'Shit,' she said. 'It's off.'

Furious, she emptied it into the sink.

'Damn!' She turned away from Jonas, put her hands on her hips as if to steady herself, and grimaced, struggling to hold back the tears.

'I don't mind it black,' said Jonas. 'The caffeine's what counts.'

Sophie forced a smile, poured Jonas a cup of coffee and handed it to him.

'Thanks.'

Jonas took a sip and went over to the big window where a radiant blue sky was flaunting itself.

'Wonderful view you have here,' he said.

'Yes.'

Sophie went to stand beside him. They were silent for a while.

'Sometimes I think I'll stay in here forever,' Sophie said. 'Not go out any more. Stockpile a few years' worth of groceries and never set foot outside again.'

'Sounds tempting,' Jonas replied with a smile.

'Doesn't it?' Sophie said. She gave a wry chuckle, then grew serious again. She turned back to look at the sky.

'Do you know what kind they are?' she asked, as two darting birds shot past the windows, making breakneck manoeuvres to dodge the roof of the house opposite.

'They're swifts,' said Jonas. 'They spend all their life in the air. They live and mate and even sleep on the wing.'

'Hm.'

Jonas watched Sophie as she looked out at the swifts, a smile on her face. She had split up with her fiancé. What did that mean? He took a sip of coffee.

'Are you going to tell me why you've come?' Sophie eventually asked, turning to him.

'Yes,' said Jonas, 'of course.' He cleared his throat. 'There's one thing I'd like to say first. I completely understand what you're going through at the moment. Really I do. But you've got to stop carrying out investigations off your own bat.'

Sophie looked at him as if he'd slapped her in the face. Belligerence flashed in her eyes.

'What makes you think I'm carrying out my own investigations?' she asked.

Jonas fought down a sigh.

'People have complained,' he said.

Sophie frowned, put her hands on her hips.

'Oh yes?' she said. 'Who?'

'Sophie, I'm telling you this for your own sake. You've got to stop. You're not only hindering the investigation, you might even be putting yourself at risk.'

For a moment only the soft noise of the dishwasher could be heard in the kitchen.

'I can't sit around doing nothing,' Sophie said at length. 'And I haven't done anything wrong. You can't ban me from talking to people.'

She turned away from him and glared out of the window.

'There are charges against you,' Jonas said.

'What?'

Sophie spun round and looked at him with big eyes.

'I don't handle those kind of offences. I found out about it by chance,' Jonas said. 'But my colleagues are bound to be in touch with you before long. There's a man claiming you pursued him and physically attacked him. Is that true?'

'Physically attacked... Sounds a bit extreme,' said Sophie. 'I held onto his arm, that was all. The bloke was a good head and a half taller than me—how could I have seriously attacked him?'

'Why did you hold onto him?' Jonas asked, although he already knew the answer.

Sophie said nothing. She stared out of the window in silence.

'You thought you'd recognised the man you saw that night,' Jonas said.

Sophie nodded.

Jonas thought of what Antonia Bug had said. *'That woman's not quite right in the head. Who knows if she saw anyone at all?'*

He tried to drive the thought away.

'I saw him,' Sophie blurted out, as if she could read his mind. 'As clearly as I see you now.'

Jonas swallowed.

'You do believe me?'

She turned round with a jerk, knocking the empty coffee cup off the windowsill with her elbow. The china smashed on the floor.

'Shit!' said Sophie.

Jonas and Sophie crouched down to pick up the pieces at the same time and banged heads. Embarrassed, they rubbed their foreheads and had to laugh. After they'd gathered it all up, they stood facing one another.

It seemed to Jonas that it was considerably warmer in the room than before. Sophie was one of those rare people who could stand there, looking at you in silence, without making you feel awkward. How on earth did she do it?

The doorbell rang and the moment ended.

Sophie ran her hand through her hair.

'That'll be my friend Karen—we were going jogging.'

'I must be getting on, anyway.'

Sophie nodded. Jonas turned to leave, but stopped in the doorway.

'I do believe you,' he said.

Then he left the flat, his heart pounding.

18

The thought that Lenzen might hurt Charlotte in some way sends a surge of nausea through my body. His threat is probably an empty one, but I can't stop thinking about it. I can tell by looking at Victor Lenzen that he's having trouble hiding his smug smile. Here he is at last: the monster from my dreams.

The rain outside has grown heavier; through the window I can see bullets of water riddling the surface of the lake. People in the real world will be grumbling about it. The more prudent among them will be going about under wind-bent umbrellas like oversized walking mushrooms. The rest will be dashing from shelter to shelter like scared animals, while the rain drenches their scalps.

'Do you like animals?' I ask Lenzen, even before he's sat down again.

Carry on. Keep things moving.

'I'm sorry?'

He sits down.

'It's my turn. Before we were interrupted, you asked me what my dog was called and I said, "Bukowski". Now I'm asking whether you like animals.'

'Oh, we're still playing this little game, are we?'

I don't respond.

'You're an eccentric woman, Frau Conrads,' says Lenzen.

I don't respond.

'All right then,' he says. 'Not especially. I never had a pet or anything, if that's what you mean.'

He glances at his notes, then looks me in the eye again.

'I don't like the tone our conversation is beginning to take,' he says. 'I'm sorry if I provoked you.'

I don't know what to say to this, so I nod.

'Let's get back to your writing. What do you like most about your work?'

'Creating my own realities. And, of course, providing my readers with something that gives them pleasure,' I say, with perfect sincerity. 'What about you? What do you like most about your work?'

'Interviews,' says Lenzen, and grins. He looks at his papers again. 'Although—or maybe because you never appear in public—there's a lot about you in the press and on the internet.'

'Oh yes?'

'Do you read articles about yourself?'

'Sometimes, when I'm plagued by boredom. Most of it is pure fiction.'

'Does it upset you to read things about yourself that aren't true?'

'No, it amuses me. The more off the wall, the better.'

That, too, is true.

'My turn,' I say. 'Two turns.'

I consider for a moment.

'Do you think you're a good person?' I ask.

I'm fishing in troubled waters. Up until now, all my questions have slid off him. I don't know what I'm angling for. I had wanted to proceed in a structured fashion—find out what he looks like when he's telling the truth, then what he looks like when he's lying. And, finally, tighten the screws. But Lenzen is as slippery as an eel. Maybe I should try to provoke him.

'A good person?' he echoes. 'My God, you don't half ask some questions. No, probably not. But I make an effort every day.'

Interesting answer. Lenzen is silent, as if probing his words before eventually approving them. Keep firing.

'What do you regret most in your life?'

'I don't know.'

'Then think about it.'

Lenzen pretends to ponder.

'The things that led to the break-up of my marriage, I suppose. What about you? What do you regret?'

'That I wasn't able to save my sister,' I say.

It's true.

'Your sister's dead?' Lenzen asks.

Bastard.

'Let's drop this,' I say.

He frowns, seems momentarily bewildered, but soon recovers his composure.

'Where was I? Ah, yes. You say that the stories about you that are circulating on the internet don't bother you. Does criticism bother you?'

'Only when it's justified,' I say. Quick, keep going. 'What do you most regret *not* having done?'

He's back on track and replies immediately.

'I should have been there for my daughter more when she was little,' he says, then presses right on. 'A critic once wrote that your characters are strong, but that your plots lack verve.'

'What's your question?' I ask.

'I'm still formulating it. What bothers me much more than the plot, you see, are some of the characters in your latest book. There are two characters in your novel who are less vivid to me than the others, and they are, interestingly enough, the murder victim and the murderer. The murder victim is—forgive me if I exaggerate—a kind, naïve country bumpkin, while the murderer is a soulless sociopath who likes killing young women. Why did you draw such archetypal figures when you're so famous for your finely drawn characters?'

Every hair on my neck is standing on end.

'That's easy,' I say. 'I don't regard those characters as clichéd archetypes.'

'Don't you?' says Lenzen. 'Take the murdered woman, for instance—Britta, as she's called in the book.'

My scalp contracts. *As she's called in the book.* He's practically admitting he knows that she really existed and that she had a different name in real life.

'Do you consider the character of Britta realistic?' asks Lenzen.

'Absolutely.'

Of course I do. Britta is Anna, Anna is Britta. She exists, she existed. I knew her as well as I know myself.

'Isn't Britta more an idealised portrait of a young woman? A lily-white dream. Sickly sweet, clever, kind, and oh-so-virtuous. I mean, that scene where she reacts to the homeless man as a little girl, wanting to fetch all the homeless off the streets…'

Lenzen makes a noise of disparagement. I find it hard to stop myself from pouncing across the table at him and slapping him in the face. But I suppress the impulse. I decide to let him ask, not to interrupt him. I'm learning more from his questions than from his answers.

'I have the feeling that Britta is an awful goody-two-shoes,' Lenzen continues. 'That flashback where she tries to persuade her sister to stop wearing leather for the sake of the animals—it seemed to me almost like a parody. Britta's constantly taking other people to task and telling them what to do. I know you depict that in a positive light in your novel, but in real life, people like that get on your nerves and certainly aren't idolised the way they are in your book—if such flawless people even exist, that is. But how do you see it?'

I gasp for breath, make a huge effort not to let him provoke me. The bastard.

'I think there *are* people like Britta,' I blurt out. 'I think there are very good and very evil people and everything in between. It's possible that we're so obsessed by the nuances and the in-between that we block out the people at either end of the scale. We call them clichés or unrealistic. But there are people like that. Very few, of course.'

'People like your sister?' Lenzen asks.

The temperature in the room soars. I break out in a sweat.

'What?'

'I have the feeling that we're talking about your sister here.'

'Really?'

The white of the wall opposite shimmers before my eyes.

'Yes, just a thought. Correct me if I'm wrong. But you've written this unbelievably idealised version of the relationship between two sisters, and you have a sister you say you weren't able to save. Maybe she's dead. Maybe you mean "save" in a figurative sense—you're a writer, after all. Maybe you weren't able to save her from drugs or from a violent man.'

'What makes you think that?'

Salty saliva collects in my mouth.

'I don't know. You're obviously very fond of this character, Britta, despite the fact that she's so awful,' says Lenzen.

'Awful?'

Suddenly I have the most extraordinary headache. The wall opposite seems to be bulging towards me as if there were something trapped in there that was trying to get out.

'Yes!' says Lenzen. 'So good, so beautiful, so pure. A proper Disney princess. In real life, a woman like that would be unbearable!'

'You think?'

'Well, I certainly find it astonishing that the older sister—what's she called again? Sorry…'

My head is bursting.

'Sophie,' I say.

'That Sophie gets on so well with the character. When Britta tells her sister that her fiancé's not good enough for her. When she goes on and on to her about her great new job. When she's constantly nagging her about her weight and her appearance. Perfect Britta—the Disney princess up on her high horse. Seriously, if I were a woman—if I were Sophie—Britta would annoy me more. I might even detest her.'

I did, too, I think.

The realisation is a blow to me. Where did that come from? It's not new—I can feel it. It's a thought I've had more than once before, but subliminally. On the far side of pain.

What kind of a person are you, Linda?

I shouldn't think the thought, but I think it again. Yes, I detested her. Yes, she was smug. Yes, she was arrogant. Yes, she was always up on her high horse—Saint Anna. Anna, who could always wear white without spilling on it. Anna, for whom men wrote poems. Anna, for whom Marc would have left me, if she had wanted him, as she never tired of reminding me. Anna, whose hair smelt of shampoo even after a camping trip. Anna, whose name you could read backwards as well as forwards—Anna, Anna, Anna.

What's going on here?

I struggle free, I surface, and I'm thinking straight again. I know what I'm up against; it's my guilty conscience—nothing but my guilty conscience, base and insidious. My guilt at not being able to save Anna. It's gnawing away at me, and to avoid being gnawed quite to pieces, my brain looks for a way out, even if it's as mean and shabby as the thought that my sister wasn't all that good.

How shabby, too, and mean, what Lenzen's just tried to do. And how shabby and mean of me to fall for it. I'm too agitated, too exhausted, too impressionable. My head is throbbing. I must pull myself together. Lenzen has taken one of my castles, but my king and queen are still in play. I try to concentrate. And, as I collect myself, I realise what I've heard, what he's said. The way he's talking: it's almost as if he harbours a personal grudge against her. Against Britta. Against Anna. And I realise something. My God.

It hadn't occurred to me. I had always assumed that the police would have caught the culprit, if there had been any connection with Anna—if she hadn't been an accidental victim. I thought that Anna

132

had died because someone had taken advantage of a beautiful young woman who lived alone in a ground-floor flat and sometimes left her terrace door open. But maybe that wasn't the case. Maybe it wasn't cruel coincidence at all. Is it possible? Did Anna know the monster?

'Be that as it may,' Lenzen continues, 'I was utterly fascinated by the description of the murder—that is to say, the chapter where Sophie discovers her sister. It's terribly painful to read, very affecting. What was it like for you writing that scene?'

My right lower eyelid twitches. I can't stop it.

'Difficult,' is all I say.

'Frau Conrads,' says Lenzen, 'I hope you're not under the impression that I don't like your book because that's not the case. The protagonist, Sophie, for instance, is a character I could wholeheartedly sympathise with for long stretches of the novel. There are, however, a few things that strike me as anomalous, so that I am, of course, thrilled to be able to take this unique opportunity to ask the author why she depicted things one way rather than another.'

'Oh yes?' I say. It takes me a moment to get my nausea under control; I have to gain time. 'What strikes you as anomalous, apart from the murder victim?'

'Well, the murderer, for example.'

'Really?'

Now it's getting interesting.

'Yes. The killer is portrayed as a soulless monster—a typical psychopath. Then the gimmick that he must leave something at the scene of the crime—from a writer of the calibre of Linda Conrads, I'd have expected a more subtly drawn character.'

'There *are* sociopaths,' I say.

I'm sitting right opposite one. I don't say that.

'Of course, sure. But they're extremely rare, even if ninety per cent of all detective stories and thrillers seem to revolve around criminals of that kind. Why did you decide on such a one-dimensional character?'

'I believe that evil, like goodness, really exists. I tried to convey that.'

'Evil? Really? Isn't there evil in all of us?'

'Maybe,' I say. 'In some measure.'

'What is it that fascinates you about criminals like the one in your book?' Lenzen asks.

'Nothing at all,' I say.

I almost spit the words.

'Nothing at all. A cold, sick soul like the murderer in my book holds no fascination for me whatsoever. Only the possibility of making sure that he ends up behind bars for the rest of his life.'

'In literature, at least, you can make sure of it,' Lenzen smirks.

I say nothing.

You wait and see, I think.

See what? another part of me thinks. How?

'Wouldn't a more complex psychological motive have been more interesting?' Lenzen continues.

It's been clear to me for some time that he's no longer talking about my book but about himself—that he's maybe even trying to justify himself. I know that, he knows that, and each of us knows that the other one knows. Maybe I should speak out, at last. Sweep all the metaphors and circumlocutions off the table.

'Such as?' I ask instead.

Lenzen's eyes change; he's seen through my crude ploy. We both know that I'm asking him for his own motive.

He shrugs. Slippery as an eel.

'I'm really no writer,' he says ingeniously. 'But tell me, why didn't you kill your main character off at the end? It would have been realistic. And dramatic at the same time.'

Lenzen stares at me.

I stare back.

He asks another question.

I don't hear it.

Love, love, love.

Oh no.

Love, love, love.

Please, no.

Love, love, love.

Please, no, I can't take any more.

I whimper. Grip the edge of the table. Look about the room in panic, searching for the source of the music. Nothing. Just a large spider crawling over the parquet; I can hear the sound its legs make on the wood. Plick-plick-plick-plick.

Suddenly Lenzen's face is very close to mine; I can see the little veins in the very white whites of his eyes. The monster from my dreams is right in front of me. I can feel his breath on my face.

'Are you afraid of death?' asks Victor Lenzen.

My fear is a deep well that I have fallen into. I'm suspended vertically in the water. I try to touch the bottom with my toes, but there's nothing there, only blackness.

I shake myself, try to keep above water, stay conscious.

'What did you just say?' I ask.

Lenzen frowns at me.

'I didn't say anything. Are you all right?'

I gasp. God knows how, but I manage to get a grip on myself.

'You know,' Lenzen continues, unmoved, 'it was the ending that surprised me the most. The fact is that I was convinced all the way through that the killer didn't actually exist and that the devastated sister would turn out to be the murderer.'

The ground is disappearing from under my feet. There's only darkness below me—the Mariana Trench—eleven thousand metres of blackness. Anna's face laughing, mocking. My fingers round the knife. Cold fury. I plunge it in.

Do I plunge it in? Me? No, no. Not that, no. It lasts only a brief, awful moment. No, it wasn't like that! It's the music! The monster's presence. It's my tense nerves! Maybe he's even given me something! I'm not with it. I wasn't with it! For a brief, awful moment I wondered whether my massive sense of guilt stemmed not from the fact that I was unable to save Anna, but from the fact that I… That I…

You know. Perhaps there was no fleeing man, after all. Just Anna and me. Perhaps the fleeing man was a story—a lovely story such as only an author's brain could come up with.

Not a bad story. The fleeing man, no more real than the fawn in the clearing. Linda and her stories.

No. This is not like the fawn story. I'm not a liar and I'm not mad. I am not a murderer. I shake off the black thought and focus my attention on Lenzen again. I nearly let him manipulate me.

I look at him. He exudes...cheerfulness. I shudder. That cold, almost imperceptible smile in his pale eyes. I don't know what's going on in Lenzen's head, but I no longer doubt that he has come here to kill me. I was wrong: he isn't a wolf. He doesn't kill swiftly and surely. He enjoys this part—he enjoys the game.

His voice echoes in my head: 'Are you afraid of death?'

Victor Lenzen is going to kill me. His hand slips inside his jacket. The knife. My God.

I have no choice.

I take the gun that I've taped to the underside of the table, ripping it loose. I point it at Victor Lenzen and pull the trigger.

22

SOPHIE

Sophie's thoughts often returned to that night. She was still tormenting herself with the question of what had seemed so odd about Britta's flat. There had been something. She had seen it at the crime scene and she saw it in her nightmares, but it kept eluding her.

She was sure this detail held the key. Her brain was simply too full of other things for her to think straight. Yesterday alone so much had happened. First the police officer had come round and reprimanded her. Then her father had been taken to hospital with a suspected heart attack, and her mother, of course, was a nervous wreck, even though it had turned out to be a false alarm.

Sophie, on the other hand, was still keyed up. No question of sleep. And the night was so silent. No Paul beside her anymore, filling the bedroom with his steady breathing. Sophie was glad he had gone, really; she was too exhausted to be in a relationship, thinking of marriage and children as Paul would have liked. She was too angry—at herself, at the world. It's a sign of grieving, her therapist said. Perfectly normal. But Sophie didn't feel normal. At the moment she felt ill-disposed towards everybody. Except, perhaps, for that young police officer who had the disconcerting knack of always saying the right thing.

Sophie felt agitated. She had once heard that many people who have suffered a great loss either break down or freeze up, only dimly aware of the outside world. Over the past weeks she had witnessed both: her father's numbness, and her mother's breakdown—although her mother was now so sedated she no longer felt much either. Sophie, however, felt everything.

Since she wasn't going to get to sleep again tonight, she got up and went to her study. She sat down at her desk, which was strewn with printouts and newspaper clippings, and switched on the computer.

Over the past days and nights, she had drawn a precise map of her sister's life. She had talked to Britta's tearful friends and to her shocked ex-boyfriend, but her queries hadn't got her anywhere. None of them could begin to imagine anyone wanting to harm Britta. Maybe Britta had surprised a burglar. Or maybe some sicko had stalked her—something like that. A stranger. Cruel chance. It was the only possibility: that was the unanimous opinion.

But Britta hadn't complained about a stalker. She hadn't been worried in any way. Britta's friends were as clueless as Sophie. There was only one avenue left to explore.

Sophie went onto the website of the internet start-up that Britta had worked for as a graphic designer. Britta's job had been the only area in her life that didn't overlap with Sophie's. If Britta had known her murderer, it could really only be a colleague; Sophie knew all the other men in Britta's life. She'd only caught a glimpse of the shadow at the terrace door before he disappeared across the terrace, but she would never forget his face. That's why she found the young policewoman's questions about their family and Britta's private life so unnecessary.

Sophie knew what she had seen: a stranger.

She glanced at the time. Almost 2am. She remembered that Britta had often stayed on in the office until late, sometimes even spending the night to meet deadlines. She wondered whether her colleagues had similar hours.

Sophie took the telephone, dialled the agency's number and let it ring. But no one picked up. Britta's colleagues were the last people she could check out; after that she'd be at a loss as to what to do next.

She had an idea. Sometimes on company homepages there were photos and brief biographies of the employees—especially with new, small companies like Britta's. She scanned the page again. Yes, there was a button labelled 'Team'. Sophie clicked on it with trembling fingers.

The photo hit her like a blow to the stomach.

Britta was looking out at her with a broad smile on her face. Blonde hair, big blue eyes, freckled nose. Britta, who had always smelt so good; Britta, who had always caught the spiders that Sophie was so afraid of, trapping them in old jam jars, carrying them carefully outside and setting them free on the grass. Sweet-toothed Britta, who was always chewing gum.

With some trouble, Sophie tore her eyes from the photo and contemplated the pictures of the other employees. Three were of women and could be ruled out immediately. Another six were of men: the two managers, the art director and three computer scientists. None of them was the man Sophie had seen in Britta's flat.

She continued to scroll down and then stopped. There were two placeholders that had names and job titles beneath them, but contained no photos. Sophie's heart beat faster and she made a quick note of the names: Simon Platzeck, Social Media, and André Bialkowski, Programmer.

Once again, Sophie glanced at the time. What were the chances that anyone would be in the office in the middle of the night? Not very high. But what was the alternative? Go back to bed and stare at the ceiling? She got dressed, took her car key and pulled the door shut behind her.

Sophie's body felt strangely light as she left the multi-storey car park adjacent to the complex where Britta had worked. Seventy-two hours without sleep. She looked about her. Of the four office buildings within eyeshot, only one had a light showing. Otherwise, the area, which would be filled with people in a few hours, was deserted: black asphalt, a few solitary street lamps, and a few taxis speeding along the road. Sophie headed for the building where the light was showing, then stopped short. It was numbered 6-10, and Britta had worked in numbers 2-4—the dark, deserted glass block next door.

Disappointed, Sophie turned back. She took the lift and went into the underground section of the car park. The air down here felt poisonous; it reeked of exhaust fumes. Sophie rummaged in her bag for the key and had almost reached her car when the feeling hit her. She was not alone.

She stopped in her tracks: she hadn't recognised the murderer, so she had assumed that he hadn't known her either.

What if that weren't the case?

He would come after her. Try to kill her, the eyewitness. There was someone there, right behind her.

She turned round, her heart thumping. No one. Her footsteps and gasping breaths echoed through the deserted car park as she hurried towards her car—nearly there now, only a few more steps. Then she froze mid-movement again. There *was* something there—a shadow crouching on the back seat. Or was there? No. It was trick of the light. Or was it?

The shadow moved. Sophie's heart skipped a beat, then started galloping again. He's going to kill me too, she thought, numbly. She wouldn't make it. She couldn't even scream; she could only stand there and stare. Then the spell broke. Out, thought Sophie. I must get out of here. And: Too close, I'm far too close. Three more steps and he'll reach me. Three more steps and he'll kill me.

At last her brain did what it was supposed to do: it tore itself free from all other thoughts and sent terror coursing through her body. The fear of death came like a surge of icy cold water, drenching her body, her clothes, her hair, and momentarily taking her breath away. Then the paralysis ended and Sophie's body switched into survival mode.

She turned and ran, and the crouching shadow emerged from her car and began to run too. He was fast and he was coming closer. How fast can you run, Sophie, how fast? She ran towards the exit, her heart pounding, her breathing shallow, the man and the knife right behind her. She crashed into the lift doors and frantically pressed the button, rapid footsteps behind her. She didn't turn round; she thought of Orpheus in the Underworld—turn round and you're dead, turn round and you're dead—and the lift didn't come, didn't come, didn't come, didn't come, didn't come, didn't come. Sophie ran to the stairs, heaved open the creaking steel door, burst through, and headed up the stairs. She heard the door slam shut behind her with a loud crash. Had the man with the knife taken the lift? What if he had taken the lift? What if the man with the knife was waiting upstairs, if...?

With a brutal shriek, the staircase door opened below and footsteps began to sound up the stairs. Sophie ran on, the taste of metal in her mouth, stumbled, struggled to her feet, carried on, the man with the knife behind her, closer and closer. Don't turn round, don't turn round. Turn round and you're dead. What if he throws the knife—just throws it? At your back?

Sophie came to the exit of the underground car park, hurled herself at the door, but it was locked. How can it be? Oh, please—if he gets you, you're dead—please, pretty please, open. Locked—and right behind her, the man with the knife, right behind her, the footsteps coming closer. Again, Sophie hurled herself at the door, and this time it sprang open. It hadn't been locked, not even jammed; she hadn't pressed the handle down firmly enough. Too stupid to open a door... Run, Sophie, damn it, don't think, run!

Sophie plunged into the open and ran. Along the front of the deserted building, along the deserted street, the footsteps and the knife behind her—black blood, Britta's open eyes, the look of surprise on Britta's face, and the figure in the shadows, the figure in the shadows. Sophie ran and ran and ran and ran, until she no longer knew where she was, until she could no longer hear anything but her own footsteps and her own breathing. Only then did she stop.

19

No, I don't pull the trigger. I draw the gun and point it at Lenzen with trembling hands, but I don't pull the trigger. I'd sworn to myself that I'd only use the gun as leverage. I am a woman of words, not weapons; I had a long, hard struggle making up my mind to get hold of a firearm, although I did, in the end, decide it was necessary.

And now I have been vindicated.

I don't pull the trigger, but the mere sight of the gun has the same effect on Lenzen as if I'd already fired it. He's as rigid as a corpse, looking at me with vacant eyes. I grip the gun more tightly; it's heavy. I stare at Lenzen. He stares at me, and blinks. He's understood: the table we're sitting at has rotated a hundred and eighty degrees.

'My God,' says Lenzen. His voice is trembling. 'Is'—he swallows—'is it real?'

I don't reply. I'm not answering any more questions. Things have reached a state of emergency. The times of neat and elegant solutions involving DNA samples or a voluntary confession are over. I do not use the word 'emergency' lightly. I am prepared to get my hands dirty.

No more skirmishing. No games.

Lenzen is sitting before me with raised hands.

'For heaven's sake!' he says. His voice sounds hoarse. 'I don't understand what's…' He falters and breaks off, struggling to retain his composure.

His forehead is beaded with sweat and I can see from his heaving chest how rapidly he's breathing. He looks as if he's in deep shock. Did it really not to occur to him that I might be armed? Surely he was aware of the possibility when he agreed to visit the woman whose sister he'd killed! The look of horror on Lenzen's face disconcerts me. What if…?

I brush aside all doubt. Lenzen is going to leave this house a self-confessed murderer. There is no alternative.

I recall what I learnt from Dr Christensen: the Reid interrogation technique. Create stress. Wear down the suspect with endless questions. Punish any inconsistencies. Intersperse banal and undemanding questions with provoking and stress-inducing ones. Resort to false evidence, blackmail, force—anything goes.

Put the suspect under stress. Wear him down. Put him under stress. Wear him down. Eventually offer him confession as a way out. Put him under stress. Wear him down. And, finally, break him.

But first of all, I must find out whether *he* is armed.

'Get up!' I say. 'At once!'

He obeys.

'Take off your jacket and lay it on the table. Slowly.'

He does so. I pick up his jacket, without taking my eyes off him, and frisk it for weapons. But there's nothing and I drop the jacket on the floor.

'Empty your trouser pockets.'

He puts his lighter on the table and looks at me hesitantly.

'Turn round!'

I can't bring myself to frisk him, but I can see that neither in his trousers nor in his belt does he have a gun.

'Push your bag across to me,' I say. 'Slowly.'

I pick the bag up and rifle through it. Nothing—just harmless stuff. Lenzen is unarmed. But that doesn't make a difference. For all I know, he might kill me with his bare hands. I grip the gun.

'Sit down.'

He sits down.

'I have some questions and I expect you to answer honestly,' I say.

Lenzen says nothing.

'Do you understand?'

He nods.

'Answer me!' I yell.

He swallows. 'Yes,' he says huskily.

I study him—the size of his pupils, the skin on his face, the throbbing of his pulse in his carotid artery. He's had a scare, but he's not actually in shock. That's good.

'How old are you?' I ask.

'Fifty-three.'

'Where did you grow up?'

'In Munich.'

'How old is your father?'

Lenzen looks at me in utter consternation.

'We can skip all this,' I say. 'Do you know why you're here?'

'Er…for the interview,' says Lenzen, his voice trembling.

He really is pretending not to know what I'm talking about.

'So you've no idea why I've asked you here?' I say. 'You, rather than anyone else?'

Lenzen looks bewildered.

'Answer me!' I snap.

Lenzen hesitates, as if he were scared I might fire the gun if he said anything wrong.

'A little while ago you said you'd chosen me because you admire my work,' he replies with studied calm. 'But it's beginning to dawn on me that that's not the real reason.'

I can't believe he's still playing the innocent. It makes me so furious that I have to make an effort to collect myself. Very well, I think. It's up to him.

'All right then,' I say, 'back to the beginning. How old are you?'

He doesn't immediately reply; I raise the gun a little.

'Fifty-three,' he says.

'Where did you grow up?'

'In Munich.'

He tries to look at me rather than into the muzzle of my gun.

'Do you have brothers and sisters?'

He fails.

'I have an elder brother.'

'Do you have a good relationship with your parents?'

'Yes.'

'Do you have children?'

His hand strays to his temple.

'Listen, you've already asked me all this!' he says, forcing himself to sound calm. 'What is this? A joke?'

'It's not a joke.'

Lenzen's eyes open a little wider.

'Do you have children?' I ask.

'A daughter.'

'What's your daughter called?'

He hesitates—only momentarily, but I sense his reluctance.

'Sara,' he says.

'What's your favourite football team?'

I note his mental sigh of relief as I move off the subject of his daughter. Good.

'1860 Munich.'

Time to hit below the belt.

'Do you like inflicting pain on others?'

He makes a sound of contempt.

'No.'

'Have you ever tortured an animal?'

'No.'

144

'What's your mother's maiden name?'

'Nitsche.'

'How old is your father?'

'Seventy-eight.'

'Do you think of yourself as a good person?'

'I do my best.'

'Do you prefer dogs or cats?'

'Cats.'

I can almost see the cogs whirring in his brain as he tries to work out where I'm going with all this and, more importantly, how he can disarm me. I'm holding the gun in my right hand, leaning on the table for support. I hold it correctly; I don't allow myself to become careless. I've been practising. The table is wide. Lenzen doesn't have a chance of getting at me or the gun. To do that, he'd have to come round the table. Not a chance. We both know that.

I ratchet up the pace.

'What's your favourite film?'

'*Casablanca.*'

'How old is your daughter?'

'Twelve.'

'What colour is your daughter's hair?'

His jaw is grinding.

'Blonde.'

The questions about his daughter are bothering him.

'What colour are your daughter's eyes?'

'Brown.'

'How old is your father?'

'Seventy-seven.'

'A moment ago you said seventy-eight.'

Punish every mistake.

'Seventy-eight. He's seventy-eight.'

'Do you think this is a game?'

He doesn't reply. His eyes flash.

'Do you think this is a game?' I repeat.

'No. It was a slip of the tongue.'

'You should get a grip on yourself,' I warn him.

Put him under stress, wear him down.

'What's your mother's maiden name?'

'Nitsche.'

'How old is your father?'

Lenzen conceals a sigh.

'Seventy-eight.'

'What's your favourite band?'

'U2. No, the Beatles.'

Interesting.

'What's your favourite Beatles song?'

'All You Need is Love.'

Touché. I try not to let anything show, but I fail. Lenzen looks at me; his gaze is shifty, inscrutable.

Time to tighten the screws.

'You lied to me, Herr Lenzen,' I say. 'But it doesn't matter. I know your daughter's name isn't Sara; it's Marie.'

I let this sink in.

'You know,' I say, 'I know a great deal about you. More than you think. I've had you watched for a long time. Your every move.'

That's a lie, but what the hell.

'You're crazy,' says Lenzen.

I ignore this.

'In fact I know the answer to every single question I've asked you and to all the questions I'm going to ask you.'

He snorts. 'Then why ask?'

Now that's predictable.

'Because I'd like to hear the answers from you.'

'The answers to what? Why? I don't understand any of this!'

At least part of his desperation sounds genuine. I mustn't go easy on him now.

'Have you ever been involved in a fight?'

'No.'

146

'Have you ever hit anyone in the face?'

'No!'

'Have you ever hit a woman?'

'I thought "anyone" included women.'

He seems back in control, damn him. Talk of violence leaves him untroubled. Cold bastard.

'Have you ever raped a woman?'

His face no longer betrays any emotion.

'No.'

The only sore point I've been able to make out so far is his daughter. I decide to embed all potentially delicate and provoking questions in questions concerning her.

'How old is your daughter?'

'Twelve.'

His jaw muscles clench.

'What year is your daughter in at school?'

'Year seven.'

'What's your daughter's favourite subject?'

I spot a vein I hadn't noticed before on Lenzen's temple. It's throbbing.

'Maths.'

'What's the name of your daughter's horse?'

And throbbing.

'Lucy.'

'Do you think you're a good father?'

His jaws are grinding.

'Yes.'

'Have you ever raped a woman?'

'No.'

'What's the name of your daughter's best friend?'

'I don't know.'

'Annika,' I say. 'Annika Mehler.'

Lenzen swallows. I feel nothing at all.

'What's your daughter's favourite colour?'

'Orange.'

His hand strays towards his temple; he's sick of all these questions about his daughter. Good.

'What's your daughter's favourite film?'

'The Little Mermaid.'

'Have you ever killed anyone?'

'No.'

The answer comes swiftly, like the others. But he knows we're getting to the heart of the matter. What is he hoping for? How's he going to get out of this one?

'Are you afraid of death?'

'No.'

'What's the most traumatic thing that's ever happened to you?'

He clears his throat. 'This.'

'Is there anything you'd kill for?'

'No.'

'Would you kill for your daughter?'

'Yes.'

'But you said…'

He loses his cool.

'I know what I said!' he shouts. 'Dear God! Of course I'd do anything to protect my child.'

He tries to calm down, but fails.

'Can you tell me what the hell's going on here?'

He's yelling.

'What the fuck is this? Is it a game? Are you thinking out a new crime novel? Am I your guinea pig? Is that it? Fuck!'

He slams his clenched fist down on the table. His fury is elemental. It scares me, despite the gun in my hand, but I contain my emotions. Outside, the sun is shining again; I can feel the warmth of its rays on my cheek.

'Calm down, Herr Lenzen,' I say and raise the gun. 'This is not a toy.'

'I can see that!' Lenzen snarls. 'Do you think I'm a choirboy? I know what a bloody gun looks like. I was almost kidnapped twice in Algeria; I've reported on goddamn warlords in Afghanistan: I am perfectly capable of telling a real gun from a water pistol, believe me.'

His face is bright red. He's losing control. I don't know whether that's a good thing or a bad thing.

'You don't like the situation,' I say matter-of-factly.

'You're damn right I don't! Can't you at least tell me…' he begins.

'But you can put an end to the situation at any time,' I say, interrupting him.

I try to sound calm. I hadn't yet been as conscious of the microphones in the house as I am at this moment.

'And how can I go about doing that?' Lenzen demands.

'By giving me what I want.'

'What do you want, for heaven's sake?'

'The truth,' I say. 'I want you to confess.'

Lenzen stares at me. My gun and I stare back. Then he blinks.

'You want me to confess,' he echoes in disbelief.

Everything in me is quivering.

'That's exactly what I want.'

Lenzen makes a deep, rumbling noise. It takes me a moment to realise that it's laughter—mirthless and hysterical.

'Then maybe you'd like to tell me what the hell I'm supposed to confess to! What have I done to you? I didn't ask for this interview!'

'You don't know what I'm talking about?'

'I haven't the faintest idea,' says Lenzen.

'I find that hard to…'

I get no further. With a swooping movement, Lenzen lunges at me across the table; he's over it in a split second, sweeping me off my chair. My head strikes the floor hard and Lenzen's on me. A shot goes off, my brain explodes, I see only mottled red, hear a whistling sound in my ears. I kick and thrash and try to heave Lenzen off me, but he's too heavy. I want to get away from him—get away—and, instinctively rather than deliberately, I bring the gun down on his skull. He screams and goes limp. I roll him off me, get to my feet, take a few steps backwards, and stumble, almost falling over my chair. I manage to stay on my feet and stand there, gasping for air. I point the gun at Lenzen. I'm perfectly calm now; there's no anger left in me—only cold hatred. I feel like pulling the trigger. Lenzen's crouching before me, motionless, staring into the muzzle of the gun. I see his wide-open eyes, the sweat glistening on his face, the rise and fall of his chest—I see everything as if in slow motion. My right hand, holding the gun, trembles. The moment passes. I regain self-control and lower the gun a little. I realise I've been holding my breath. Lenzen's gasping for air; we're both gasping for air. He's bleeding from a wound on his head. He gets onto his knees, looking out at me from behind metallic eyes—a wounded animal.

'Get up,' I say.

Lenzen gets up. He puts his hand to his head and looks aghast when he feels the blood. I fight back my nausea.

'Turn round and walk towards the front door.'

He looks at me uncomprehendingly.

'Go on,' I say.

I follow him with raised gun, steering him on wobbly legs towards the guest bathroom which, as luck will have it, is right next to the dining room. I get him to take a towel, wet it, press it to the bleeding. It's soon clear that the wound is tiny; I didn't hit him properly at all. Neither of us says a word; only our heavy breathing is audible.

Then I steer Lenzen back to the dining-room table. Thick clouds cover the sun and dusk is falling; we're on the narrow ridge between daytime and evening. Far off, there's a rumble. The storm that Charlotte had prophesied is coming. It may be some time coming, but the air in the room is already electrically charged.

'Please,' said Lenzen, 'let me go.'

I stare at him. What is he thinking?

'I don't know what you want from me,' he says. 'And I don't know what kind of a game you're playing. But you've won.'

Tears are gleaming in his eyes. Not bad. The blow on his head really was good for something.

150

'You don't know what's going on here?' I ask.

'No!'

He almost screams the word.

'Why did you say earlier on that you had the impression the sister in my book was the murderer?' I ask. 'Were you trying to provoke me?'

'Why should that provoke you? I don't understand you!' Lenzen shouts. 'You were the one who wanted to talk about the book!'

Not bad.

'And the carry-on with Charlotte?'

He looks at me as if I were speaking a foreign language.

'Charlotte?'

'Charlotte, my assistant. What was all that about?'

Lenzen gives a tortured sigh and forces himself to reply calmly.

'Listen. Your assistant was flirting openly with me; I'm not to blame for that. I was just trying to be friendly; you can't hold that against me, I...'

'What was the idea behind the questions about my dog?'

'I wasn't hoping to achieve anything with those questions, Frau Conrads,' he says. 'Please try to remember that I'm here at your behest. You invited me. I'm being paid to talk to you. I've treated you politely throughout. I've done nothing that would justify your behaviour towards me.'

'What was the idea behind the questions about my dog?'

'We're here for an interview, right?' says Lenzen.

He looks at me as if I were a dangerous animal that might pounce on him at any moment. I can sense how much strength it's costing him to keep calm.

I don't reply.

'You'd mentioned that you had a dog,' says Lenzen, 'so it's only natural that I should ask about it.'

By now he probably thinks I'm completely nuts—totally unpredictable. That's good. With a bit of luck, I'll soon have him where I want him.

'Why did you ask me if I was afraid of death?'

'What?'

'Why did you ask me if I was afraid of death?' I repeat.

Again I hear thunder, far, far away—a menacing rumble, like the scolding of a morose giant.

'I didn't,' he says.

He looks bewildered. Not for the first time, I am on the point of getting up and applauding him.

'Please let me go,' he begs. 'I'll forget this has happened. Only...'

I interrupt him. 'I can't let you go.'

His hypocritical posturing, his crocodile tears, his yammering—it all makes me feel sick. I find it hard not to puke at his feet. Seven stabs—and he goes to pieces over a little cut.

I take a deep breath.

'Do you have children?' I ask.

Lenzen groans and buries his head in his hands.

'Please,' he says.

'Do you have children?' I ask again.

'Please leave my daughter out of this,' Lenzen moans.

I notice that he's crying.

'What's your daughter called?' I ask.

'What do you want from my daughter?'

He says it almost pleadingly. And I twig. Is it possible that he thinks I mean to harm his daughter in some way? That it's why I keep asking about her? That it's a kind of threat? I'd never have come up with that, but all right. I decide to ignore his whining. Maybe he's ready to give me what I want now.

'You know what I want,' I say.

Give me what I want and I'll leave your daughter alone, I'm saying between the lines. Lenzen knows that and I know it. I don't have the time to feel bad about it.

'A confession,' says Lenzen.

The surge of adrenalin, which had flooded my body when Lenzen attacked me, is suddenly back with a vengeance. I feel its heat.

'A confession,' I confirm.

'But I don't know…'

Here we go again. How long is he going to keep this up?

'Then I'll help you,' I say. 'Where were you living twelve years ago?'

He considers for a moment.

'In Munich,' he says. 'That was my last year in Munich.'

'Do you know an Anna Michaelis?'

There's nothing in his eyes—nothing.

'No. Who's she?'

Liar. I almost have to admire him. Considering there's a gun involved, he's holding out pretty damn long. Maybe he really isn't afraid of death.

'Why are you lying to me?'

'Okay, okay, okay,' he says. 'Let me think. The name does ring a bell.'

What kind of a game are you playing, Victor Lenzen?

'I found out during my research that your real surname is Michaelis. Conrads is a nom de plume. After Joseph Conrad, one of your favourite authors, right?'

I'm having trouble keeping my temper. He's still acting.

'Is Anna Michaelis a relation of yours?' Lenzen asks.

'Where were you on 23 August 2002?' I retaliate.

He looks confused. You could clean pity the man, the way he's sitting there, bleeding and snivelling.

'Where were you on 23 August 2002?' I repeat.

Put him under stress, wear him down, break him.

'Bloody hell, how am I supposed to remember that?' he asks.

'Think about it.'

'I don't know.' Again he buries his head in his hands.

'Why did you kill Anna Michaelis?'

'What?'

Lenzen leaps up, knocking his chair to the floor. The sudden movement and the clatter make me start. For a moment, I think

Lenzen's going to make a second attempt to attack me, and I too leap up, and back away a few steps. But he only looks at me aghast.

'I want to know why you murdered my sister,' I say.

He looks at me. I look at him. I feel nothing. Everything about me is cold and numb; only the gun in my hand is red hot.

'What?' says Lenzen. 'Have you finally…'

'Why did you do it? Why Anna?'

'Oh God,' Lenzen says wearily.

He's reeling.

'You think I murdered your sister,' he murmurs.

He seems dazed. He's not looking at me any more; he's looking at the floor, staring into space.

'I *know* you did,' I correct him.

Victor Lenzen looks up and stares at me with wide-open eyes. Then, grasping the edge of the table, he turns away from me and breaks into spasms of vomiting. I look at him in horror: he's bleeding, he's crying, he's throwing up.

Lenzen rallies himself. He coughs, gasping for breath, and looks at me, his upper lip beaded with sweat, that curious expression on his face like a child that's been given a hiding. For a moment, I see a human being instead of the monster and my stomach tightens with pity. I feel his fear—the fear he feels for himself, but more than anything else the fear he feels for his daughter. It's written all over his face.

That face. I notice again that he has a sprinkling of freckles. I can imagine what he must have looked like as a little boy—before life, before the wrinkles. Interesting wrinkles. I catch myself thinking that I'd like to touch his face, just to know what it feels like. I remember my beautiful grandma and her lovely lined face. Lenzen's face would feel different beneath my fingers—firmer.

I brush the thought aside. What am I doing? I'm like a child at the zoo who wants to stroke the tiger even though she's quite old enough to know that it would tear her limb from limb.

Get a grip on yourself, Linda.

I mustn't let myself get carried away by my pity.

Lenzen is retching again.

'You're a murderer,' I say.

Lenzen shakes his head.

I'm perplexed. Either Victor Lenzen has no breaking point, or else... I hardly dare think it through. What if I'd long since reached the point at which Victor Lenzen would break down under pressure? If the only reason he hasn't yet confessed is that he doesn't have anything to confess?

No!

I realise how dangerous this train of thought is. I must pull myself together, remember what I learnt from Dr Christensen: that thinking this way might lead to a breakdown. The situation is not only a strain on Victor Lenzen's nerves but on mine too. I mustn't budge an inch, mustn't show any pity and I certainly mustn't start doubting now. Victor Lenzen is guilty. Everyone has a breaking point; Lenzen just hasn't yet reached his. He's used to extreme situations; he said as much himself. Maybe now is the time to offer him the famous way out: a tangible incentive to confess.

'Herr Lenzen,' I say. 'If you give me what I want, I promise I'll let you go.'

He coughs, gasping for breath, then looks at me.

'Give me what I want—and this nightmare will be over,' I say.

I hear him swallow.

'But you want a confession!' he says, turning from me, his hand clutching at his stomach.

'That's right.'

I know what he's going to say next: *But if I were to confess, you'd shoot me straight away! Why should I believe you?* Of course my only answer to that could be: *Right now, you have no alternative, Herr Lenzen.*

He says nothing. Then he gives me a steady look.

'I have nothing to confess,' he says.

'Herr Lenzen, you're not thinking straight. You have two options.

Option one: you tell me the truth. That's all I want. I want to know what happened to my younger sister that night twelve years ago. You tell me—and I'll let you go. That's number one. Option two is this gun here.'

Lenzen stares into the muzzle of the gun.

'And,' I add, 'my patience won't hold out forever.'

'Please,' Lenzen says, 'you've got the wrong man!'

I stifle a groan. How long can he continue to deny it? I decide to change tactics.

'Would you like a tissue?' I ask, taking care to make my voice sound brighter, softer.

He shakes his head.

'A glass of water?'

He shakes his head.

'Herr Lenzen, I understand why you're denying it,' I say. 'It must be hard for you to believe that I really will let you go if you tell me what I want to know. That's perfectly understandable for someone in your position. But it's the truth. If you tell me what I want to know, I'll let you go.'

It is quite still again; only Lenzen's shallow breath can be heard. Standing there, hunched over, he seems a lot smaller.

'I'm not going to lie to you,' I say. 'I will, of course, inform the police. But you will leave this house unscathed.'

Now I have his attention. He looks at me.

'I'm not a murderer,' he says. Tears glisten in his eyes. I don't know whether it's because of the retching or because he really is on the point of crying again. At this moment, I feel sorry for him, in spite of everything.

Lenzen straightens up, taking his hand off his stomach. He turns to face me once more. His eyes are red; he looks older. His laughter lines have vanished. I can see him fight the impulse to wipe his mouth on the sleeve of his smart shirt. I can smell the pool of vomit at his feet.

I squash my pity and tell myself it's a good thing. The more ill at ease he feels, the better. His situation is humiliating and that rankles—good! I hold the gun so tight that my knuckles stick out white. Lenzen stares at me in silence. A trial of strength. I'm not going to be the first to speak. I want to see how he turns the situation now. The way out is clear; the cards are on the table. He has to confess.

It is silent. Outside, the sky flickers. I hear my breathing and I hear Lenzen's, gasping and fitful. Thunder follows. Apart from that, it is quite still.

Lenzen closes his eyes, as if by so doing he could release himself from this nightmare. When he opens his eyes, he begins to speak. At last.

'Please listen to me, Frau Conrads,' he says. 'There's been some mistake! My name is Victor Lenzen. I'm a journalist. And a family man. Not a particularly good one, but…'

He's losing focus.

'I abhor violence. I'm a pacifist. I'm a human-rights activist. I've never harmed anyone in my life.'

His gaze is penetrating. I waver.

'You have to believe me!' he says.

But I must not doubt.

'If you lie to me once more, I'll pull the trigger.'

My voice sounds strange. I don't know whether I really mean it.

'If you lie to me once more, I'll pull the trigger,' I repeat.

Lenzen says nothing—he simply stares at me.

I wait, as the storm grows closer and the wind gets up. I wait a long time and I realise that he's decided not to talk to me anymore.

It's over to me.

23

JONAS

A feeling for whether a case would be solved quickly or not at all always took hold fast. Jonas's gut instinct told him that the case concerning the elfin woman who had been found stabbed to death in her

157

flat was not going to be solved as rapidly as his colleagues assumed. They expected either the jealous lover or the piqued ex to be charged, especially as there had been an eyewitness.

But a sense of unease was creeping over Jonas, so black and heavy that it left no room for optimism. True, everything smacked of a *crime passionnel*, and there was an identikit picture of the culprit. But no one from the victim's circle of friends and relations had recognised the picture. How was that possible, if it was a crime of passion? Of course, a secret affair was a possibility. But that wouldn't have been like Britta Peters.

Jonas took a deep breath and entered the conference room. It smelt of a peculiar mixture of PVC flooring and coffee. The entire team had already assembled: Michael Dzierzewski, Volker Zimmer, Antonia Bug and Nilgün Arslan, a much-loved colleague recently returned from maternity leave. The room was filled with murmurs as they discussed yesterday's football match, trip to the cinema or evening in the pub. The inevitable fluorescent lighting was on, even though it was broad daylight.

Jonas switched it off and stepped in front of the group.

'Good morning all,' he said. 'Let's hear what you've got to say. Volker!' He pointed to the man in jeans and a black polo shirt.

'I had a word with the victim's landlord,' Zimmer said. 'We'd heard from a neighbour that Britta Peters had complained about the man gaining access to her flat without her agreement.'

'We remember all that,' said Jonas impatiently.

'Well, the only crime this landlord—a certain Hans Feldmann— has committed is boring his son and daughter-in-law to death with three hours of photos from his recent trip to Sweden.'

'He has an alibi?' Jonas asked.

'Yes, his son and daughter-in-law stayed the night with him.'

'Couldn't he have slipped out briefly?'

'It's possible,' Zimmer replied. 'But if the eyewitness's statement is to be believed, it wasn't Hans Feldmann she saw: he's over seventy.'

'Okay,' said Jonas. 'Michael?'

'The ex-boyfriend can be ruled out too,' said Dzierzewski.

'Britta's teenage sweetheart?' asked Bug.

'That's the one. The two of them had been together for a long time and it seems it wasn't a pretty break-up. But he split up with her, not the other way round.'

'Okay, that makes him less suspicious,' said Jonas. 'Doesn't mean he's off the hook.'

'I'm afraid he is. He was away, you see—with his new flame, a certain Vanessa Schneider. A romantic holiday to the Maldives.'

'Okay, keep going—what else?' asked Jonas.

'A quick question about the ex-boyfriend first,' said Nilgün. 'Does anyone know why he dumped her?'

'He thought she was cheating on him,' Dzierzewski replied. 'But her sister and all her girlfriends swear that that's nonsense and that he was only looking for an excuse because—I quote—"he's a cowardly bastard".'

'All right,' Jonas replied. 'Cowardly bastard or not—he's out. Anything else?'

'Not much,' said Antonia. 'No other partners, no ex-boyfriends, no trouble at work, no debts, no enemies, no rows. You could pretty much say that Britta Peters was an incredibly dull person.'

'Or an incredibly good one,' said Jonas.

The team was silent.

'Okay then,' he said. 'The only thing we can do now is carry on looking for the mystery man observed by the eyewitness at the scene of the crime.'

'*Allegedly* observed,' said Antonia Bug. 'I think the sister's lying. I mean, please, even the identikit artist says she sounded as if she was making the face up as she went along.'

Jonas sighed.

'Some people aren't good at faces,' he said. 'Especially not in stressful situations. And why should Sophie Peters have killed her sister? She alerted the police as soon as she found her. There was no blood on her clothes. Even the stab wounds inflicted on the victim suggest the culprit was much bigger than Sophie Peters—and, in all probability, a man. Besides...'

'I know all that,' said Antonia Bug, interrupting him, 'and I didn't say I thought Sophie Peters killed her sister. But what if she's covering for the murderer? You're not telling me you believe this story of the mystery man.'

'Who do you have in mind?'

'I don't know—maybe her fiancé. Do you remember how Sophie Peters reacted when I asked her the reason for the row she'd had with him?'

Jonas thought of the removal boxes in Sophie's flat. Her fiancé was moving out. What were the implications of their break-up?

'Sophie Peters and her fiancé have split up since,' said Jonas.

A murmur went round the room. Antonia Bug slapped her thigh.

'There you are,' she cried. 'There you are!'

Jonas held up his hands in a conciliatory gesture.

'Do we have any reason to believe that Sophie Peters' fiancé was having an affair with the murder victim?' he asked.

Volker Zimmer was about to say something, but Bug was faster.

'A good friend of Britta Peters told me that said fiancé, Paul Albrecht, was madly in love with Britta, and that Sophie Peters knew it. Britta Peters apparently told her herself.'

'Sorry, folks,' said Zimmer, finally making himself heard, 'but I'm afraid I have to take the wind out of your sails. I checked on the fiancé yesterday. He did indeed have a row with Sophie Peters on the night of the crime. But after she'd gone off in a huff to be consoled by her sister, he took himself to the pub and went on such a bender with two colleagues from his solicitors' office that the landlord had to kick all three of them out and call them a taxi. It can't have been him. He's definitively out.'

'Damn,' said Bug.

Helpless silence filled the room.

'All right,' said Jonas. 'Antonia and Michael, please talk to the victim's colleagues again. Find out if she was really planning to move away—had she perhaps already handed in her notice? You might hear something. Volker and Nilgün, please have another word with the victim's ex-boyfriend. Maybe we can find out from him whether there had been a new man in Britta Peters' life after all. Ask him if he *really* thinks Britta Peters was cheating on him. Meanwhile, I'll get in touch with forensics again.'

As the team scattered, Jonas fought the urge to go out and light up. It was getting more and more obvious: if they really didn't find the murderer anywhere in the victim's circle of friends and relations, it was going to be very, very hard. He wouldn't be able to keep the promise he had made to Sophie.

20

Victor Lenzen looks at me with bowed head and says nothing. I stare back. I'm going to stand my ground, no matter what happens.

We're sitting down again. I had asked him—with raised gun—to return to his seat.

'Where were you living twelve years ago?' I ask.

Lenzen lets out a tormented noise, but says nothing.

'Where were you living twelve years ago?'

I don't raise my voice, I don't shout; I simply ask, the way I've learnt.

'Do you know Anna Michaelis?'

It is disconcerting looking somebody in the eyes for a long time. Lenzen's eyes are very pale—grey, almost white. But the grey contains some tiny speckles of green and brown, and is edged with a black circle. Lenzen's eyes look like an eclipse of the sun.

'Do you know Anna Michaelis?'

Silence.

'Where were you on 23 August 2002?'

Silence.

'Where were you on 23 August 2002?'

Nothing—just a frown. As if the date reminds him of something that is only now coming back to him.

'I don't know,' he says faintly.

He's talking. Good.

'Why are you lying to me, Herr Lenzen?'

In a film, I would release the safety catch at this point to drive my words home.

'Where were you living twelve years ago?' I repeat. 'Talk, damn it!'

'In Munich,' says Lenzen.

'Do you know Anna Michaelis?'

'No.'

'Why are you lying, Herr Lenzen? There's no point.'

'I'm not lying.'

'Why did you kill Anna Michaelis?'

'I've never killed anyone.'

'Have you killed other women?'

'I've never killed anyone.'

'What are you?'

'I beg your pardon?'

'What are you? Are you a rapist? A robber and murderer? Did you know Anna?'

'Anna,' Lenzen says, and the hairs on the back of my neck stand on end. 'No.'

It does something to me, hearing him speak Anna's name out loud like that—the name she was so proud of being able to read backwards as well as forwards. I tremble. I see Anna lying in a pool of blood, although blood gave her the creeps, and I know that I'm not going to let Lenzen go: Victor Lenzen will confess or die.

'Do you know an Anna Michaelis?'

'No, I don't know any Anna Michaelis.'

'Where were you on 23 August 2002?'

Silence again.

'Where were you on 23 August 2002?'

'I…' He hesitates. 'I'm not sure.'

That annoys me. He knows perfectly well where he was on 23 August 2002. He knows perfectly well what I'm driving at. The cat's been out of the bag for ages. So what's all this about?

'What's that supposed to mean?' I ask, unable to conceal my impatience.

'Frau Conrads, please listen to me. Please. Do me a favour.'

I'm sick of him. I'm supposed to be breaking him and instead I'm the one who's being worn down. I can't bear his look anymore, his voice, his lies. I no longer believe he's going to confess.

'All right then,' I say.

'I didn't know you'd lost your sister,' says Lenzen, and his hypocrisy makes my gun hand tremble.

Lost. The way he says that—as if no one were to blame. I feel like hitting him again, but harder and more than once.

He sees it in my eyes and holds up his hands beseechingly. Look at him, cowering there, cringing like a beaten child, trying to appeal to my pity. It's pathetic.

'I didn't know,' Lenzen repeats, 'and I'm very sorry.'

I'd like to shoot him, to see what it feels like.

'You really think I did it.'

'I know you did,' I correct him, 'yes.'

Lenzen is silent for a moment. 'How?' he asks at last.

I can't help frowning.

'How can you know?'

What kind of a game is this, Victor Lenzen? You know that I know.

'How can you know?' he asks again.

Something inside me rips. I can't take any more.

'Because I fucking well saw you!' I yell. 'Because I looked you in the eye the same way I'm looking at you now. So save your lies and your posturing because I can see you. I can see you.'

My heart's pounding and I'm gasping as if I'd run a sprint. Lenzen stares at me in disbelief. Once again he holds up his hands.

I'm trembling. I force myself to remember that I'll never find out why Anna had to die if I shoot him now.

'That's not possible, Frau Conrads,' says Lenzen.

'And yet it's the case.'

'I didn't know your sister.'

'Then why did you kill her?'

'I didn't kill her! You've made a mistake!'

'I have not made a mistake!'

Lenzen looks at me as if I were a stubborn child refusing to listen to sense.

'What happened back then?' he asks.

I close my eyes briefly. Specks of red dance on my retina.

'What were the circumstances of your sister's death? Where did she die?' Lenzen asks. 'If I knew a bit more about it, maybe I could convince you...'

Dear God, give me the strength not to shoot him.

'I recognised you straight away, when I saw you on television.'

I spit the words at him.

'Maybe you really did see somebody...'

'You're damn right, I did! Of course I saw somebody!'

'But not me!'

How can he say that? How *can* he? We were both there, in that room, on that hot summer's night, with the smell of iron in the air. How can he say that and seriously hope to get away with it?

I give a start when Lenzen swoops to his feet. Instinctively, I get up and point my gun straight at his chest. No matter what he does, I want to be able to stop him in time.

He puts up his hands.

'Think about it, Linda,' he says. 'If I had anything to confess, I'd have confessed long ago.'

The gun is heavy.

'A human life is at stake here, Linda. You're the jury; I've grasped that now. You think I'm a murderer and you're the jury. Is that right?'

I nod.

'Then at least grant me the right to defend myself,' says Lenzen.

I nod again, reluctantly.

'Do you have any other evidence against me, apart from the fact that you think you saw me?'

I don't reply. The answer is galling: no.

'Think about it, Linda. It's twelve years ago, isn't it. Isn't it?'

I nod.

'Twelve years. And, quite by chance, you see your sister's murderer on TV? What are the odds?'

I'd like to ignore the question. I've put it to myself often enough, in the long nights since the earthquake struck. I feel sick. My head is bursting. Everything's spinning.

'What are the odds?'

I don't reply.

'Are you sure I'm guilty, Linda? Not fairly sure, not ninety-nine per cent sure, but absolutely sure, beyond a shadow of a doubt? If you are, then shoot me right here on the spot.'

Everything's spinning.

'Be careful. Two human lives are at stake here—yours and mine. Are you sure?'

I don't reply.

'Are you absolutely sure, Linda?'

I feel sick, my head is bursting. The room rotates in languid ellipses and I remember that the Earth is moving at an incredible speed through a cold and empty universe.

'Is 23 August 2002 the day your sister was killed?' asks Lenzen.

'Yes,' is all I can say.

Lenzen seems to be thinking. There's more silence. He seems to come to a decision.

'I think I know where I was that day,' he says.

I stare at him. He stands before me with raised hands—a

166

good-looking, intelligent man, whom I would probably like if I didn't know what was hidden behind the charming exterior. I mustn't let him fool me.

'Where was your sister killed?' Lenzen asks.

'You know very well where,' I say.

I can't help it: my self-control is beginning to crack.

'I don't know,' says Lenzen. 'My research didn't turn up anything about a sister who was murdered.'

'Do you want to know where my sister was murdered?' I ask. 'In her flat. In Munich.'

Lenzen gives a sigh of relief.

'I wasn't in Munich at that time,' he says. 'I wasn't in Munich at the time and I can prove it.'

He gives a short laugh of relief, a humourless sound, and then says again, almost incredulously, 'And I can prove it.'

He sits down.

I forbid myself to let him take me in with this cheap bluff. Lenzen laughs again, hysterically. He's like a man who's been through hell, like a man who'd already given his life up for lost, and suddenly sees a glimmer of hope.

What's going on here?

'If you weren't in Munich at that time then where were you?'

Lenzen's eyes are bloodshot. He looks exhausted.

'Afghanistan,' he says. 'I was in Afghanistan.'

24

SOPHIE

The events of the past night seemed like a dream to Sophie. The shadow crouching in her car, the footsteps hard on her heels, her pure, primeval fear. It must have been the same fear Britta had felt in the last minutes of her life.

Sophie wondered whether she should tell the police that she was being followed. But what could she say to them? Even to her, it all seemed so unreal. How could she explain it all to that arrogant young policewoman she was always put through to, even when she asked to speak to Superintendent Jonas Weber? (A fact that wounded Sophie more than she cared to admit.) It was true that the charges against her had been dropped, but she wouldn't have the best reputation at the police station right now. She could, of course, hope that the man who had pursued her in the underground car park had been caught on a surveillance camera. That, at least, would finally prove his existence.

The only problem was that now, in broad daylight, in the safety of her flat, it seemed like a dream. What if the police were to go through the surveillance tapes and find no one? Wouldn't that completely undermine Sophie's credibility?

She'd sort things out somehow, even without any help.

She sat down at her desk. It was covered in notes and newspaper cuttings on the case—a welter of contradictory information and false trails. An impenetrable jungle.

Sophie buried her face in her hands. She could feel her life falling apart. She hadn't noticed at first; she'd had too much to do and had been running and running to avoid having to stop and think. But now there was nothing left to be done, and she had been forced to come to rest.

Sophie had talked to everyone in Britta's life. She had painstakingly reconstructed Britta's last days and looked into the two new employees from Britta's company, but neither of them remotely resembled the man she had surprised in her sister's flat. She had even checked up on every single guest at the party Britta had thrown for a friend shortly before her death. All without success.

She had sifted through Britta's social media profiles for new friends—nothing. Whenever she had the feeling she was getting somewhere, her hopes were always dashed. And the police were becoming obsessed with their stupid theory of a row with a violent lover. They'd even questioned Paul, but that had soon been proved idiotic, just like that business with Britta's landlord, who was perhaps a little senile but nothing more. It was hopeless. The police would never find the murderer.

*

Sophie's mobile was ringing and she recognised her parents' number. She didn't have the slightest inclination to take the call. The last time her mother had rung, she'd accused her of being unnatural for not crying over her sister and told her she ought to be with them rather than running all over town playing James Bond.

The ringing stopped. Sophie stared at the improvised pin board with all the information and evidence she had gathered in connection with the murder; it took up nearly her entire study. There was so much that she didn't understand. How was it possible that nobody else had seen the murderer? Why hadn't he attacked her, the eyewitness? What would he have done if she hadn't turned up? Why hadn't he run away as soon as he heard somebody in the flat? Was he a burglar? If so, why hadn't he stolen anything? And what the hell was the detail that had struck such a false note but that she couldn't now lay her finger on, no matter how hard she racked her brains?

Of the countless agonising questions, the worst was: why? Why did her sister have to die? Who had hated Britta that much? Britta, who was always ready to listen to everyone; Britta, who took such good care of others—perfect Britta! Sophie clung to her conviction that it must have been a stranger. But how was she supposed to find a stranger?

The flat seemed unbearably airless to Sophie. She slipped on her trainers, left the house, stepped onto the street and set off. It was a Saturday, and there must have been some football match on that afternoon because it was crowded when Sophie reached the underground station. Without knowing where she was actually going, she allowed herself to be carried down the escalator by the crowd and eventually came to a stop on the platform where the trains left for the town centre. It reeked of sweat and trouble; the football fans were everywhere, with their beery breath and aggressive singing.

Sophie was borne onto a train by the stream of people. She stood there, squashed between three giants, and the train set off with a jolt. The rucksack of the man in front of her was in her face; the zip scratched her cheek as the train took a bend. The windows were steamed up and there were no longer people in the carriage, only a heaving, homogenous mass, breathing the humid, unwholesome air.

Sophie tried to elbow herself a bit of space, but the crowd around her didn't budge a millimetre. The air was no longer air; it was hot and doughy and solid. Someone switched on a ghetto blaster; 'Seven Nation Army' blared out and the mass broke into a delighted roar.

Sophie clenched her teeth. She felt like a nail bomb.

At the next station, she was thrown out of the damp heat of the train onto the platform; the crowd carried her towards the exit. Sophie fought her way through the swarms of people, broke free and began to run.

Only when she had entered the museum did she breathe freely again. This was what she needed if she was to stay sane: a few hours with her favourite artists, with Raphael and Rubens and van Gogh. A little beauty, a little time to forget.

Sophie bought herself a ticket and wandered about, eventually coming to stop in front of one of van Gogh's *Sunflowers*. She marvelled at the radiant colours and at the vitality that always seemed to emanate from the painting, and for a moment she forgot her fears and worries. Then it came back to her—that detail in Britta's flat that had struck such a frighteningly false note.

21

Once again the weather has changed, and again the balance of power threatens to tip. Victor Lenzen is no longer cowering before me like a thrashed dog; he's regained some of his self-confidence.

'I have an alibi,' he says.

We're sitting in semi-darkness. The storm's on its way. I can hear the thunder coming closer and closer, and I have a terrible feeling that something dreadful is going to happen when the storm reaches us. I brush the thought aside, telling myself that my grandmother was afraid of storms and communicated her fear to me; that it's superstition and nothing more.

Lenzen is lying. He must be lying. I saw him.

'I have an alibi,' he repeats.

'How are you going to prove it?' I ask.

My voice sounds husky. Fear is creeping up on me, cold and merciless.

'I remember that summer,' Lenzen says. '2002. World Cup in Japan and South Korea. Brazil and Germany in the final.'

'How are you going to prove that you have an alibi?' I repeat impatiently.

'I flew to Afghanistan on 20 August,' Lenzen says. 'I remember it very well, because my ex-wife's birthday is 21 August, and she was pissed off because I was going to miss her party.'

My world begins to totter.

I grasp the pistol, steadying myself. Just another trick.

'How are you going to prove it?' I ask, forcing myself to breathe steadily.

'I was reporting daily at that time, on the ground. The deployment of German troops in Afghanistan was still relatively recent; people were interested in what was going on in the Hindu Kush. I accompanied some soldiers at close quarters; the reports should still be on the internet—even today.'

I stare at him. Gooseflesh spreads over my body. I won't believe him. He's bluffing.

'Look it up,' says Lenzen with an encouraging glance at my smartphone, which is lying on the table in front of me, and I see through his trick. The bastard. He's hoping for a brief moment of distraction to attack me again, to take the gun off me.

I shake my head and point my chin at Lenzen's phone without loosening my grasp on the gun. I haven't forgotten the rapid swooping movement with which Lenzen got over the table; I won't be giving him another opportunity to do that.

Lenzen understands and picks up his phone. He begins to tap around on it.

I grow nervous. What if he wanted to get to his phone to call the police?

'Any funny business and you won't leave this house alive.'

Scarcely have the words left my mouth before I give a mental start. Why should he want to ring the police if he's Anna's murderer?

You've stopped thinking straight, Linda.

Lenzen frowns at me and goes back to tapping. At length he looks up, an inscrutable expression on his face, and pushes his phone across the table to me. I pick it up, without taking my eyes off Lenzen. Then I lower my gaze and read.

Spiegel Online. I read, scroll, read again, scroll up, scroll down. Compare the names, the dates. *Spiegel Online.* Archive. Victor Lenzen. Afghanistan. 21 August 2002, 22 August 2002, 23 August 2002, 24, 25, 26, 27, 28 August 2002.

I read and read, over and over again. My brain's searching for a way out.

'Linda?'

I scroll up and down.

'Linda?'

I hear his voice as if through cotton wool.

'Linda?'

I look up.

'How was your sister killed?'

My hands are trembling like an old woman's.

'How was your sister killed?' Lenzen repeats.

'She was stabbed seven times,' I say, as if in a trance.

So much anger. And the blood—blood everywhere.

I don't know whether I say it out loud or only think it.

'Linda,' says Lenzen, 'you've got the wrong man. Please think about it.'

I can hardly concentrate on what Lenzen is saying; it's all going too fast for me; I'm lagging three steps behind, still trying to come to terms with the fact that Lenzen has just come up with an alibi. It's not possible, it's just not possible.

'Get it clear in your head what that means,' Lenzen says, speaking slowly and quietly, as if he were trying to charm a poisonous snake. 'You're not seeing justice served if you shoot me. On the contrary: no matter what you do to me, the true murderer is still out there somewhere.'

That hits me like a bullet. But who was it, if it wasn't Lenzen?

No. No. No. I saw Lenzen.

'Linda?' says Lenzen, jolting me out of my thoughts. 'Please put the gun down.'

I look at him. At last I begin to understand.

From 21 August 2002 until at least 28 August 2002, Victor Lenzen was in Afghanistan. He had no opportunity to kill my sister.

My head aches, I feel dizzy, and I think to myself that it's been going on for such a long time now: the pain, the dizziness, the hallucinations, the song—that damn song—the shadow in the corner of my bedroom, the sleeplessness, the blackouts. I understand, and the realisation is incredibly painful.

I am mad.

Or well on the way to becoming so.

That is the truth. That is my life.

The effects of extended isolation include sleeping disorders, eating disorders, cognitive impairment and even hallucinations. I read a lot—I know that kind of thing.

The panic attacks, the trauma, my tendency to lose myself in stories, my guilty conscience at not having been able to save Anna, my years of loneliness. It all makes sense. But that doesn't make things any better.

The man facing me is innocent. All the things he said that I interpreted as references to the murder were no more than comments on fictional characters and a work of literature.

What have you done, Linda?

My throat aches. It's tears rising—I remember the feeling, even though I haven't cried for a good ten years.

I give a dry sob. Everything is spinning. The ceiling is suddenly full of insects, like a creeping, teeming carpet. I'm losing control. For a moment I forget who I am, or what I'm called and what's going on. I'm so confused. But there is a voice.

'Put the gun down, Linda.'

Lenzen. It's only now that I become aware of the weight in my hand again, the gun.

Lenzen gets up, approaching me cautiously.

'Put the gun down.'

I hear him as if through cotton wool.

'Keep calm,' he says. 'Keep calm.'

It is over. I have no more strength. My horror at what has happened—at what I have done—overwhelms me. The phone drops from my hand and clatters to the floor. I'm trembling all over. My muscles no longer function; I slide off the chair—I would fall, but Lenzen catches me, holds me, and we go down together and sit there on the floor, gasping, sweaty, frightened. Lenzen holds me and I let him; I am numb, I am stunned; I have no choice but to let it happen. I wait, sitting it out. I am a knot—a woman-shaped knot, hard and tight. But then something happens: the tectonic plates of my brain shift and, slowly, the knot loosens, and I begin to cry. I sob and tremble in Victor Lenzen's arms, I dissolve in his arms, salt in the sea. My brain is racing, it can't process physical proximity; it isn't used to it, although it's been hankering after it for a good ten years. Lenzen's body is warm and firm, he is taller than me, my head fits into the hollow between his throat and his chest. I whimper. I don't understand why he's doing what he's doing. I let him hold me, I feel connected, alive, and the feeling almost hurts. Then he eases himself away from me, and once more I feel the ground disappear from beneath my feet.

Lenzen gets to his feet, looks down at me. I'm drifting, trying to get a hold on the shore.

'But I saw you!' I say feebly.

He watches me with complete composure.

'I don't doubt that you believe that,' he says.

We look each other in the eye and I see that he is sincere. I see his fear and his relief, and something else that I can't put a name to—maybe pity.

We are silent again. I'm glad I don't have to say anything. My brain has ceased its unrelenting deliberation and has fallen quiet from exhaustion. A good thing, too—I don't want to have to think about criminal charges and scandal and prison or the psychiatric ward right now. I only want quiet, for as long as possible.

I look at the face of the man before me. I seldom have the opportunity to have a really good look at a face. So I look at Lenzen and watch as the monster turns into a perfectly normal man.

I sit there, sniffing, and listening to my tears falling on the parquet. Then Lenzen takes a step towards the table and makes a grab for the gun. I watch him, but it's not until he's holding the gun that I realise I've made a huge mistake.

'You still don't believe me,' he says.

It's not a question; it's a statement of fact. He looks at me for a moment, then says, 'You really do need professional help,' and turns and leaves.

Deep in shock, I stare after him. It's a few moments before I am able to ease myself out of my stupor. I hear him open the front door, and the noise of the storm swells, as if someone had turned an invisible control knob. I hear his footsteps recede down the gravel path.

I get up onto legs that scarcely bear my weight and I go after him. When I see the front door wide open, my heart begins to race. What is he doing? I glance cautiously out of the door. I have no idea what the time is, how long we've been talking, how long we've been circling one another, but it's been dark for ages.

I spot Lenzen in the moonlight, walking purposefully towards the lake, the gun in his hand. Between the lake and the edge of the woods he stops and seems to hesitate. Then he raises his arm and throws my pistol into the water. It seems to me that I hear the sound it makes as it hits the smooth surface, but that is impossible; I'm too far away. In the black and white of the moonlight I see Lenzen turn to face me. I can't make out his features—he is only a silhouette—but I can feel his gaze. I wonder what I must look like for him from out there, a small blur in the doorway of my enormous, brightly lit house. We look at each other across the distance, and for a moment I think that Lenzen is going to turn and walk away. But he does the opposite: he begins heading towards me. He's coming back of his own free will.

Stockholm syndrome is the name given to a psychological phenomenon in which hostages develop a positive emotional relationship to their aggressors. I know things like that; I've had a lot of time to read over the past decade.

I shudder—not only because of the cold that's blowing in from outside, but because I realise that in this scenario I am the aggressor.

My God, Linda.

I have threatened an innocent man with a gun, hit him and detained him in my house. What's more, I've recorded everything. I will never find my sister's murderer. The best thing to do would be to put a bullet in my head. But Lenzen's sunk my gun in the lake.

He's standing right in front of me.

'Now do you believe that I'm not going to hurt you?'

I nod feebly.

'Why don't you call the police?' I ask.

'Because I want to talk to you first,' he says. 'Where can we sit?'

I lead him into the kitchen. The coffee cups and newspapers that the photographer arranged on the table in another age, another lifetime, are still there. As if the birds hadn't fallen from the sky after all.

'Why did you throw the gun in the lake?' I ask.

'I don't know,' Lenzen replies. 'A displacement activity.'

I nod. I know what he means.

'I…' I begin, and immediately falter. 'I don't know what to say. I don't know how I can apologise.'

'You're trembling,' says Lenzen. 'Sit down.'

I do as he says and he sits down opposite me. Once again we are silent for a long time. The silence is no longer a trial of strength; I simply don't know what to say. I count the wrinkles on Lenzen's forehead. When I've almost reached twenty, he jolts me out of my thoughts.

'Linda? If I may call you Linda…'

'Anyone I've held at gunpoint has the right to call me by my first name,' I say.

I cringe at my pathetic attempt at a joke.

Lenzen ignores it.

'Do you have anybody you could ring up?' he asks. 'Family? Friends?'

It's only now that I realise what a mellifluous voice he has. It sounds

177

like the dubbing voice of an aging Hollywood actor, but I can't think who.

'Linda?'

'Why do you ask?'

'I have the feeling you shouldn't be on your own right now.'

I stare at him. I don't understand. I attacked him; he has every right to call the police. Or retaliate.

'Unless he really does have something to hide and would rather not get involved with the police.'

It's not until after the last word is out of my mouth that I realise I didn't think that; I said it out loud.

Lenzen takes that on the chin too. He seems to have resigned himself long ago to the fact that I'm completely insane. And I am, too—insane, mad, a public menace.

Bestselling author, 38, shoots journalist, 53, during interview.

Lenzen has an alibi. Lenzen is innocent. It's going to take me some time to get used to this new state of affairs.

'Maybe your parents,' he says.

'What?'

'Maybe you could give your parents a ring. So you're not on your own.'

'No, not my parents. My parents and I, we…'

I don't know the end of that sentence.

'We don't talk much,' I say eventually, although I had been going to say something else.

'How unusual,' says Lenzen.

His suntanned hands lie on my kitchen table and I feel a terrifying urge to touch them. I tear my gaze away. His pale eyes are resting on me.

'What do you mean?' I ask, when his remark finally gets through the membrane that surrounds me.

'Well, you told me your sister was murdered. And, of course, I'm no expert, but a tragedy like that normally welds a family together rather than driving them apart.'

I shrug. The word 'normally' has no meaning in my world. 'With us, it's different,' I say.

It's no business of his, but it does me good to say that. My parents aren't interested in me; they're not interested in my books. They won't even let me buy them a bigger house. All they're interested in is their dead daughter.

Lenzen sighs. 'I have a confession to make, Linda,' he says.

Every hair on my neck stands on end.

'I wasn't entirely honest with you regarding the premise of this interview.'

I swallow hard, can't say a thing.

'I knew about your sister.'

I'm gobsmacked.

'What?' I croak.

'Not the way you think,' Lenzen says quickly, holding up his hands in a conciliatory gesture. 'I came across the murder case when I was researching for the interview. In fact, I'm surprised no one had unearthed it before, but then the internet wasn't as crazy at that time as it is nowadays. There wasn't such detailed documentation of everything.'

I can't follow him.

'Well, at any rate, I know about your sister's case—a dreadful affair. I understand you, Linda; it's not easy coming to terms with a thing like that.'

'But you pretended you didn't even know I had a sister.'

'I'm a journalist, Linda. Of course I didn't start by laying all my cards on the table; I wanted to hear what you had to say first. Put yourself in my position. A woman who was the main suspect in a murder case many years ago writes a book in which that very murder is described down to the last detail. It's a bloody sensation! But if I'd known that you're so'—he falters—'that you're so fragile, then...'

His words seep into my consciousness.

'The main suspect?' I say flatly.

Lenzen looks at me in surprise.

'I was never under suspicion.'

'Hm,' says Lenzen. 'Well, I suppose that whoever finds the corpse is automatically one of the main suspects to begin with, and that it doesn't have anything to do with you as such.'

I swallow. 'What do you know?' I ask.

Lenzen squirms. 'I don't think I...'

'What do you know? Who have you spoken to?' I yell. 'I have a right to know! Please,' I add softly.

'All right then,' he says. 'I spoke to the policeman who led the investigation. And you were indeed the main suspect for a long time. Didn't you know?'

'Which policeman?' I ask.

'I don't know whether I can tell you,' Lenzen replies. 'Is it really that important?'

I see a face before me—one eye green and the other brown. No, it's not possible!

'No,' I say, 'not that important.'

I'm hot; the air is electrically charged. I long for rain, but there's no rain coming. The storm has simply passed us by; it will break elsewhere. Only the wind can still be heard, whistling round the house.

'In any case, it's clear that you're innocent,' says Lenzen. 'They were never able to prove anything against you. You didn't have the hint of a motive.'

I can't believe we're talking about whether *I'm* guilty or innocent.

'And, of course, it's really not your fault that you can't leave the house,' Lenzen adds.

'What?'

Again, I feel a jolt of fear.

'What's that got to do with any of this?'

'Nothing, of course,' Lenzen hastens to assure me.

'But?'

'It was only a casual remark.'

'You're not the kind to make casual remarks,' I reply.

'Well, some of the people investigating your sister's murder case back then interpreted your…retreat as, well, how can I put it…as an admission of guilt.'

'My retreat?' My voice cracks with anger and despair; I can't help it. 'I didn't retreat! I'm ill!'

'What I'm telling you isn't my opinion. But there are people out there who don't believe in this obscure illness; they see a murderer who has fled from society. There are those who think you live in a kind of self-imposed solitary confinement here.'

I feel dizzy.

'I shouldn't have told you,' Lenzen says. 'I thought you'd heard it all long ago. It's a good story, that's all.'

'Yes,' I say.

I've run out of words.

'The worst is the doubt. A vestige of doubt always remains,' Lenzen says. 'That's the awful thing. Doubt is like a thorn you can't get a hold on. It's terrible when a thing like that destroys families.'

I blink.

'Are you trying to tell me that my family—my parents—think I'm a murderer?'

'What? No! God… I would never…'

He doesn't finish the sentence.

I ask myself when I last spoke to my parents—really spoke to them, not just the I'm-fine-how-are-you? farce. I can't remember. Lenzen is right. My parents have distanced themselves from me.

And there are people out there who have told Victor Lenzen they think I killed my sister.

I remember how nervous Lenzen seemed when he arrived, and I understand why. He wasn't unsure of himself because he felt guilty, but because he was wondering how mad, how dangerous, the woman he was about to interview was.

Victor Lenzen didn't come to my house to interview a world-famous, bestselling author. He came to find out whether said author is not only eccentric but also a murderer.

We were both after a confession.

A painful burning sensation spreads through my abdomen, rises up to my throat and breaks out of my mouth in a hollow and utterly humourless laugh. It hurts, but I can't stop; I laugh and laugh until the laughter segues into sobs. I am overcome by the fear of being stark raving mad.

My fear is a deep well that I have fallen into. I'm suspended vertically in the water. I try to touch the bottom with my toes, but there's nothing there, only blackness.

Lenzen watches me, waiting until the fits of laughter subside. Only the pain remains. I suppress a whimper.

'Why don't you hate me?' I ask when I can talk again.

Lenzen sighs. 'I've seen wars, Linda. Fighting, the aftermath of fighting. I've seen what it looks like when nothing will ever be right again, prisoners of war, children with their limbs blown off. I know what it looks like when someone is deeply traumatised. Something in you has broken, Linda; I can see it in your eyes. We're not so different, you and me.'

He is silent for a moment, appearing to deliberate.

'Linda, do you promise me you'll leave me in peace?'

I can hardly speak for shame. 'Of course,' I say. 'Of course.'

'If you promise me that you'll leave me and my family in peace, and if you'll promise me to seek psychiatric treatment'—he seems to hesitate before making up his mind—'if you can promise me those two things, then no one need know about what's happened today.'

I look at him in disbelief.

'But...what will you tell your editor?' I ask stupidly.

'That you didn't feel well. That we had to break off the interview. And that there won't be a repeat.'

My brain can no longer keep pace.

'Why?' I say. 'Why are you doing this? I deserve to be punished.'

'I think you've been punished enough.'

I look at him. He looks at me.

'Can you promise me those two things?' Lenzen asks.

I nod.

'I hope you can make peace with yourself,' he says.

Then he turns and leaves. I hear him take his coat from the hook in the hall and go into the dining room to fetch his jacket and his bag.

I know he'll be out of my reach as soon as he crosses the threshold. I know I'll never see him again and that there will be nothing more I can do.

And what were you thinking of doing?

I hear Victor Lenzen's footsteps in the hall, hear him open the front door. I stand in the kitchen and know I'm not going to stop him. The door falls shut behind him. Silence spreads through the house like floodwater. It is over.

22

The rain has come after all. Again and again, the wind flings it at the kitchen window as though it were trying to break the glass. But it tires, and eventually ceases altogether, and soon the storm is no more than a memory, a mute flash of summer lightning in the distance.

I stand there, propped up at the kitchen table, trying to remember how to breathe. My body has stopped doing it for me automatically, so I have to focus all my attention on it. I don't have the strength for anything else; I think of nothing. I stand like that for a long time.

But then a thought does reach me, and it gets me moving, and while I'm wondering at the fact that my arms and legs and everything else function the same as ever, I'm walking through rooms and climbing stairs and pushing open doors. Then I find him. He's asleep, but wakes up when I sit down beside him. First his nose, then his tail, then the rest of his body. Bukowski's tired, but he's pleased to see me.

Sorry to wake you, mate. I don't want to be on my own tonight.

I curl up in a ball beside him on the floor, half on his blanket. I snuggle up to him, trying to get some of his warmth, but he wriggles free; he doesn't like it, needs his space. He isn't a pussy cat after all; he wants freedom, room to move. Soon he is asleep again, dreaming his doggy dreams.

I lie there alone for a moment longer, trying to keep thinking of nothing, but an animal impulse stirs in my chest and I remember Lenzen's embrace—the firmness, the warmth—and I have a feeling in my stomach as if I were in free fall, and again I try to think of nothing, but still I think of Lenzen's embrace and the beast in my chest and its terrible name: desire. I know how pathetic I am, but I don't care.

I know too that this isn't about Lenzen; that it isn't his embrace I desire, that my desire isn't for him. I know who it's for, but I mustn't think about that.

Lenzen was merely the trigger, but now it hurts to remember what it could be like to live among people—the looks, the physical contact, the warmth. I don't want to think about it, but I'm drawn into my memories, and then the rational part of my brain starts up again. The grace period is over, and I think: any minute now the police will arrive.

I know that I have committed a crime, documenting it myself fastidiously—all those microphones and cameras here in the house. I have done terrible things and the police will come and arrest me, no matter what Lenzen said. As soon as he can think straight again, he'll call them. But it won't make much difference whether it's here or in some prison, that I sit on my own and vegetate with a knot of desire in my chest.

So I do nothing. I don't go round the house destroying all the tapes and cameras that have so mercilessly documented my madness. I lie down on my bed and wait, glad that nothing of the past hours surfaces in my consciousness, because I know that there is such a lot there that could distress me. As I'm thinking this, it happens, and a thought pops up, clothed in Lenzen's voice, although it's my thought too: 'The worst is the doubt. Doubt is like a thorn you can't get a hold on. It's terrible when a thing like that destroys families.'

I think of my parents, of what they were like in the aftermath of that terrible night—and, indeed, have been ever since. Subdued, as if someone had turned the volume down. They treated me gingerly, as though I had been made of glass. Gingerly and guardedly. Courteously, too, as if I were a stranger. I have always tried to interpret it as consideration, but deep down I've known that it is something else. It has taken Victor Lenzen for me to work out what that something is: it is doubt.

Linda loved Anna. No, Linda doesn't have any motive at all. No, Linda wouldn't be capable of a thing like that, and in any case, why would she? Impossible. No, never, definitely not, not a chance. But what if she had?

After all, we live in a world in which anything is possible: in which babies come into being in test tubes, and robots explore Mars, and tiny particles are beamed from A to B. So why not that? A vestige of doubt always remains.

I can't bear it. I sit up in bed, reach for the telephone, dial my parents' landline number that's been the same for about thirty years, and wait. When did we last speak? How many years has it been? Five? Eight? I think of the drawer in the kitchen that is full of Christmas cards from my parents, because that's the way we celebrate Christmas—we send each other cards. We haven't spoken properly since Anna's death. We ran out of words. Conversations became sentences, sentences became single words, words became syllables, and then we stopped talking altogether. How could it come to this? And can we ever get back from postcards—the only thing keeping us from total communication breakdown—to conversations? What if my parents seriously think I'm a murderer?

Do you really want to know, Linda?

Yes, I do.

It's not until the ringing tone sounds that I remember that in the other world, where my parents live, time matters so much more than in mine. On the second ring I cast a hasty glance at the clock: it's three in the morning—that late, damn it. How long did I stand in the kitchen, staring into space? How long did I spend watching my

sleeping dog? How long did I lie there with the cold eyes of my surveillance cameras looking down on me like indifferent gods?

I'm about to hang up, having decided it's too late for this, when I
hear the alarmed voice of my mother.

'Hello?'

'Hello, it's Linda.'

My mother lets out a noise that I can't place—a deep, distressing
groan. I don't know what it means, and I'm searching for the right
words, words to explain why I've got her out of bed in the middle of
the night and to tell her that there's something I must ask her that's
terribly difficult for me to ask, when there's a crackle on the line followed by a drawn-out bleep. It's some time before I realise that my
mother has simply hung up.

I put down the phone and stare at the wall. Then I sink back into
bed.

My name is Linda Conrads. I am thirty-eight years old. I am an
author and a murderer. Twelve years ago I killed my younger sister
Anna. No one can explain why. I probably can't explain it myself. I'm
probably quite simply mad. I am a liar and a murderer. That is my
life. That is the truth. At least, it is for my parents.

A black thought that has been swirling around in my subconscious
drifts to the surface, big and heavy, stirring up a maelstrom of other
thoughts in its wake. Lenzen's voice.

*'The Disney princess up on her high horse. If I were a woman—if I
were Sophie—I would detest Britta.'*

And I think: I did too.

The pain of that realisation. The memories. Yes, I did detest her;
yes, I hated her; yes, I was jealous; yes, I thought it was wrong that
my parents always favoured her—the younger one, the prettier one,
the one who knew how to manipulate them, who looked so sweet
and innocent with her blonde hair and her round child's eyes that
she had everyone wrapped round her little finger. Everyone except
me, because I knew what she was really like; I knew how hurtful she
could be, how inconsiderate, how cruel, how incredibly mean.

Mum and Dad will believe me, want to bet?

Do you like that bloke? I can make him come home with me, want to bet?

No wonder Theo reached the point where he couldn't stand her any more; after all those years of their relationship, he'd had a glimpse behind the scenes; he knew her almost as well as I did.

Oh no, Anna wouldn't do a thing like that, Anna wouldn't say a thing like that, you must have got it wrong—she's only little. You're trying to tell me Anna did that? There must have been some misunderstanding; that doesn't sound like her at all. Honestly, Linda, why do you always come up with such lies?

Anna, Anna—Anna, who could always wear white without spilling on it—Anna, who had mix tapes made for her by the boys—Anna, who inherited our grandmother's ring—Anna, whose name you could read backwards as well as forwards, whereas my name backwards is a joke.

If you read your name backwards, you get Adnil. Sounds like Adolf or Arsehole. Now don't go and get angry again, Adnil, I was only joking. Adnil—hahahahaha.

Saint Anna.

Yes, I detested my sister. That is the truth. That is my life. I don't want to think about it. I don't want to think about the police, who aren't here although they ought to be by now, or about my parents, or Victor Lenzen or my own black thoughts.

I reach out for the bedside table, pull open the drawer, take out a packet of pills (a bumper pack from the USA—I love the internet), shake a few into my hand, wash them down with stale water, retch and then notice I'm hungry. My stomach rebels—my stomach full of pills. I curl up in a foetal position and wait for the cramps to stop. I want to sleep. Tomorrow is another day. Or, with a bit of luck, not. My stomach feels like a fist. Liquid collects in my mouth and I can't help thinking of the pool of shock and poison and gall that Victor Lenzen left on my dining-room floor. Everything is spinning around me.

Pressing my hand to my mouth, I slip off the bed and totter towards the door. Bukowski glances up, sees that I'm beyond help and leaves me to my own devices. I stagger to the upstairs bathroom and just make it to the basin before throwing up. I turn on the taps, wait a moment and retch again, suddenly sweating—suddenly cold.

I stand in front of the mirror and contemplate my reflection. The woman looking back at me is a stranger. I frown, and examine the wrinkle that divides my forehead down the middle like a crack, and I realise that it's not my face but a mask. I raise my eyebrows and more cracks appear, branching out, further and further. I press my hands to my head in an attempt to stop the pieces from falling and shattering, but it's too late; I've started a process that I couldn't stop even if I wanted to.

I let go. My face falls to the floor with a clatter, and behind it is emptiness.

Am I mad?

No, I'm not mad.

How can you tell you're not mad?

You just can.

How can you tell if you are mad?

You just can.

But if you really are mad—how can you know? How can you know anything with absolute certainty?

I listen to the voices arguing in my head, and I no longer know which of them is the rational one.

I'm back in bed. I'm lying quite still, but my thoughts are racing. I'm scared. I'm still cold.

Then a peculiar noise penetrates my consciousness: a buzz. No, a drone. It swells, subsides, starts up again. It's throbbing, alive and menacing, and it's getting louder. I hold my ears and almost fall out of bed. When I take my hands away, I realise that what I'm hearing is silence. That is all that remains, after this day that should have decided everything. Silence.

I sit up and listen until it dies away. Now there's nothing—only the cool of the night. Everything is muted. My heart is beating dully, as if it no longer believes that this Sisyphean work is worth it. My breathing is quite shallow, my blood is flowing wearily, and my thoughts have almost come to a standstill. I think of nothing except a beautiful pair of different-coloured eyes.

All of a sudden I'm sitting up with the phone in my hand, although I can't remember having made a decision, and I'm dialling a number.

My heart is now beating like mad and my breathing is galloping and my blood has started flowing again and my thoughts are coming thick and fast, because I'm finally making the call I've put off for eleven years. I know the number by heart; I've dialled it often enough only to cut off the connection immediately, every time.

The first ringing tone is nearly more than I can bear; I almost hang up again from pure reflex—but I push on. The second ring sounds, the third, the fourth, and with a kind of relief I'm beginning to think he's not there. Then he picks up.

25

JONAS

Jonas Weber's mobile was vibrating for the third time in half an hour. He took it out of his trouser pocket, looked at the display, saw that it was Sophie and cursed himself for having given her his number. After a brief internal struggle, he answered.

'Jonas Weber.'

'It's Sophie Peters. I have to talk to you.'

'Listen, Sophie, this isn't a good time,' he said, sensing Antonia Bug and Volker Zimmer turn to look at him as he spoke her name. 'Can I ring you back?'

'It won't take a second and it's really, really important,' said Sophie.

Something in her voice alarmed Jonas. She sounded odd—manic.

'Okay. Hang on.'

With an apologetic glance at his colleagues, he left the scene of the crime they'd been called to, extremely glad, in fact, to step outside for a bit.

'Okay, I've got away for a moment,' he said.

'Are you in a meeting or something?'

'Something.'

'I'm sorry. It's just that I was in the museum a moment ago. I was looking at van Gogh's sunflowers. And...you know that I told you it must have been a stranger? That no one who knew Britta would have hurt her in any way? You said I made her sound like an angel? That's what she was, you see. A kind of angel.'

'Sophie,' said Jonas, 'slow down a bit. I can't keep up!'

He could hear her nervous breathing at the other end of the line.

'I knew straight away that I'd seen something in Britta's flat that didn't belong there. I told you, do you remember? That the culprit had left something behind, like a serial killer in a film. Something was out of place—I just didn't know what. But now I do!'

'Keep calm, Sophie,' said Jonas as patiently as he could. 'Take a deep breath. That's the way. Now, carry on.'

'Okay, so I said it must be a serial killer—a lunatic—and you said that there aren't serial killers in real life; that most crimes are committed by the victim's partner. All that stuff.'

'Sophie, I remember very well. Where are you going with this?'

'You said it couldn't be a serial killer because, for one thing, there wasn't a series because there's no comparable case. But what if Britta's the beginning? The first in a series? What if he keeps going?'

Jonas was silent.

'Are you still there? Jonas?'

'I'm still here.'

Her story was a muddle, but he realised that he was going to have to let her talk.

'Good. Well, in any case... I told you I was in the museum, in front of van Gogh's sunflowers. Do you remember how I told you that something wasn't right in Britta's flat? Now I know what it was. No idea why I didn't think of it before—it's as if my brain had been blocked. Probably because it was far too obvious and somehow, for whatever reason, I was looking for something subtle, something obscure. But I knew it, damn it, I knew it!'

'It was the flowers,' said Jonas.

There was a moment of shocked silence.

'You knew?' Sophie asked.

'Not until just now,' said Jonas, trying to sound calm. 'But listen, Sophie, I really should be getting back.'

'Do you know what that means, Jonas?' Sophie asked in excitement, ignoring his last words. 'The murderer left flowers in Britta's flat! What normal murderer, acting in the heat of the moment or out of base motives, would leave flowers next to his victim?'

'Let's talk this over in peace some time, Sophie,' said Jonas.

'But...'

'I'll ring you as soon as the meeting's over, I promise.'

'The murderer left them there, do you see? They weren't Britta's flowers! Britta didn't like cut flowers! Everyone knew that! The flowers are probably a kind of trademark of his! If that's the case, he'll do it again! That's the direction your investigations must take. Maybe it's not too late to stop him!'

'Sophie, we'll talk later, I promise.'

'But there's something else I must te—'

'Later.'

He hung up, put his mobile back in his pocket and returned to the airless flat.

The scene of the crime, which his colleagues were going over with a fine-tooth comb, was similar to the scene in Britta Peters' flat. On the living-room floor lay a blonde woman. She was wearing a white dress that was now almost saturated with her blood. As far as appearances went, she could have been a sister of Britta Peters. Like her, she too lived alone; like her, she had a ground-floor flat. When the police officers had arrived, the door had still been open.

Sophie's words went through Jonas's head: 'The flowers are probably a kind of trademark of his.'

Jonas looked about the flat as he went back to join his colleagues. There was one big difference between the crime scenes: here the flowers he'd brought with him weren't strewn about.

Again, Jonas heard Sophie's voice: 'He'll do it again! But maybe it's not too late to stop him!'

He looked at the corpse of the blonde woman. She was holding a small, neat bunch of white roses, which stood in lurid contrast to the dark dried blood in which she was lying.

It was too late.

23

I am sitting at the window looking out onto the lake. Sometimes I spot an animal at the edge of the woods, a fox or a rabbit—even a deer, if I'm very lucky. But there's nothing there now.

I've been watching the sun rise. I haven't slept. How could I have slept the night my world collapsed all over again? After the phone call?

I could hear him sit up in bed when I said my name. First there was a rustling down the line, and then his fraught voice.

'Frau Michaelis!' he said. 'My goodness!'

I had to swallow.

'It's six in the morning,' he said, alarmed. 'Has something happened? Do you need help?'

'No,' I said. 'Not really. I'm sorry to disturb you…'

There was a brief silence.

'That's all right. I'm just surprised to hear from you.'

I could hardly believe he'd called me 'Frau Michaelis'. And then his professionalism—the practised composure that immediately took over, crowding out his surprise and his…his…

'How can I help you?'

Hey, Julian, I've written a book in which you're one of the main characters. How are you?

I force myself to be as formal with him as he is with me. Has he really forgotten me? It's probably for the best.

'I don't know how much you remember—you investigated the murder of my sister some years ago,' I say.

'Of course I remember you,' he replies after a moment. He sounds neutral. I swallow my disappointment.

What did you expect, Linda?

I try to recall my original intention.

This isn't about you, Linda.

'I have to ask you something,' I say.

'Please do.'

Entirely neutral. There's…nothing there.

'Well, it's about my sister's case. I don't know whether you remember, but I found my sister, and…'

'I remember,' he says. 'I promised you I'd find the murderer and I wasn't able to keep my word.'

That, too, he says neutrally. But he does remember *that*.

Go on, Linda, ask him.

'There's something on my mind.'

'Yes?'

Ask him!

'Well, first of all, I'm sorry if I woke you; it's a stupid time to ring anyone, I know… It's… Well, back then…' I swallow. 'It wasn't clear to me for a long time that I was the main suspect.'

I pause, waiting for him to contradict me, which he doesn't.

'And, well, I have to know whether you…' I can hear him breathing. 'Did you think I was the murderer back then?'

Nothing.

'*Do* you think I'm the murderer?'

Still nothing. Is he thinking about it? Is he waiting for me to carry on talking?

Silence.

He thinks you're finally going to confess, Linda. He's waiting for your confession.

'Herr Schumer?' I ask.

I miss our conversations and I can't think of anything I'd like more than to sit down and let you convince me that poetry can be wonderful. I want to know what became of that tedious colleague of yours and did your wife really move out in the end and do you still have that whorl of hair on the back of your head? And, anyway, how are you? I've missed you, Julian. I had the feeling we were from the same star.

'Herr Schumer,' I say, 'I have to know.'

'The correct procedures were followed. We investigated every avenue to try to find the murderer.'

Evasive.

'But I'm afraid we were never able to pin him or her down.'

'Him or her'. Why not 'the sister'?

Fuck.

'You'll have to excuse me: this isn't the best time. I don't know if it's a good idea to speak now. Why don't we talk more another day?'

After he's conferred with his colleagues on how to deal with the fact that the main suspect from a decade-old case has got in touch with him out of the blue. After he's worked out the best way to wring a confession out of you, Linda.

'Thank you,' I say lamely and hang up.

Julian—no, Superintendent Schumer—thinks I'm guilty. I'm on my own. I stand in my big living room, staring out at the lake. Everything is still—inside me, too. Then a switch is flipped and I remember.

It is summer. It is hot—a midsummer's heat that even the approaching night can't cool down. The air tastes stale and insipid, nighties stick to thighs, children everywhere toss and turn in their sheets, only to get up after all: Mummy, I can't sleep. Terrace doors stand open, curtains gently flutter, mosquitoes are plump and contented. The air is charged, babies fret, couples row. I have had a row, too: I've screamed and raged, I've thrown things—ashtrays, books, cups, flower pots, my mobile, his mobile—everything I could lay my hands on. Shoes, cushions, apples, a can of hairspray, my sunglasses. And there was Marc, laughing uncontrollably—you've completely lost it, princess, you're completely crazy, seriously, you should stop drinking so much—and there was I, even angrier because he was laughing at me, laughing off my anger and jealousy. My God, how can you even think such a thing, your own sister, that's absolutely ridiculous, completely barmy, princess, I met her by chance, it's a small town, and Christ, it was only a cappuccino, I didn't know it was forbidden to have a coffee with your own fiancée's sister, wow, she was right, you crack me up, there was I thinking she was completely nuts but she was right, you crack me up!

I run out of ammunition. I'm hot and my T-shirt sticks to my back and between my breasts, and I stop and stand there, panting, and I say, 'How do you mean?'

Marc looks at me. He stays put—no more missiles for him to dodge—but snorts with laughter.

'How do I mean what?' he asks.

'How do you mean, "she was right"?'

Marc shakes his head and, briefly, raises an eyebrow in exasperation.

'Well, if you really want to know, Anna said it would be better if I didn't tell you we'd met because you'd go ballistic.'

For a moment I am quite weak with anger. I try not to look at him; if I look at him now, I'll explode. I fix on the newspaper lying on the dining table, concentrating on the headline—German troops in Afghanistan—and then on the photo of the columnist. I stare at the weather-beaten face with unusually pale eyes. I try to calm down. The face flickers before my eyes and I stare at it, but it's no help at all.

Marc snorts again. 'And, idiot that I am, I say, "Come on, Anna, what rubbish. Linda is cool." And Anna says, "You'll see, Marc. You'll see."'

He's not grinning any more. He's staring, as if seeing me for the first time—as if he'd only now realised that his fiancée isn't cool after all. Cool: the word he always uses to describe me to his mates. Linda is cool, Linda loves football and beer, Linda doesn't cause any trouble if I spend a night away. Jealousy? Oh, please. Not Linda. Even when I had that thing going with the woman from the marketing department, Linda understood. It was purely physical. I confessed and she understood, because she's cool. We talk about everything. Linda's up for anything: lads' films, cans of beer, porn. Linda has the best sense of humour in the world. Linda is cool.

Marc stares at me. 'Why are you being so uncool?' he asks.

My anger is clenched tight like a fist, and I grab the car keys and am gone.

Outside, it's even warmer; the summer night is hot and throbbing. I get in my car and speed off, breathless with rage, my foot pressed down on the accelerator. I find my way; it's not far. The streets are empty and shimmer blackly, and suddenly I'm at her door, leaning on the bell. She opens up to me in a short dark dress, cellulite-free skin, pearl-necklace smile, gum in mouth. What's the matter, Linda? And I'm in the flat. What the hell's going on, Anna? What the hell is this? Are you trying to drive a wedge between me and Marc? Is that it? Are you trying to steal my fiancé, you manipulative little cunt?

She laughs her little laugh, because she knows I never get truly angry, and because swearwords sound ridiculous coming from my mouth—wrong, somehow, and put on, as if I were imitating some actor. She blows a chewing-gum bubble—*pop*—and says, 'In my experience, men don't let you steal them if they don't want you to,' and then she laughs this laugh and heads off for the kitchen, leaving me standing there, and it's only then that I notice the music—the Beatles, on vinyl—*my* Beatles record that the little cunt stole from me; you never listen to it anyway, Linda.

I can't believe it—she simply buggers off and fucking makes herself a fucking salad, and I have no choice but to trot along after her like a fool, still yelling my head off: What is this, Anna? What is this? You already have everything you want. You're not interested in Marc. She ignores me until I grab her by the arm and say it again: You're not remotely interested in Marc. He's not even your type, so what's all this about? What is this, Anna? You're not fifteen anymore. It's not funny to steal my boyfriend for the hell of it. We're not teenagers now and, let's be honest, it wasn't funny when we were.

But this is different. She tears her arm free. You're crazy, Linda. I don't know what you want from me. You and your stories: you always have to make such a drama out of everything. Snap out of your fucking victim role. I can't take anything from you that you don't let me take. I can't steal any man from you that you don't let me steal. Your whingeing is really getting on my nerves—nobody understands me, nobody likes me, I'm so fat, I'm so ugly, nobody reads my stories, I'm so broke, I'm so miserable, boo hoo hoo...

For a moment, everything goes black—black with anger—but I fight the anger. I'm not fifteen any more; I said so myself. I'm not a fifteen-year old loner. I don't have spots or spare tyres or ridiculous glasses: I have money, I write, I'm making a name for myself, I have a fiancé, I'm a grown-up woman. I don't have to let my sister bait me; I can simply breathe away my anger, take the wind out of Anna's sails, turn round and go home. I don't have to play along with her, I don't have to let her provoke me. I can simply go home before this gets out of hand—and these things always get out of hand and Anna always ends up winning, and I always end up being blamed, because Linda tends to exaggerate a bit; Linda can be melodramatic, she's always been like that; Linda and her stories.

I breathe in and out, in and out. It works well; I manage to calm down. The colours return to normal; the world loses its reddish hue, and all is well. Then Anna says, 'How do you know what my type is anyway?' And when I say, 'What?' she repeats her question with exaggerated clarity: 'How...do...you...know...what...my...type... is...anyway?'

I stare at her—her round eyes and pointy canines—and she's finished chopping the tomatoes and wipes her damp fingers on a tea towel and looks me in the face: 'Marc is an attractive man.'

I can only stare at her, and when I do eventually manage to choke something out, my voice is hoarse: 'But you're not interested in Marc.'

'Maybe not.'

Anna shrugs her narrow shoulders. She smiles, blowing a chewing-gum bubble. Pop.

'Maybe I just want to see if I can.'

All at once, an unbelievable pain shoots through my head—keen and piercing. I see red, and the knife finds its way into my hand, and I don't remember exactly what happened next—no, I don't really remember, I quite honestly don't remember. The rest is silence, and the smell of iron and bone. I am stunned, truly stunned. I don't understand, my brain refuses to understand, and I wipe away fingerprints and then we're in the living room; Anna has staggered into the living room—not far, a few metres; it's a small flat. I open the terrace door (air, I need air) and the world is red, deep red, and I'm not breathing air; I'm breathing something red, something thick and gelatinous, and I hear an awful tune: *All you need is love, la-da-da-da-da*—sweet and mocking—*love, love, love.* The world looks peculiar—sharp-edged and hard. I'm in a photograph, and somebody has turned up the colour saturation as high as it will go. I'm disorientated. What has happened? Why is Anna lying on the floor? What's that blood doing there? Blood gives Anna the creeps—how can she be lying in a pool of blood that is spreading almost to the tips of my shoes?

I take a step back; I stare at Anna on the floor, dead or dying. My God, what has happened? Somebody must have been here—where is he?

A breath of air wafts across my face and I look up, sensing a movement, and give a start. There *is* somebody there, disappearing through the terrace door. Oh my God, oh my God, oh my God, oh my God, there's somebody there. Don't turn round. But he does turn around, and our eyes meet, and I know he killed Anna. The moment drags on, and then the man's gone and all I can see are the curtains at the terrace door blowing in the wind like willow branches, and I avert my eyes and see Anna in a pool of blood—and my brain doesn't understand what's going on—how could it? I let myself in, because Anna didn't answer, and I came into the flat and found Anna like this, dead and bleeding, and there was this man at the terrace door—oh my God, oh my God—and I thought he was going to kill me too—that I would die, like Anna—oh my God, please, please, dear God, I'm so scared, it smells of blood, there's blood everywhere.

I pick up the phone and call the police. I'm trembling and whimpering, and I think of the man at the terrace door, in the dark, barely visible. I only saw him briefly, but those eyes—those cold, pale eyes— I'll never forget, not as long as I live.

The police come. I sit there and stare at Anna, and the police ask me questions and wrap me up in a blanket. There's this good-looking police officer with different-coloured eyes, and I can't speak at first, not at all. I don't know what's going on. But I make an effort—such a nice man, I'd like to help him, and I pull myself together and tell him about the cold, clear eyes in the dark and the terrace door and how it's not possible that Anna's lying there in a pool of blood, because Anna freaks out at blood. I ask him why and he promises to find out, and at some point there's a stretcher and a photographer and more police, and then I'm in a police station and then I'm in bed and my parents are there—oh my God, oh my God, no.

Marc is there too. He sits down beside me and strokes my hair mechanically—it's all so awful, my poor princess, oh my God. Later he makes a statement—the same statement as everybody else, the same statement my parents make, and all our friends. The story they have spun around themselves and would defend with their lives: a happily married couple and two inseparable sisters who adore one another. No, they never quarrelled, never, not even when they were little, and certainly not as adults. Little fits of jealousy between sisters? Goodness, no, nothing like that—what nonsense, what a cliché. They loved each other, got on well, thick as thieves, the pair of them— adored one another, inseparable.

I repeat the story about the man with the pale eyes and forget it's a story; I'd forgotten that, even as I was making it up. I tell my story and

I'm good at telling it (Linda and her stories). I tell my story over and over again, I tell it for my life, and I get drawn into it, I become one of the characters—the murder victim's sister, desperate and broken, lonely and withdrawn—'She never really recovered, poor thing, the two of them adored one another. Inseparable, they were.'

But the truth is gnawing away at me, struggling inside, hurling itself about in me like a caged beast trying to break free. Still I believe in my story. I am my story; it's a good story. And I grow ill; I can no longer leave the house, and I keep the beast locked away and continue to believe in the cold eyes and the stranger.

But the caged beast doesn't give up, and one day it summons up all its strength—all its brute force—and makes one final attempt. I see a man who resembles the character in my story, and I'm forced to reflect, to return to that night, and I grapple with the man with the cold eyes and fight for a confession, but I will not get it into my head, I will not accept—will not, will not, will not accept—that the confession I am fighting for is my own.

That I am a murderer.

And the rest no more than a good story.

That's how it could have happened. Something like that.

I stand at the window and look out onto the edge of the woods and the lake.

26

SOPHIE

Sophie stared at the telephone, willing it to ring, but it remained doggedly silent.

She went into the kitchen, took a wine glass from the shelf, filled it to the brim and sat down. She gave a start when she heard a creaking sound.

Only the floorboards. She tried to calm down, taking a gulp of wine and beginning to put her thoughts in order.

She had the feeling she was being followed. But was she really, or was it her nerves, which were now in tatters? No, there had been someone there that night, in the underground car park. And who knows how often he had pursued her since without her noticing.

Sophie looked at her mobile. Still no message from Jonas Weber. She let her index finger hover over the call button, then left it. What was the point? Jonas would only give her a lecture on how she should leave police work to the police and have a bit of confidence in them.

If any kind of progress were to be made, she would have to take the matter into her own hands—that much was clear. She got up and reached for her jacket, but then hesitated and sat down. She switched the TV on—and then off again.

If only she'd got to Britta's a couple of minutes earlier. If she'd let herself in instead of wasting time ringing the bell. If she'd administered first aid straight away. If, if, if. Sophie knew it was her guilty conscience driving her to keep busy. She simply had to find the man. But how?

Suddenly, it came to her.

It was essentially easy. She'd seen the murderer and he'd seen her. But while it was true that she hadn't recognised him, he certainly seemed to know who she was. Somehow he must have found out, for he was following her—trying to catch her on her own so he could do away with the eyewitness to his crime. He wasn't going to stop. The perfect opportunity hadn't yet presented itself to him.

What if Sophie served herself up to him on a silver platter? What if she didn't run the next time she sensed him behind her but stayed put instead?

No, that was completely crazy. Self-destructive.

Sophie leant back on the sofa and took another gulp of wine. She reflected on the fear Britta must have felt in the last minutes of her life and told herself that fear was not a valid excuse for inaction.

She drank more wine and lay down, staring at the wall. She turned over and stared at the ceiling. The white grew whiter and whiter, gleaming and shimmering before her eyes. But there was something else. Sophie could make out microscopic dark spots, smaller than fruit flies, and yet more than mere specks of colour, for when she looked more closely, she saw the black growing before her eyes, puncturing the white and getting thicker and blacker, until all at once she realised what was going on. There was hair sprouting out of the ceiling, thick and black like pubic hair, growing towards her. The ceiling was becoming porous; it would cave in on her if she continued to lie there like that, doing nothing.

Sophie leapt up, drained her wine, and went along the hall to the bedroom, grumbling at the removal boxes that Paul still hadn't collected. She was furious—at herself, at the world—and would have liked to take one of the stupid golf clubs that were sticking out of the box labelled 'Misc.' and bash something with it. She rummaged around in her hold-all for the pepper spray she had bought a short while ago, put it in her handbag along with her wallet, keys and mobile, left the flat and stormed down the stairs.

The darkness was velvety and smelt autumnal. Sophie realised that the stifling hot summer had given way to a moody autumn.

She walked along the night streets, moving further and further from the busier parts of town, deeper and deeper into the shadows. She hadn't really stopped to think about her plan.

A trap for a murderer. With her as bait.

Perfect, provided you weren't overly attached to life.

Sophie realised that she was thinking in the terms of a TV crime drama, with the murderer, the victim, the pesky eyewitness, the nice police officer. Somehow it was easier that way: to view the affair not as a genuine tragedy, not as a real part of her life, but as just another case.

Sophie walked and walked. Fewer and fewer people passed her. It turned chilly—cold, even—and the wind was biting. Sophie unbuttoned her jacket; she wanted to be cold, to shiver, to feel something other than grief or anger at last, even if it was only coldness. Or pain.

Something inside her understood how self-destructive such thoughts were, how crazy this plan was, driven only by her overwhelming feelings of guilt. But Sophie silenced the warning voice and turned into the dark park that lay before her.

She sat down on a bench and waited. She stared into the shadows, growing colder. It wasn't long before she saw him.

24

'm drinking tea in small sips. I had put on music in the hope it would drive away the voices in my head, but it's not working. Ella Fitzgerald is singing to me about the summertime and easy living, but summer is a long way off and my life feels hard and the voices in my head are still arguing about the truth. In the morning sun, the lake gleams indigo, violet, deep red, orange, yellow, and then pale blue.

I saw Victor Lenzen on that terrible, hot, deep-red night—I'm sure I did.

Linda and her stories.

I saw him.

The way you saw that fawn in the clearing all those years ago?

I was only a child then. All children tell fibs, make things up.

And you're still at it now.

I know what I saw. I'm not mad.

Oh, aren't you?

Those pale eyes, the shape of his eyebrows, the look on his face—that mixture of fear and belligerence—all those things I saw twelve years ago, and all those things I recognised when he stood before me yesterday.

He has an alibi.

I saw him.

A bombproof alibi.

Still, it was him. I saw him.

Then why didn't the police catch him?

The police didn't 'catch' me either. If everyone thinks I'm crazy and murdered my own sister, then why haven't the police arrested me?

You were lucky.

I've never been lucky.

You're a good liar.

I didn't lie. I saw him. At the terrace door.

You've been telling your stories for so long that you've come to believe them yourself.

I know what I saw. I remember that evening. I remember it precisely.

You're mad, Linda.

Nonsense!

You hear music that isn't there.

But I remember.

You see things that aren't there, you're constantly dizzy, your head's almost bursting with pain—you can't even help yourself.

I remember it precisely. He was there. I saw it in his eyes; he recognised me as well. And he hated me for bringing it all back to him. He was there. He killed Anna. Maybe I was wrong all along. Maybe Anna wasn't an accidental victim. Maybe the two of them knew each other. Just because I didn't know anything about an affair doesn't mean there was no affair. Who knows? Perhaps a jealous lover. A stalker. A lunatic.

It's YOU who's the lunatic. Maybe you're schizophrenic. Or have a brain tumour. Maybe that's what's causing the pain—and the dizziness and the music.

That ghastly music.

I look out the window. The water glistens and sparkles, and a fair distance away, on the eastern shore of the lake, something stirs. There's a movement of branches, and it steps out from between the trees, majestic and incredibly big: a red deer—dignified and beautiful, its head held high. I catch my breath and watch it as a painter might, drinking in its movements, its grace, its vigour. For a few moments it stands motionless in the light mist that is rising from the lake, and then it vanishes again between the trees.

So often have I sat here in the hope of seeing an animal, and so seldom have I actually seen one. And a red deer? Never. The animal seems to me like a sign.

There's no such thing as signs. You see things that aren't there.

For a long time, I remain sitting at the window in the big peaceful house that is my entire world, looking out, hoping that the red deer will return—knowing full well that it won't, but sitting and waiting all the same. I wouldn't know what else to do. I sit there, and the sight of the lake, its surface rippled by the wind, soothes my mind. The sun rises higher and higher, unmoved by the chaos that has descended on my world. It has its own world to shine on.

The sun is about 4500 million years old. I know that kind of thing; I've had a lot of time to read over the past ten or eleven years. It's already shone on a great deal of things. Its morning rays warm me through the glass. It's as if somebody were touching me and I relish it.

It's a lovely day. Maybe I can forget what I've been through and simply be grateful for this day, for the edge of the woods and the lake and the sunshine. The sun rises higher; it's not tired, even after 4500 million years. There's nothing I have to do, and I'm thinking that I could sit here forever, calm and serene—that it's best if I don't budge so much as an inch, because even the slightest change might destroy everything—when I hear it. The music.

Love, love, love.

No. Please, please, no.

Love, love, love.

Not again. Please, I can't stand it anymore.

I let out a dry sob, curl up on my chair and press my hands to my ears.

The music vanishes. I whimper and hold my head so tight that it hurts, while my heart pumps fear through my body. I don't know whether it was the despair or the pain or my extreme physical and mental exhaustion, but it's only now that it occurs to me: if I'm only imagining the music—if the music is only in my head and has only been in my head all along—then how is it possible that it's silenced as soon as I put my hands over my ears? I take my hands off my ears and listen. Nothing. I'm almost disappointed. I was beginning to think...

Love, love, love.

There it is again. I feel dizzy, like every time I hear it. But this time it sounds different. It swells and fades away and...moves about. The music is moving.

I get up from the chair with aching joints and try to get my bearings. Then, all of a sudden, I understand. The tilted windows all over the house... The music is coming from outside. It's not a recording of the Beatles; it's...whistling. Somebody is creeping round the house whistling.

My heart begins to race. Is it Victor Lenzen, come back to kill me after all? That doesn't make sense, I immediately correct myself; he had ample opportunity.

What a thought. Victor Lenzen is innocent and has proved it, however hard I may be finding it to concede the fact.

Then who was it? On numb legs I step closer to the window, press my face up against the cold glass and try to peer round the corner. I can't see anybody. The whistling grows fainter—whoever it is has moved away from me. I hurry next door to the dining room, telling myself I'm going to miss him again, fling open the door—and our eyes meet.

27

SOPHIE

Sophie couldn't stop her teeth chattering as she walked home through the night streets, chilled to the bone and soaked through. She had sat for a long time on that park bench. Several times she had thought she'd seen a shadow break ranks and come towards her, but it had always turned out to be her nerves playing tricks on her. There was nothing there; the only shadow she had set eyes on had been her own.

Sophie turned into her street. It frightened her to think of going into her flat and spending another sleepless night with those horrible pictures in her head.

She unlocked the door to the building, stepped into the hall and started to climb the stairs. She could hear something on the next floor. Her pulse quickened. There was a rustling noise on the landing above her. Somebody was outside her flat.

Sophie's heart fired a few painful volleys; she could feel the weight of the pepper spray in her coat pocket and she forced herself to keep her nerve—only a few more steps, then she'd be able to see round the corner and the landing outside her flat would come into view. Another eight steps: what would she see? Another seven: the shadow tampering with the lock? Another six: a neighbour dropping off a parcel she'd taken in for her? In the middle of the night? Another five: the annoying little dog from downstairs that often got out? Another four: no, the shadow. Another three: the shadow with his white eyes. Another two... Sophie collided head-on with a man hurtling down the stairs towards her.

'Sophie!' said Jonas Weber.

'Sorry,' gasped Sophie. 'Oh God!'

'No, I'm sorry. I didn't want to scare you. I rang you about a dozen times, and when you didn't pick up, I got worried.'

'I'd put my phone on silent,' said Sophie. 'How long have you been waiting here?'

'Not long. Maybe ten minutes. Where have you been?'

Sophie didn't reply.

'Would you like to come in?' she asked. 'If we talk out here on the stairs we'll wake the whole building.'

A little while later, they were facing one another across the kitchen table, Sophie in clean dry clothes, both of them with a hot cup of tea.

'Those damn flowers,' she said. 'I can't believe I didn't twig sooner.'

'We should have realised sooner. It's our job, not yours.'

Sophie sipped her tea, studying Jonas over her cup. He avoided her gaze.

'What are you keeping from me, Jonas?'

He looked at her with his green eye and his brown eye.

'You need to call it a day, Sophie.'

Furious, Sophie slammed her fist down on the table.

'I can't, damn it!' she screamed. 'Since my sister was murdered, I've been suffocating! I can't breathe again until I've found him!'

She fought back her tears. Jonas gently took her hand.

'You know, Sophie,' he said, 'I understand you. If this had happened to me, I'd want to do something too. I understand that you feel guilty. All survivors feel guilty. But it's not your fault.'

Sophie's eyes filled with tears again.

'Everyone thinks it's my fault. Everyone!' she sobbed.

It did her good to say it out loud at last.

'My parents and...'

'No one believes that,' Jonas interrupted her. 'Only you.'

'If only I'd got there sooner...'

'Stop it. You couldn't have helped your sister. And you're not helping yourself now by putting yourself in danger. I don't like the way you wander around the neighbourhood at night all by yourself. It's almost as if you wanted to lure him to you.'

Sophie withdrew her hand.

'Do you want to get yourself killed? Is that it?' Jonas asked.

Sophie averted her gaze.

'I'd like you to go now.'

'Don't do it, Sophie,' Jonas said. 'Don't put yourself in danger.'

She was silent, close to tears again, but didn't want him to see.

'You'd better leave,' she said.

Jonas nodded and turned to go.

'Please take care of yourself.'

Sophie struggled with herself. Should she tell him? That she had the feeling she was being followed?

'Wait,' she said.

He turned round and looked at her expectantly.

Sophie's brain was working overtime.

'Nothing,' she said eventually. 'It's nothing. Goodbye, Superintendent Weber.'

When Sophie was alone again, she confessed to herself that she was no longer sure.

When she had been running through the underground car park with her lungs on fire, she had heard the heavy footsteps behind her so clearly; she'd been convinced that her sister's murderer had lain in wait for her on the back seat of the car. But when she had gone to fetch her car the next morning, the streets full of people, the whole thing had seemed like no more than a bad dream.

Out jogging in the park recently, she had thought she'd seen someone dart behind a tree. But when she stopped and stared at the damn tree, nothing had stirred.

Am I going mad? she wondered.

No, of course you're not, a voice inside her replied.

How can you tell if you're mad? another voice asked.

You just can.

But if you really are mad, the voice of doubt persisted, how are you supposed to know?

Sophie tried to shake the thought off. She'd been out of it lately — the break-up from Paul, because she couldn't stand to be around him, her inability to talk to her parents, and then this ghastly, keen red feeling that had struck for the first time at her gallerist's party and that she now knew to be a panic attack. Sophie no longer felt herself.

She returned to the kitchen, past Paul's stupid removal boxes, made herself another cup of tea and looked out of the window, though there was nothing to see except a few murky figures and the odd passing car.

In the end she sat down at the kitchen table, took up her sketch-book and a pencil and, for the first time in a while, began to draw. It was lovely. The quiet of the night, the velvety darkness—and Sophie, alone at the kitchen table with pencil, paper, cigarettes and tea under her old-fashioned hanging lamp in a small island of yellowy light. She drew with ease.

The different coloured eyes that had been looking at her so gravely only a short while ago were rendered monochrome by the lead pencil, but she was satisfied with her quick sketch. Jonas.

On an impulse, Sophie took her mobile out of her trouser pocket and found his number. She had to tell him.

Then she remembered that it was late; the middle of the night. She put the phone away. She was cold, so she got up, filled the kettle, fished another teabag out of the packet—and jumped when she heard the creaking noise in the hall.

25

I stand like stone in the middle of the room and stare out of the window.

My gardener is looking in at me; the expression on his face is almost cheerful. The spell breaks and my anger is back, as if someone had flicked a switch—the anger and the piercing headache. Those Siamese twins.

'Why are you doing that?' I yell.

He frowns. He doesn't seem to have heard me, but he can see my angry face. I fling open the window.

'What the hell is this?' I ask him.

'What's what?' Ferdi asks, puzzled, looking at me with his big, brown boy's eyes that are both out of place and touching in his wrinkly face.

'That song you were whistling…'

I don't know how to finish the sentence; I'm afraid that Ferdi's going to say, 'What song?' or something like that, and then I'd have to scream—scream and scream and scream and never stop.

'Don't you like the Beatles? It's a great tune!'

I stare at him.

'What exactly were you whistling by'—my mouth is dry—'by the…by the Beatles?'

Ferdi looks at me as if I were completely off my head. Perhaps he's right.

'It's called *All You Need is Love*. Everyone knows it!'

He shrugs.

'It's funny,' he says. 'Since I heard it coming from your house yesterday, I've had it stuck in my head.'

Now I'm wide awake.

'You were here yesterday?' I say. 'But you're never here on a Thursday.'

I can feel my knees trembling.

'Yes, but you said the other day that I could arrange my time to suit myself, so I thought it would be okay to come on a Thursday just this once.'

For a few seconds, I gape at him.

'Should I have let you know?' he asks.

'No, rubbish,' I stutter. 'Of course not.'

I don't know what to say. My face feels numb.

'Ferdi, I need to speak to you. Would you mind coming in for a moment?'

He looks confused. Maybe he's worried I'm going to sack him.

'Well, I was actually about to pack up. I've got to be getting on to another client.'

'Just for a second. Please!'

He nods uneasily.

On the way to the front door I try, without success, to put my thoughts in order. When I reach the door and fling it open, Ferdi is already on the doorstep.

'Did I frighten you or something? With my whistling?' he asks.

'No, you didn't, but—' I stop short, not wanting to go into it standing in the doorway. 'Come on in first, Ferdi.'

He wipes his feet, leaving big clods of dirt on the doormat, and steps into the house.

'Sorry,' he says, rolling his R in that inimitable way of his, and I wonder at the fact that I've never got round to asking him where his dialect is from. Ferdi's been looking after my garden for many years now and it must be making him nervous that today, for the first time, I didn't greet him with a smile. He's not as young as he was—must be well past retirement age, despite his dark hair and dark brown bushy eyebrows. I like him a lot, and apparently he either needs the work or enjoys it because he's never shown any sign of wanting to give up. That's for the best: it would break Bukowski's heart if I lost Ferdi and had to look for a new gardener. Bukowski loves Ferdi more than he loves almost anyone else.

As if on command, I hear a noise upstairs. Bukowski has woken up and, at the sound of our voices, he comes shooting down the stairs and jumps up at us—first at me, then at Ferdi, then at me again, and I almost have to laugh at him—my dog, my mate, this bundle of fur and energy.

I pick him up, take him in my arms and hug him to me, but he has no truck with my sentimentality, and twists and turns until I let him down again, then begins to scamper up and down the hall, chasing invisible rabbits.

Ferdi shifts his weight from one leg to the other, like a schoolboy expecting trouble.

'It's nothing serious, Ferdi,' I say. 'Take a break and have a cup of coffee with me.'

My knees are like rubber. I go on ahead into the kitchen. If Ferdi really did hear the music, then maybe it means that... And then everything else might also...

Not so fast, Linda.

I offer my gardener the kitchen chair I sat on yesterday (was it really only yesterday?) to have my photo taken. He lowers himself with a groan, but only because sitting down with a groan is the done thing at his age; it's all put on. In actual fact, Ferdi is fitter than I am.

As the coffee machine gurgles, I grope for words.

'So you were here yesterday and got a song stuck in your head?' I say.

Ferdi looks at me, his head on one side. Then he nods, as if to say: *Yes—so what?*

'You really heard that song?'

He nods.

'Where?' I ask.

'Through the window. I didn't want to bother you, I really didn't. I saw you had visitors.'

I can see Ferdi hesitating.

'Why do you ask?' he finally says.

How much should I reveal?

'Just wondering,' I say.

'Wouldn't want you to think I'd been eavesdropping,' Ferdi adds.

'Don't you worry yourself,' I say. 'That's not why I'm asking.'

The coffee's ready.

'Well,' he says, 'the windows were open yesterday and I was digging in the bed outside the dining room when I heard the song. The music was quite loud. But you'll know that.'

I want to laugh and cry and rage all at once. Instead I take two cups out of the cupboard.

'Yes,' I say. 'Of course. I was there.'

As if on autopilot, I pour the coffee into the cups. This new piece of information is more than my brain can cope with.

'No milk or sugar for me,' says Ferdi.

I hand him his cup and, clasping mine, I take a sip, then put the cup down when Bukowski comes bounding up to me and starts licking my hand.

I play with him for a while, almost forgetting that Ferdi is there until he says, 'Thanks for the coffee. I'd better be on my way.'

Bukowski runs off after Ferdi, yapping and wagging his tail, leaving me to sink back onto the chair in a daze.

What kind of game are you playing, Herr Lenzen?

So the music *was* real. I wasn't imagining things.

But if it was real, who was behind it? Victor Lenzen? Because he'd read my book and come to the conclusion that I'd react to the song in the same way as my literary alter ego Sophie? Yes, if the music was real—and real it was, because I wasn't the only one to hear it—then Victor Lenzen must have been behind it. Because he had a plan. He was lying when he said he couldn't hear it.

Hang on a second. Thoughts are fluttering inside my head like a flock of startled birds. The photographer was there too! He must have heard the music and should have reacted to it in some way!

Unless Lenzen had an accomplice.

That's too weird, Linda.

It's the only possibility.

It doesn't make sense. You're not thinking straight.

What if one or both of them put something in my water or in my coffee?

Why in God's name should the photographer be involved?

He must have been.

A conspiracy? Is that what you're thinking? Lenzen's right; you need help.

Maybe the photographer tried to warn me. 'Take care of yourself,' he said on his way out. 'Take care of yourself.'

It's just a turn of phrase.

I get up. I cross the hall and dash upstairs—trip over, stumble, struggle to my feet, take the last steps up, run along the passage and reach my study.

I boot up my laptop and, still standing, begin to type with trembling hands—type and click and search—searching, searching, searching for the homepage Victor Lenzen showed me on his phone. *Spiegel Online*, August 2002: 'Our correspondent in Afghanistan.' I search and search. It's not possible—how did he do that? But it's true. I can't find it; it's vanished—the archive page with Lenzen's reports—with Lenzen's alibi.

It's not there.

28

JONAS

Jonas relished the feeling that spread through his stomach as he sped along the dark road. He was exhausted and wanted to get home.

His head was buzzing with all the facts his team had gathered that day concerning the second murder victim. Apart from the physical similarity, there was no connection whatsoever with Britta Peters. The search for a culprit from the small circle of shared acquaintances had been called off for the time being. They would have to come up with another method of approach. It wouldn't be easy.

After work, Jonas had let off steam as best he could with some boxing practice and had felt a bit better afterwards. Since seeing Sophie Peters, however, the relaxation that goes with hard physical training had been blown away. She was the reason he was taking this case so personally. He wondered whether it was having an adverse effect on him—whether it made him overlook things, make mistakes.

Sophie had been different this evening. She had seemed gloomier and more vulnerable. It was only a feeling, but Jonas instinctively reduced the speed at which he was hurtling along the road. He'd seen Sophie's face before him—her look of resignation. The way she'd said, 'Goodbye, Superintendent Weber.' So sad, so final.

Should he drive back? Rubbish.

Sophie wasn't the kind to harm herself.

Less than a quarter of an hour later, Jonas was lying fully clothed on his bed. He wanted to have a rest before going over the case again in his study. He could sense the emptiness beside him that his wife had left when she'd gone to live with her best friend to 'get a few things clear in her mind'. Jonas closed his eyes. He had the feeling that he was at last stepping off the carousel of thoughts he'd been riding round on all day.

When his mobile pinged with a text message, he gave a groan.

Maybe it was Mia? Picking the phone up from the bedside table, he didn't immediately recognise the number, but eventually it dawned on him. Sophie.

Jonas sat up and opened the message.

It consisted of only two words: *He's here.*

26

The website containing Lenzen's alibi has disappeared.

I blink dazedly and recall that I looked at it on his phone, not mine. It was Lenzen who typed in the address, not me. Whatever I saw, I can't find it now. I stare at the screen for a while. Then I take my laptop in both hands and hurl it at the wall. I rip the telephone out of the socket and throw that too. I yell, I kick my desk. I feel no pain. I grope about, blind with rage and hatred, grabbing everything I can lay my hands on—pens, stapler, ring binders—and fling them at the wall. I beat the wall with my fists until the white runs red. I feel nothing.

My study lies in ruins. I slump to the floor, in amidst the chaos. The heat in my body gives way to cold, and I start shivering. I've been turned inside out, my organs are turning to ice, shrivelling up, growing numb.

Lenzen duped me.

I don't know how he did it, but how hard can it be to set up a fake website?

Not much harder than playing a Beatles song on a small mobile device and pretending not to hear anything.

Not much harder than dosing yourself with an emetic to lend credibility to your shock.

Not much harder than spiking a woman's coffee to make her amenable and disorientated and susceptible to alien ideas.

That must be what happened. It explains the hallucinations, the strange blackouts and the fact that I was suddenly open to absurd ideas—almost without a will of my own. It explains why it's only now that I am beginning to see clearly again. Perhaps a small dose of bufotenine. Or DMT. Or mescaline. That would make sense.

How could I have thought even for a second that I might have harmed Anna?

The sun is falling onto the study floor. There is blood dripping from my hand. My ears are buzzing. I think of Anna; I see her before me quite clearly: my best friend, my sister. Just because Anna could sometimes be inconsiderate and vain and selfish doesn't mean she wasn't also naïve and sweet and innocent. Just because Anna could sometimes be incredibly hurtful doesn't mean she wasn't also capable of being selfless and generous. Just because I sometimes hated Anna doesn't mean I didn't love her. She was my sister.

Anna wasn't perfect. Not Saint Anna, just Anna.

I think of Lenzen. He was so much better prepared than me.

I have nothing I can use against him and now he knows it. That's why he came—to find that out. He didn't have to come and talk to me. But Victor Lenzen is a wise man. He knew that if he didn't, he would never find out how much I really knew—whether I had any concrete evidence against him, and whether I'd told anyone about him. How relieved he must have been when he realised that he was dealing with a woman who was lonely and unstable. His strategy was as simple as it was inspired: deny everything at all costs and make me feel as insecure as possible. It was enough to plunge me into doubt.

But now I have no more doubts. I listen. The voices have stopped arguing. There's only one now. And that voice is saying it is unlikely that I saw my sister's murderer on the TV after twelve years—highly unlikely—but not impossible. It is a highly improbable truth. Victor Lenzen killed my sister.

My anger is clenched tight like a fist.

I have to get out of here.

29

SOPHIE

He stood before her. He had a knife.

She had turned to stone when she heard the noise in the hall, but she'd had the presence of mind to tap a message into her phone and send it to Jonas. Then she had held her breath and waited, listening.

Whoever was in the hall had done the same. There was no sound—not a creak, not a breath—but Sophie could sense someone's presence. Please, let it be Paul, she thought, quite against her better judgement. Paul, come to pick up his stupid boxes at last, or to blubber and tell me he misses me. But please, please, let it be Paul.

It was then that she saw him. He loomed tall and menacing in the doorway, almost filling it, less than two metres away. Sophie caught her breath.

'Frau Peters,' he said.

She saw it all before her. He must have watched her as she walked through the dark streets and parks, and decided that it was too risky to approach her. She saw him outside the big block of flats where she lived, waiting for one of the other residents to come or go, and then slipping through the front door before it fell shut. She saw him almost noiselessly opening her door, perhaps with a credit card. She hadn't locked it, as usual, although she was always promising herself she would.

Sophie was still rigid with fear. She'd heard the voice before but couldn't say where.

'You killed my sister,' she gasped.

It was all she could think of to say, her brain was working so very slowly, and then, without meaning to, she said it again.

'You killed my sister.'

The man laughed a mirthless laugh.

'What do you want from me?' Sophie asked.

Even as she said it, she realised how stupid the question was. The shadow didn't reply.

Sophie searched feverishly for a solution. If she didn't do anything now, she wouldn't leave the room alive. She must at least gain time.

'I know you,' she said.

'Ah, so you do recognise my voice?' the man replied.

Sophie stared at him. Then the penny dropped.

'You're Britta's landlord's son,' she said in stunned shock. 'The one with the brother who had an accident.'

'Bingo.' He sounded almost cheerful. 'It was great fun talking to you on the phone,' he added, while Sophie ran through possible plans of action in her head.

She had no way of escaping. She thought of the kitchen knife in the drawer, but it was too far away, and then of the pepper spray in her handbag—but the bag was hanging on a hook at the front door.

'I'm afraid the car crash story wasn't true,' the man added. 'Don't hold it against me. I thought it was a nice touch.'

He smiled at his own ingenuity, then all amusement drained from his face.

'Come on,' he said. 'We're going to the bathroom. You lead the way.'

Sophie didn't move.

'Why did you do it? Why Britta?' she asked.

'Why Britta?' the man repeated, and pretended to ponder the question for a moment. 'That's a good question—why Britta? To be perfectly honest with you, I don't know the answer. Can any of us say why we find one person attractive and another repulsive? Do any of us really know why we do what we do?'

He gave a shrug.

'Any more questions?' he asked sarcastically.

Sophie swallowed.

'What were you doing in the car park the other night? Were you following me?' she asked. Gain time, no matter how little.

'What car park?' the man asked. 'I've no idea what you're talking about. Now, enough mucking around. Get in the bathroom.'

Sophie's throat tightened. 'What are we going to do in there?' she croaked.

'You couldn't handle your sister's death. Tomorrow they'll find you in the bath. You just couldn't carry on. Everybody will understand.' And then, more impatiently: 'Hurry up.'

But Sophie couldn't move. She'd always made fun of the way people in horror films simply stand there when they're threatened, instead of doing something. Like lambs to the slaughter. But she too was rooted to the spot. Then she came out of her stupor and screamed as loud as she could.

In a split second the man was on her, pressing a hand over her mouth.

'One more scream and it'll all be over, here and now. Do you understand?'

Sophie let out a gasp.

'Nod if you understand.'

She nodded.

The man let go of her. 'Now get in the bathroom,' he said, raising the knife menacingly.

Sophie's body began to obey her again. She set off with shaky steps, feverishly racking her brains. To get to the bathroom, they'd have to walk down the long cluttered hall in the direction of the front door. She took a step or two out of the kitchen; she could sense the man with the knife following her. Paul's removal boxes lined the way. 'Winter things' it said on one box, 'DVDs' on the next. Sophie took another step, and then another, past 'Books' and 'Shoes'. The front door was getting closer but it still felt infinitely distant, down there at the end of the hall. Another step. She wouldn't make it. But perhaps...

It would only take a second—a short moment of distraction. Another step. But the murderer wasn't taking his eyes off her; she could sense him behind her, alert. Three or four more steps to the bathroom, and then it would all be over. Two more steps. 'CDs', 'Misc.'. One more step...

When Sophie reached the door, she could see the man from the corner of her eye, knife raised, and she was about to push down the door handle, when the bell rang, long and shrill. The man glanced towards the door, momentarily distracted, and she took her chance, tearing Paul's golf club out of the removal box and wielding it above her head.

27

Eleven years is a long time. When I wake up at night and stare at my bedroom ceiling, I sometimes wonder whether I've dreamt the world out there. Maybe this world isn't really *my* world; maybe it's the only one there is. Maybe I should only believe in the things I can see and touch. Maybe I made up all the rest. After all, I've always made up stories. I remember doing it.

I imagine that this is all there is—my house, the world. I imagine that there is nowhere else for me to go; that I will grow old and die here. That I will somehow have children here, children who are born into my world and know nothing but the ground floor and the first floor, the attic and the cellar, the balconies and the terraces. I imagine myself telling them fairy tales, in which marvellous things happen, tales teeming with wonders and fabulous beings.

'There is a country,' I will say, 'where there are enormous great trees.' 'What are trees?' they will ask, and I'll tell them that trees are magical things that grow up, up, up out of the ground, when you bury tiny seeds in the earth—wondrous things that look different in every season, and change as if by magic, putting out blossoms, or green or coloured leaves. 'And there aren't just trees in this country; there are feathered creatures too, big ones and little ones, that sit in the trees and sing songs in a foreign language. And there are enormous creatures, the size of our house, that live under the water and spew fountains as high as a steeple. And there are mountains and fields and deserts and meadows.'

'What are meadows, Mummy?' my children will ask.

'Meadows are great tracts of land, very green and very soft, and covered all over with grass—cheeky stalks that tickle children's legs as they skip across them. They are so big that you can run until you're quite out of breath without getting anywhere near the edge.'

'But they can't be that big, Mummy,' one of my children will say. 'No, Mummy, they can't be that big. Nothing's as big as that.'

When I think of the world out there, I am overwhelmed by infinite longing. It is a feeling I know well; I have felt it while writing, on the running machine and in my dreams—even when talking to Lenzen.

I want to stand on a market square in a small town, and I want to look up into the summer sky, shade my eyes from the sun and watch the breakneck manoeuvres of the swifts as they race around the church tower. I want the smell of wood and resin on a forest ramble. I want the distinctive movement of a butterfly—that blithe aimlessness. I want the cool feeling you get on your sun-warmed skin, when a small cloud thrusts itself in front of the summer sun. I want the slimy feeling of waterweed tickling your calves when you're swimming in a lake. And I think: I can have those things again.

Yes, I am afraid. But if there's one thing I've learnt over the past weeks and months, it's that fear is no reason for inaction. On the contrary.

I have to return to the real world. I'm going to be free.

Then I'll deal with Lenzen.

JONAS

Superintendent Jonas Weber stood at his office window watching the last of the swifts as they played in the sky. It wouldn't be long until they too left for the south.

He'd had to get a grip after receiving Sophie's text. He had stepped on the accelerator, sped through town and arrived even before his colleagues in the patrol car, whom he'd alerted on his way. He'd run the last few metres to Sophie's flat and leant on the bell, forcing himself to keep calm when no one opened up. He'd rung the neighbours' bells until a furious old lady let him into the block—it's okay, it's the police—and he'd run up the stairs, pounded at the door and been on the point of forcing an entry, when it had swung open.

Jonas tried not to think of that terrible moment when he hadn't been sure whether he'd got there in time.

Sophie had opened the door to him, white as a sheet, but calm. With relief, he had registered that she was unhurt. Then he'd seen the man lying dead or injured on the floor. He had felt for his pulse and established that he was still alive, then called an ambulance. His colleagues had arrived, the ambulance had come, and everyone had set to work. It had turned out all right, after all.

Jonas moved away from the window and sat down at his desk. He wondered what Sophie was doing now. For days, he had been resisting the temptation to give her a call. She would get over the shock, he was sure of that; she'd soon be her old self again. People like Sophie always landed on their feet. But he was struggling with himself; he felt like hearing her voice. He took his phone, entered her number, hesitated—and gave a start when Antonia Bug stormed into his office.

'Dead man in a wood,' she said. 'Are you coming?'

Jonas nodded. 'Be right with you.'

'What's the matter?' Bug asked. 'You've got a face like a wet week.'

Jonas didn't answer.

'Are you still thinking about our young friend?' she asked.

It annoyed Jonas that Bug should speak so matter-of-factly about the murderer. After all, the man had gone on to kill another woman after Britta Peters. But they all talked like that.

'We should have got him,' Jonas replied. 'He shouldn't have been given the opportunity to strike a second time. When Zimmer found out that Britta Peters had complained about her landlord letting himself into her flat, we should have pursued it.'

'We did pursue it.'

'But we shouldn't have just accepted the old man's denial. If we'd been more persistent, we might have realised that it wasn't him who'd let himself into the flat; it was his son.'

'You're right,' said Bug. 'Maybe things would have turned out differently. But what use is it now?'

She shrugged. She had dismissed the entire case astonishingly quickly.

Jonas, however, was still coming to terms with the murderer's coldness. He hadn't borne any kind of grudge against Britta Peters; he hadn't really known her at all. He'd simply seen her one day on a visit to his father, and she'd happened to be his type; she'd triggered something in him. So pure, so innocent. He had killed her 'because he wanted her and because he could'. There had been no other motive. He had thought the white roses in the victims' flats 'a nice touch', something 'original'—'like in the movies'.

Jonas Weber was going to be plagued by thoughts of this man, whose trial was soon to begin, for a long time to come.

'Are you coming?' Antonia repeated.

Jonas nodded again and put his mobile away. It was for the best. Sophie had got what she wanted; her sister's murder had been solved. That was what it had been about—that and nothing else.

28

By the time Charlotte shows up in the early morning and starts to unpack my shopping, I have already put in several hours of hard work. I have watched the surveillance technicians with their impassive faces remove the microphones and cameras from my house. I have cleaned up. I have eliminated all traces of Victor Lenzen. I have seen the videos of the crazy author and the bewildered reporter. I have kept my anger in check—no more rooms laid to waste, no more bloody fists. Instead, I have prepared myself.

Now all that remains is to get Charlotte on board, but it's not that easy. We're standing in the kitchen. Charlotte is putting fruit and vegetables and milk and cheese in the fridge, and gives me a suspicious look. I can sympathise; my request must seem odd to her.

'How long do you want me to keep Bukowski?' she asks.

'A week? Would that be all right?'

Charlotte scrutinises me, then nods.

'Sure—why not? Love to. My son will go wild. He adores dogs; he'd like one of his own.'

She hesitates, casting a stolen glance at the bandage on my right hand—the hand I smashed against my study wall like a madwoman and injured so badly that I had to ask my GP to come and attend to it. I know there's something else Charlotte wants to say: that she's worried about this peculiar employer of hers, who never sets foot outside, has been through at least one depressive crisis recently, and is now asking her to take care of her dog. It sounds as if I'm planning my suicide and want to make sure that somebody will take care of my beloved pet when I'm dead. Of course it does—normal people don't give their pets to other people to look after unless they're going on holiday, and the idea that I might have plans to travel is absurd.

'Frau Conrads,' she says falteringly, 'are you all right?'

I feel such immense fondness for Charlotte that I can barely stop myself from hugging her, which would surely unsettle her even more.

'Everything's fine—really it is. I know I've been strange these last weeks and months, maybe even depressed, but I'm better now. I just have an awful lot to get done in the next few days and Bukowski needs so much attention at the moment...'

I pause. I know I sound ridiculous, but there's nothing I can do about it.

'It would be really great if you could take him for a few days. I'll pay you, of course.'

Charlotte nods, nervously scratching her tattooed lower arm.

'Okay.'

I can no longer restrain myself and I fling my arms round her neck. Earlier today, I had asked her whether the journalist who had interviewed me had been in touch with her and she said no. In any case, I don't believe that Lenzen would harm Charlotte. He's not stupid.

Charlotte suffers my embrace. I hold her tight for a few seconds, then let her go.

'Er, thanks,' Charlotte mumbles, embarrassed. 'I'll go and pack the dog's things then.' And she takes herself off upstairs.

I'm immensely relieved, almost cheerful even. I'm about to go in my study when I stop in the hall and stare in amazement at the little orchid I fetched in from my conservatory a few months ago. I've tended it with care, fed it fertiliser, watered it once a week, given it frequent attention. But it is only now that I see the new stem it's put out. The buds on it are tiny, unspectacular and tight, but already they hold the lush splendour of exotic blooms. It seems a miracle. I decide to entrust the plant to Charlotte's care as well. I wouldn't want it dying while I'm away.

The rest of the day I've spent at my laptop in my study, reading. I've discovered that orchids can survive practically anywhere—in soil, on rocks and stones, on other plants. They can, in theory, continue to grow indefinitely, but almost nothing is known about how long they can live.

At some point, Charlotte left. Bukowski made a scene when she put him in her car, as if he feared that something awful was in store. He knows Charlotte's car because she's the one who drives him to the vet, but he was still distraught. I stroked him a bit and ruffled his fur, but only a little. I didn't want him to think we were parting for good.

Hope to see you again, mate.

After Charlotte and Bukowski had left, I went into the conservatory and watered my plants. When I'd finished, I made myself some coffee. Then, cup in hand, I wandered into my library, breathed in its soothing smell and looked out of the window for a while, until my coffee began to grow cold and the world outside began to grow dark.

It is night. There's nothing left to do. I am ready.

EPILOGUE

SOPHIE

She had bumped into him quite by chance. She had gone to a pub she'd never been to before and, although it was pretty full, had spotted him at once.

He was sitting at the bar on his own, a drink in front of him. Sophie could hardly believe it. Then it occurred to her that he might think she was stalking him, and was on the point of walking out again when he turned and spotted her. She gave an embarrassed smile and went over.

'Are you following me?' Jonas Weber asked.

'Pure coincidence, honest,' Sophie replied.

'I've never seen you here before,' he said. 'Do you come here often?'

'I often walk this way, but today's the first time I've been inside.'

Sophie swung herself onto an empty barstool.

'What are you drinking?' she asked.

'Whisky.'

'Okay,' said Sophie and turned to the barman. 'I'll have what he's having.'

The landlord poured her a glass and set it in front of her.

'Thanks.'

Sophie contemplated the clear brown liquid, making it slosh back and forth a little in the glass.

'What shall we drink to?' she asked at last.

'I'm drinking to the official failure of my marriage,' said Jonas. 'How about you?'

Sophie hesitated, unable to digest what she'd heard. She wondered whether she should comment but decided against it.

'I always used to say: to world peace,' she said. 'But the world isn't peaceful and isn't ever going to be.'

'No toast then,' said Jonas.

They looked into each other's eyes, clinked their glasses together and knocked back the whisky.

Sophie dug a banknote out of her trouser pocket and placed it on the bar.

'Keep the change,' she said to the barman.

She turned to Jonas. He looked at her with his strange eyes.

'You're leaving already?' he asked.

'I have to.'

'Really?'

'Yes. I have someone waiting for me at home,' said Sophie.

'Oh. You and your fiancé are...back together?'

His voice was neutral.

'No, I've found somebody else and I don't want to leave him on his own for long. Would you like to see him?'

Before Jonas could reply, Sophie had pulled her mobile from her jeans pocket. She made a few hasty taps on the display and then thrust a photo of a tousled pup under his nose.

'Isn't he gorgeous?' she asked.

Jonas had to smile.

'What's he called?'

'I'm thinking of calling him after one of my favourite authors. Maybe Kafka.'

'Hm.'

'You're not convinced?'

'Kafka's definitely a good name. But he somehow doesn't look like a Kafka.'

'What does he look like then? And don't come with any of your poets; I'm not calling him Rilke.'

'I think he looks like a Bukowski.'

'Like a Bukowski?' Sophie asked, indignant. 'Wasted and boozy?'

'No, unkempt. And kind of cool.'

Jonas shrugged. He was about to say something when his phone rang. He didn't answer, and a brief buzz announced the arrival of a voicemail.

'You need to call back,' Sophie said. 'A new case.'

'Yes.'

'Well, I have to be going anyway.'

Sophie got down off the barstool. She looked Jonas in the eyes.

'Thank you,' she said.

'What for? You're the one who caught him.'

Sophie shrugged.

'Thanks all the same,' she said. She planted a kiss on Jonas's cheek and disappeared.

29

My world is a thousand-square-metre disc and I am standing on the edge. Out there, on the other side of my front door, lurks my fear.

I push down the handle, open the door. Before me is darkness. For the first time in many years I'm wearing a coat.

I take a tiny step and the stabbing pain in my head is back. But I have to get through this—through the fear. The front door falls shut behind me; there's something final about the sound it makes. Night air hits me in the face. The stars twinkle in a cold sky. All at once, I'm unbelievably hot; my guts seize up. But I take another step, and another. I am a lonely seafarer on foreign waters. I am the last human being on a deserted planet. I stumble on—ever onward. I reach the edge of the terrace. It is black all around me.

This is where the grass begins. I set one foot in front of the other, feeling the soft meadow beneath my feet. Then I stop, out of breath. The darkness is inside me. I feel sweat on my forehead.

My fear is a dark well that I have fallen into. I'm suspended vertically in the water. I try to touch the bottom with my toes, but there's nothing there, only blackness. I close my eyes and let myself fall. I'm sinking in the dark, my body is drifting down, swallowed by the water; I'm being sucked down. The well is bottomless; I'm sinking deeper and deeper and I let it happen: my eyes closed, arms waving above me like waterweed. Then, all of a sudden, I reach the bottom of the well, cool and firm. I feel it brush my toes, and soon my weight is resting on it and I'm standing.

I open my eyes and notice in amazement that here, in the heart of darkness, I can stand and breathe effortlessly. I look about me.

The lake is still. A light breeze whispers at the edge of the woods. There are crackling, rustling noises all around me. Birds in the undergrowth, perhaps, or a busy hedgehog or prowling cat, and I realise how much life there is here, even if I can't see it. I am not alone—all those animals in the woods, on the meadow, in the lake and on the shore—all the roedeer and red deer, all the foxes and wild boars and martens, all the little owls and tawny owls and barn owls, the trout and the pike, the grasshoppers, ladybirds and gnats. So much life.

A smile steals onto my lips. I am standing at the edge of the meadow. There's nothing left of my fear. I set off again. I step out into Van Gogh's starry night. I look about me; the stars make streaks and the moon is a smudge in the viscous, gleaming night sky.

I think to myself that the night is not just mysterious and poetic and beautiful.

It is also dark and frightening. Like me.

30

After Anna's death, everything was too much for me. The looks, the questions, the voices, the lights, the noise, the speed—and the panic attacks, which at first only struck when I saw a knife or heard a certain song but were soon triggered by all sorts of things. A passer-by wearing Anna's perfume, bloody meat on display in a butcher's window—pretty much anything. That glare in my head, the pain behind my eyeballs, that keen, red feeling. And no control.

It did me good to stay at home for a while: to be alone, getting some peace and quiet, writing a new book. Getting up in the morning, working, eating, working some more, sleeping. Making up stories where nobody had to die. Living in a world in which there was no danger.

People think it's hard not to leave your house for over a decade. They think it's easy to go out. And they're right; it is easy to go out. But it's also easy not to go out. A few days soon become a few weeks; a few weeks become months and years. That sounds like an immensely long time. But it's only ever one more day strung on to those that have gone before.

At first, nobody noticed I'd stopped leaving the house. Linda was around; she made phone calls and wrote emails, and when do we actually find time to see each other, we all have such an awful lot to do. But at some point my publishers asked whether I wanted to give a few readings again, and I said no. Friends were married or buried and I was asked to the weddings and funerals, and I said no. I won prizes and was invited to the award ceremonies, and I said no.

In the end, people caught on. When the rumours about a mysterious illness started, I was thrilled. Until then, I had tried to overcome my fear; I had stood and battled with myself at the front door, willing myself across the threshold and failing miserably.

But this wonderful illness, invented and spread about by some big, lying daily paper, released me from all that. The invitations ceased. Suddenly I was no longer rude and antisocial but, at worst, to be pitied—and at best, brave. The whole thing was even a boon to my literary career. Linda Conrads, the author with the mysterious illness, who lived cut off from society, sold better than the flesh-and-blood Linda Conrads, who shook your hand and talked to you at readings. So I never denied the rumours. Why should I? I certainly wasn't interested in talking about my panic attacks.

Now I have the feeling I am being drawn into a book of fairy tales that I haven't looked at for eleven years. I'm sitting in a taxi, speeding through the night, my head against the window and my eyes drinking in the world as it flashes by.

I look up. The night sky is an inky black curtain with pink clouds drifting past it like acrobats. Every now and then, stars sparkle. The real world is so much more magical, so much more incredible than I remembered it. I feel dizzy when I think of the almost infinite possibilities it offers me.

It's almost more than I can bear—the wild, restless feeling that spreads through my chest when it becomes clear in my mind: *I am free.*

It is dark, but the lights and the oncoming cars, the speed and the movement and the life around me are mesmerising. We're coming into town; the traffic's growing heavier and the streets are filling up, even though it is late. I am on safari, watching the passers-by as if they were exotic animals; as if I'd never seen anything like it in my life. Here is a mother and her young; she carries the creature strapped to her belly, its plump legs idly kicking. There is an elderly couple holding hands; they make me think of my parents and I swiftly avert my gaze. Over there, a horde of animals—five, no, six of them—are walking along the pavement, heads bowed, eyes fixed on the mobile phones that they're tapping away at distractedly. These teenagers filling the streets were still toddlers when I was last here.

I recognise the town, and at the same time I don't. I knew there was nothing left but chains—supermarket and discount-store and fast-food and coffee-shop and bookshop chains. I read the papers; I know things like that. But I hadn't seen them with my own eyes.

The taxi stops with a jolt and I give a start. We're in a quiet residential area on the edge of town—pretty little houses, well-kept front gardens, bicycles. If it were Sunday, I'd be able to glimpse the last minutes of a crime series through most of the living-room windows.

'We're there,' the driver says drily. 'That's twenty-six twenty.'

I pull a bundle of notes out of my trouser pocket. I'm not used to handling cash; I've done all my shopping online for so long. I find a twenty euro note and a tenner and relish the feel of real money. I give the notes to the man and tell him: 'Keep the change.'

I'd like to stay sitting here a bit longer and delay things, but I know I've already gone too far tonight to turn back.

I open the door of the car. I ignore the impulse to shut it again straight away. I ignore the pain in my head and pulling myself together, I get out and stumble to the door of number eleven, which looks exactly the same as number nine and number thirteen. I ignore the feelings that well up inside me at the familiar crunch of my footsteps on the gravel path. I trigger the motion detector and jump when a lamp lights up the path and announces my arrival. I see movement behind the curtains and hold back a curse; I'd like to have had the time to collect myself.

I climb the three steps to the front door, put my finger on the bell, and even before I can push it, the door swings open.

'Linda,' the man says.

'Dad,' I say.

My mother appears behind him—roughly five foot three of shock. My parents stand in the door and stare. Then, both at the same time, they come out of their stupor and clasp me to them, and all three of us are locked in one big hug. My relief tastes of the sweet cherries in our garden—of sorrel and daisies and all the smells of my childhood.

A little while later, we're in the front room drinking tea, my parents sitting next to one another on the sofa, and me opposite them in my favourite armchair. The way to this armchair led along a hall covered in photographs from my childhood and teenage years—Linda and Anna camping, Linda and Anna at a sleepover, Linda and Anna at Christmas, Linda and Anna at Mardi Gras. I tried not to look.

Out of the corner of my eye, I can see the flicker of the TV that my mother switched on as a kind of displacement activity. I have tried to explain to my parents how it's possible that I'm here, suddenly leaving the house again. I've told them that I'm better and have something important to deal with and, surprisingly, that seemed to satisfy them for the time being. Now we're sitting here. We look at each other shyly; we have so much to talk about that we don't know what to say.

On the coffee table are sandwiches that my mother rustled up. She still feels the need to feed me. I'm in a daze; it's all far too surreal—the woodchip, the cuckoo clock, the carpet, the family photos, the familiar smells—incredible. And incredible that I'm here at all.

I cast a stolen glance at my parents. They have aged in different ways. My mother looks almost the same—perhaps a little more delicate than she used to be, but otherwise not much changed. She is short, thin, sensibly dressed, her trim, old-fashioned hairdo newly dyed a reddish brown. Dad, on the other hand, has grown old. All those years. The left corner of his mouth droops limply. His hands tremble and he tries to hide it.

I grip my teacup as if it were a lifeline and let my gaze wander around the room. It comes to rest on the bookcases to my left. One row of books in particular catches my attention—that special typeface. It looks familiar. I have a closer look and realise that they're my books standing there on the shelf—two copies of each of my novels in strict chronological order. I swallow. I'd always thought my parents weren't interested in my books, and I certainly didn't think they read them. They never mentioned my writing—neither the short stories I concocted as a teenager, nor the novels I wrote in my early twenties. We never talked about my unsuccessful early work or the subsequent bestsellers. They never enquired about them or asked me to send them copies. It was a disappointment to me for years, until, in the end, I forgot about it. But now I see that they had my books all along—every one of them—and in duplicate. Maybe a set each—or spares, in case any were mislaid.

I'm about to ask, when my mother clears her throat—her surreptitious way of opening the conversation.

I had intended to be the first to talk and get it over and done with. But I can't find the words. How do you do it? How do you ask your parents if they think you're a murderer? And how do you bear the answer?

'Linda,' my mother begins, and immediately breaks off, swallowing a lump in her throat. 'Linda, I'd like you to know that I understand you.'

My father nods emphatically.

'Yes, me too,' he says. 'I mean, it came as a shock, of course. But your mother and I have talked it over and we understand why you're doing it.'

I don't understand.

'And I'd like to apologise,' my mother says. 'For hanging up when you rang the other night. I felt awful about it—as soon as I'd done it, in fact. I even rang you back the next day, but I couldn't get through.'

I frown. My first impulse is to disagree. I always know when someone rings. I am—in the truest sense of the word—the biggest stay-at-home on the planet. But then it comes back to me—my wrecked study, my shattered laptop, the ring binder torn to shreds in a fit of rage, the telephone ripped from the wall and dashed to pieces on the floor. Okay. But what are they talking about?

'You can do what you want, of course; it's your story,' my mother says. 'At the end of the day, it's your experience. Only it would have been nice if you'd given us some warning. Especially'—she falters, clears her throat and continues more softly—'especially, of course, about the bit with the murder.'

I stare at my mother. She looks exhausted. But I really don't know what she means.

'What are you talking about, Mum?' I ask.

'I'm talking about your new book,' she says. 'About *Blood Sisters*.'

I shake my head, bewildered. My book's not coming out for two weeks. So far, only a few advance copies have been sent to booksellers and the press. There's been no coverage of any kind, and my parents have no contact whatsoever with the publishing industry. How do they know about my book? A dark feeling spreads through my stomach, thick and syrupy.

'How do you know about my novel?' I ask as calmly as I can.

Of course, I should have been the one to let them know. But it would be a lie to pretend I'd thought of warning them. I simply forgot.

'We had a journalist here,' my father says. 'Nice bloke, from a respectable paper, so your mother asked him in.'

I can feel the hairs on my neck stand on end.

'Sat right where you're sitting now and asked us what we thought about our famous daughter making literary capital out of her sister's murder in her next book.'

I'm falling.

'Lenzen,' I gasp.

'That was the name!' my father shouts, as if he's been trying to remember it all along.

'We didn't believe him at first,' my mother says, joining the conversation again. 'Until he showed us a copy of the novel.'

242

I feel dizzy.

'Victor Lenzen was here, in this house?' I say.

My parents look at me with alarm in their eyes. I must look very pale.

'Are you all right?' my mother asks.

'Victor Lenzen was here, in this house, and told you about my book?' I ask.

'He said he was meeting you for an interview and wanted to find out a bit about your background first,' says my father. 'We shouldn't have let him in.'

'That's why you hung up when I called,' I gasp. 'You were cross about the book.'

My mother nods. I'd like to fling my arms round her neck in relief, because she's there, because she's my mother, because she never for a second believed I could be a murderer—not for a second. The very idea is absurd. Now that I'm sitting face-to-face with her, that is quite clear to me. But alone in my big house, it seemed entirely logical. I've been living in a hall of mirrors that have distorted everything in my life.

Victor Lenzen came here to find out what I knew, what my parents knew. When he realised that Mum and Dad knew nothing and that we were barely in touch with one another, he brilliantly turned the situation to his advantage.

My anger takes my breath away. I need a moment's peace to gather my thoughts.

'Excuse me for a second,' I say, getting up.

I leave the room, feeling my parents' eyes on my back. I lock myself in the guest bathroom, sit down on the cool tiled floor, bury my face in my hands, and try to calm down. The euphoria I had felt at finally managing to leave the house is slowly evaporating, giving way to the urgent question: What am I to do about Lenzen?

There is no evidence against him. He would have to confess. And he didn't do that even when he was looking into the muzzle of my gun.

But that, of course, was in my house, and he had to reckon on everything being recorded. What if I were to look him up now—now that he feels safe?

I hesitate for a moment, then I take my phone and enter Julian's number. It rings once, three times, five times, then the answering machine starts up. I leave a few words asking him to call me back and giving my mobile number, then I hang up. Might Julian still be at work? I ring the police station. A policeman I don't know takes the call.

'This is Linda Michaelis,' I say. 'Is Superintendent Schumer there?'

'No, sorry,' the man replies. 'Not till tomorrow.'

Damn! I'm tempted to go ahead anyway. But I don't want to screw things up again. I need help.

I flush the chain and run the tap, in case my parents are still sitting tensely in the living room and can hear me. Then I leave the bathroom and go back to them. Their faces brighten when I step through the door. I notice what trouble they're taking not to scrutinise me, not to scan my face for traces of the past years.

I sit down again. I take a sandwich, because I know it will please my mother. It's not until I start to eat that I realise how hungry I really am. I'm about to take another when my phone rings. I don't recognise the mobile number. Could it be Julian ringing me back? Hurriedly, I take the call.

'Hello?'

'Good evening. Is that Linda Conrads?' a male voice asks.

It's a voice I don't know. I'm on instant alert. I get up, casting an apologetic glance at my parents, and go into the hall, closing the door behind me.

'Yes. Who's speaking?'

'Hello, Frau Conrads, I'm glad I've got hold of you. My name is Maximilian Henkel. I have your number from my colleague, Victor Lenzen.'

I'm reeling.

'Oh?' I say lamely.

I have to prop myself up against the hall wall so as not to lose my balance.

'I hope you don't mind my disturbing you so late,' the man says, but he doesn't wait for a response. 'It's about the interview. We were all thrilled, of course, when we received your offer of an exclusive interview. Such a shame it didn't work out first time round. Are you better now?'

What's going on here?

'Yes,' I say, swallowing.

'Great,' says Henkel. 'Victor said you hadn't felt well and that the interview couldn't take place. But we'd still love to have you in one of our next issues. I wanted to ask you if it would be possible to repeat the interview at a more opportune time. The sooner the better.'

I catch my breath.

'Repeat it?' I exclaim. 'With Lenzen?'

'Oh, yes, I should perhaps have mentioned that to begin with. I'm afraid Victor Lenzen won't be available. He's made a spur-of-the-moment decision to leave for Syria tonight on a lengthy research trip. But if you wouldn't mind making do with me or one of my other colleagues...'

'Victor Lenzen's leaving the country tomorrow?' I gasp.

'Yes, the crazy fellow,' Henkel says in an offhand manner. 'It was probably only a matter of time before he got itchy feet again. I know he was your preferred interviewer, but perhaps we can...'

I hang up. My head is ringing.

Tonight is all I have left.

I'm so sunk in thought that I jump when the living-room door opens and my mother pops her head round the side.

'Is everything all right, love?'

My heart leaps with joy. She hasn't called me that for years.

My father's face appears behind her. I smile, in spite of my panic.

'Yes,' I say. 'But you'll have to forgive me; I'm afraid I've got to be going again.'

'What—now?' my mother asks.

'Yes. I'm very sorry, but something's cropped up.'

My parents look at me in horror.

'But we've only just got you back. You can't leave again straight away,' my mother says. 'Please stay the night.'

'I'll be back soon. Promise.'

'Can't it wait till tomorrow?' my father asks. 'It's late.'

I can see the concern on their faces. They don't care what I write or how I live; they only want me to be with them. Linda. Their elder daughter, their only remaining daughter. My parents look at me in silence and I almost cave in.

'I'm sorry,' I say. 'I'll come back, I promise.'

I hug my mother and feel like bursting into tears. Gently, I free myself from her embrace. She lets me go, reluctantly. I hug my father—remember him spinning me through the air when I was little, so big and strong; a laughing giant. Now he feels fragile. I ease myself away from him. He looks at me with a smile, takes my face in his trembling hand and strokes my cheek with his thumb, the way he used to.

'See you tomorrow,' he says, letting me go.

'See you tomorrow,' my mother says.

I nod, forcing a smile.

I take my bag, leave my parents' house, step onto the street and feel the night swallow me up.

31

I am sitting in a taxi outside his house. To my immense relief, there are lights on; he's at home. He's divorced now, but he still lives here. That much, at least, I know. Not that his marital status should be a matter of interest to me in the present situation.

I am breathing a mixture of smells: leather seats, sweat and pungent aftershave. I let my gaze rest on the front steps, and remember how we sat there in the darkness sharing a cigarette, an infinitely long time ago.

I haven't seen Julian for almost twelve years. At the beginning of those twelve years, I had been convinced that couldn't be all; that he would get in touch sooner or later—give me a ring, drop me a line, turn up on my doorstep, make some kind of sign. But there was nothing. Superintendent Julian Schumer. I remember the bond between us, as invisible and as real as electricity.

I have missed him. Now I'm sitting here in a taxi outside his house, a classical music station on the radio, the driver drumming the beat on the steering wheel, and time running through my fingers as I try to summon up the courage to get out of the car.

I pull myself together. I stride towards the front door, dazzled partway by the light triggered by the sensor. I climb the steps, ring the bell, brace myself to meet Julian. My feelings are irrelevant. What matters is that he believes me—that he helps me. I manage one deep breath, then the heavy wooden door opens.

A very tall, very beautiful woman stands before me and looks at me enquiringly.

'Yes?' she says.

For a moment I am speechless. What an idiot I am. Why had this possibility never occurred to me? The world has carried on turning.

'I'm sorry to bother you,' I say. 'Is Julian Schumer in?'

'No, he isn't.'

The woman folds her arms across her chest and leans back against the door jamb. Her auburn hair falls in loose waves over her shoulders. She glances at the waiting taxi, then turns her attention back to me.

'Will he be home tonight?' I ask.

'He should have been back ages ago,' she replies. 'Are you a colleague of his?'

I shake my head. I can feel the woman's mistrust, but I have no choice but to ask her for a favour.

'Listen, I urgently need help. Can you try to get hold of him on his mobile?'

'He doesn't have his mobile with him.'

Oh, Linda. So much for your plans.

'Okay. Then…could you give him a message when he gets back?'

'Who are you anyway?'

'I'm Linda Michaelis. Julian investigated my sister's murder many years ago. I urgently need his help.'

The woman frowns. She seems unsure whether or not to ask me in to hear what I have to say—and evidently decides against it.

'Tell him I was here. Linda Michaelis. Tell him I've found him—the man from back then. His name's Victor Lenzen. Can you remember that? Victor Lenzen.'

The woman stares at me as if I've gone mad, but doesn't reply.

'Tell him to come to this address as quickly as possible,' I say, rummaging in my bag for my notebook and tearing out the page where I'd jotted down Lenzen's address.

'As quickly as possible, okay? It's really important!'

I look at her imploringly but only succeed in making her back away from me.

'If it's as important as all that, why don't you ring the emergency number?' she asks. 'Julian isn't the only policeman on the planet, you know.'

'It's a long story. Please!'

I hold out the scrap of paper. She stares at it. Without stopping to think, I grab her arm and thrust the paper into her hand, ignoring her startled gasp.

Then I turn and leave.

In the light of the street lamp, the taxi is glowing orange like the setting sun. I make my way back to it on wobbly legs and get in. No more detours. I give the driver the address and brace myself. Lenzen's face appears before me and adrenalin surges through my belly and mingles with my anger. My body is so full of energy that I find it hard to sit still. I take some deep breaths.

'Everything all right back there?' the driver asks.

'Everything's fine,' I say.

'Do you feel ill?'

I shake my head.

'Can you tell me what we're listening to?' I ask, to distract myself.

'It's a Beethoven violin concerto,' the driver replies. 'But I couldn't tell you which. Do you like Beethoven?'

'My father loves Beethoven. He used to play the Ninth at full blast whenever he got the chance.'

'The most fascinating piece of music ever written, if you ask me.'

'Really?'

'Absolutely! Beethoven composed the Ninth Symphony when he was already stone deaf. That wonderful music, all the different parts, the instruments, the choir, the soloists—all those divinely beautiful sounds—came from the head of a deaf man.'

'I didn't know that,' I lie.

The driver nods enthusiastically and his enthusiasm makes me happy.

'When Beethoven conducted the Ninth for the first time and the final notes died away, the audience behind him went wild with excitement. But Beethoven couldn't hear them. He turned round to face the audience, unsure how his symphony had been received. It wasn't until he saw the ecstatic faces that he knew it was good.'

'Wow,' I say.

'Yes,' the driver replies.

Then the taxi gives a jolt and we stop.

'Here we are,' the driver says.

He turns round and looks at me. I look back.

'Good,' I say.

I leave the protective cocoon of the car and it immediately vanishes into the darkness. I'm on the edge of town, in a quiet, well-heeled residential area. Bigger houses than in my parents' street. Avenues of chestnut trees.

I recognise Lenzen's house. I know it from photographs taken in the early stages of my plans by a private detective I had charged with finding out as much as possible about Lenzen, his family and his social milieu.

For the third time on this strange evening, I'm walking up a gravel path. But this time my knees aren't trembling, my heart isn't racing. I am calm. The sensor goes off and lights up my way. I climb the two steps to the front door. Inside, a light is turned on, and even before I have time to ring the bell, Victor Lenzen opens the door to me.

Those pale, clear eyes.

'I should have known you'd come,' he says, and lets me in.

250

32

have reached the end of my journey. Victor Lenzen is standing before me, only an arm's length away.

He has closed the front door behind him, shutting out the world. We are alone.

Lenzen seems changed. He is wearing a black shirt and jeans. He looks like an aftershave ad. Those pale blue eyes that I knew I would never forget, when I saw them for the first time, all those years ago in Anna's flat—how could I ever have doubted myself?

'What are you doing here, Linda?' asks Lenzen.

He seems to me a touch shorter than when we last met. Or do I feel taller?

'I want the truth,' I say. 'I deserve the truth.'

For a second or two, we stand there, looking at one another. The air between us seems to vibrate. The moment drags on painfully; I endure it. Then Victor Lenzen looks away.

'Let's not talk here,' he says.

He sets off down the hall and I follow him. His house is large and empty. It looks as if he were about to move out—or as if he's never really moved in.

I wonder what he's thinking as he walks ahead of me, feeling my presence behind him. The fact that I'm here means that I've seen through him, that it's not yet over for him, that it's going into the next round.

He's making an effort to appear calm. But his thoughts must be going haywire. We walk along a corridor hung with large-format grainy black-and-white photographs. The sea at night, the back of a woman's curly head, a snake shedding its skin, the Milky Way, a black orchid and the astute-looking face of a fox accompany me on my way. Then we climb a short flight of free-standing stairs to Lenzen's living room.

A designer lamp in metal and Perspex bathes the room in cool light. There is no television. There are no bookshelves, no plants. Just leather, glass and concrete. Designer furniture, two leather armchairs, a glass table and abstract art in blue and black. A faint smell of cold smoke hangs in the air. There is an adjoining open-plan kitchen. The room leads onto a balcony that is shrouded in darkness.

'Please,' Lenzen says. He indicates an armchair. 'Sit down.'

'You should be aware that other people know I'm here,' I say.

It is my only trump.

'If I don't get in touch with them, they'll come and look for me.'

Lenzen's cold eyes narrow. He nods ponderously.

I take a seat. Lenzen sits down opposite me on the other armchair. We are separated only by the coffee table.

'Would you like a drink?' Lenzen asks.

He seems confident that I am unarmed. Presumably because he sank my gun in Lake Starnberg.

'No, thanks.'

I won't let myself be distracted—not this time.

'You aren't surprised to see me,' I say.

'Not really.'

'How did you know I'd come?'

'I guessed you weren't anything like as ill as you made out,' he says.

He shakes a cigarette out of a packet that's lying on the coffee table and lights up.

'Would you like one too?' he asks.

'I don't actually smoke,' I say.

'But the main character in your book—she smokes,' says Lenzen and places a cigarette on the coffee table between us, along with his lighter.

I nod, take the cigarette, light up. We smoke in silence. A cigarette-long grace period (it seems we're both thinking the same) before we bring this to an end. I smoke mine down to the last millimetre before stubbing it out, steeling myself for the answers to my questions.

I don't know why, but I have the feeling that Lenzen is going to give them to me now that the time for games is over.

'Tell me the truth,' I say.

Lenzen doesn't look at me; he's staring at an indeterminate spot on the floor.

'Where were you on 23 August 2002?'

'You know where I was.'

He lifts his gaze. We look each other in the eyes, like all those years ago. Of course I know where he was. How could I ever have doubted it?

'How did you know Anna Michaelis?'

'Are we really going to carry on like this? With these stupid questions?'

I swallow. 'You knew Anna,' I say.

Lenzen lets out a deep rumble—his mirthless version of a laugh. 'I loved Anna,' he says. 'But did I "know" her? To be perfectly honest, I have no idea. Probably not.'

He snorts, grimaces, then throws back his head and lets it circle, making his vertebrae click. He lights another cigarette. His fingers are trembling. Only slightly. I try to digest his words.

I hear Julian's voice in my head: 'A crime of passion. So much anger, so many knife wounds, always point to a crime of passion.'

And my reply: 'But Anna wasn't in a relationship. I'd have known.'

Oh, Linda.

'You were…' I find it hard to say it, as if it were incredibly lewd. 'You were in a relationship with my sister?'

Lenzen nods. I think of the small, flat smartphone, taped to my chest in a makeshift fashion and now recording everything, and I wish he'd reply. But he shows no sign of doing so. Only sits and smokes. Still he avoids looking me in the eye. And I realise that things have changed. Now *he's* the one who can no longer endure *my* gaze.

'May I ask you a question?' I begin.

'That's what you're here for,' says Lenzen.

'Why did you come to my house?'

Lenzen stares into space. 'You can't imagine what it was like,' he says.

I twist my mouth wryly.

'The call to my editor: a famous author wanting to be interviewed by me. I didn't know what was going on. I was vaguely familiar with the name Linda Conrads from the cultural pages, but apart from that it meant nothing to me.'

Lenzen shakes his head.

'The literary editor was offended at being ignored. He wanted to interview you himself, of course. I didn't care. I was looking forward to the interview.'

Lenzen gives a bitter laugh. He takes a nervous drag on his cigarette and carries on talking.

'Ah well. Our trainee arranged a date for the interview and I got an advance copy of the book to prepare myself.'

I'm quivering.

'So I read it. You know, the way you read something you have to read for work. Whenever I could snatch the time: on the train, on the escalator, a few pages in bed before going to sleep. I skipped a lot. I don't much rate crime novels—the world is brutal enough as it is; I can do without books full of…'

He realises how wrong that sounds coming from him and breaks off.

'I didn't notice,' he says at length. 'Until the chapter where it happens, I didn't notice.'

I despise him for avoiding the word 'murder'. He says nothing for a moment, gathering his thoughts.

'When I read that chapter… It was funny. I didn't understand at first. I expect my brain didn't want to understand and put it off for as long as it could. The setting seemed familiar to me, in an unpleasant, disturbing way. Like something I might have seen in a film once—completely unreal. I was on the train at the time. When I realised—when it became clear to me what I'd read—it was…funny. It's odd, when you suddenly remember something you'd repressed. At first I wanted to put the book down and think of something else—forget all about it. But the first domino had fallen and, one by one, the memories were coming back. Then I got bloody furious.'

He looks at me. His eyes scare me.

'I had tried so hard to forget that night. So hard! And I had almost succeeded. I…you know…you live. You work. You don't sit around thinking about the past. At least, not all the time.'

He loses the thread, buries his head in his hands, plunges into thought, surfaces again and forces himself to carry on talking.

'I haven't been walking around all day every day for twelve years thinking to myself that I've killed somebody. I…'

He's said it. My hands are trembling so much I have to press them flat on my thighs to keep them still. He's said it! He said that he killed somebody.

Lenzen breathes in and out.

'But I did. I did. And the book reminded me that I had. I had almost forgotten. Almost.'

In stunned shock, I watch Lenzen bury his head in his hands once more, chastened and self-pitying. Then he straightens up again. I don't know why, but he seems to have made up his mind to answer all my questions. Maybe because he thinks no one would believe me anyway. Or because it does him good to talk. Or maybe because he made up his mind a long time ago that he wasn't going to give me the opportunity to tell anyone.

No. He can't do that! He wouldn't get away with that and he knows it.

'Once I'd realised what the book was about, I did some research into you. It didn't take me ten minutes to find out that you were Anna's sister.'

He looks at me when he says Anna's name, as if he were searching for her features in my face.

'I had to come,' Lenzen says simply.

'You wanted to know what evidence I had against you,' I say.

'I didn't think you had any evidence against me. If you had, you'd have called the police. But I couldn't be sure.'

He laughs his mirthless laugh.

'A nice little trap,' he says.

'You didn't come unprepared.'

'Of course I didn't. I have everything to lose—really, everything.'

I sense the threat contained in these words. I endure it. I wonder whether he'd reply if I asked him what happened that night.

'Where was the music coming from?' I ask instead.

He knows at once what I mean.

'The first time, it came from a small mobile device in the photographer's bag. The second time, from my other phone—the one not on the table.'

I should be getting worried that he's so willing to answer all my questions, but I keep going.

'How did you get the photographer to play along?'

Lenzen raises the corner of his mouth, as if he'd like to smile but has forgotten how.

'He owed me a favour. A big favour. I sold him the whole thing as a harmless prank—the crazy author who never leaves the house freaks out a bit and we get a great story. Don't think too badly of him. He wasn't at all keen. But he had no choice in the end.'

I remember the frosty atmosphere between Lenzen and the photographer.

'Why did you do it in the first place?' I ask. 'Why the whole show?'

Lenzen sighs and stares at the floor. He looks like a magician whose marked cards have just fallen out of his sleeve in full view of the audience.

'I had to play safe. So that you wouldn't go to the police and send them after me.'

I see. Sowing doubt in my mind was a sure-fire way of getting me to keep silent—the nutty writer who never leaves the house—lonely, eccentric, unstable, almost completely cut off from society. I look at Lenzen, this grave, quiet man. No wonder I was taken in. Certain things I might have expected of him—lies, violence, denial at all costs, maybe even an attempt to kill me. But I'd never imagined him capable of this great show—walk-on parts and props and musical numbers and all. Masterly. Because who'd suss a thing like that? And who'd believe me if I told them?

'You tried to make me think I'd murdered my own sister,' I say, spitting out the words.

Lenzen ignores me.

'How did you know that I'd fall for it? How did you know that Anna and I didn't always...'

I falter. The thought is incredibly painful.

'Anna told you about me,' I say.

Lenzen nods. It's like a punch in the stomach.

'What did she say?'

'That you'd always quarrelled, even as children—like fire and water, the two of you. That she thought you were selfish and was sick of your arty airs... That you had called her a smart alec and—excuse me—a manipulative little slag.'

My mouth feels horribly dry.

'But even if Anna hadn't told me all that,' Lenzen adds, 'what sisters don't hate each other, at least every now and then? And what survivor doesn't feel pangs of guilt?'

257

He shrugs, as if to say it was almost too easy.

We're silent for a moment. I try to put my thoughts in order and Lenzen wreathes himself in cigarette smoke.

Now I have to ask the question. I've been putting it off, because once he's answered it, everything will have been said and I don't know what will happen next.

'What happened that night?' I ask.

Lenzen smokes and says nothing. He's silent for so long I'm afraid he'll never answer. Then he stubs out his cigarette and looks at me.

'August 2002,' he says. 'God, it's a long time ago. Another life.'

I try not to nod. That summer twelve years ago. Anna still alive. Me engaged. Suddenly successful. Suddenly rich. My third book a bestseller. My parents' silver wedding anniversary. The summer Ina and Björn got married—the party by the lake where we got drunk and went skinny-dipping with the newlyweds. Another life.

Lenzen takes a deep breath. My mobile, still in record mode, burns on my skin.

'Anna and I, we'd been…we'd known each other for about a year. I'd just become a father, and I'd just been made editor-in-chief. I had the feeling that I was somebody. There were envious people, sure—people who claimed I'd only got the job because I'd married into the family who owned the company. Voices who thought I was only after my wife's money and clout. But I knew that wasn't true. I was good at my job. And I loved my wife. I had found my niche in life. But then I go and fall head over heels with this young girl. It's ridiculous, but these things happen. We kept our relationship secret, of course. She thought it was fun to begin with, and kind of exciting—forbidden love. I thought it was dangerous right from the start. A few times her boyfriend almost caught us. He knew something was up and he dumped her. She didn't care. But it frightened me, because I was afraid we'd be found out. Only I couldn't give her up. Not at first.'

He shakes his head.

'Idiotic, completely idiotic. And so banal. Such a cliché. Because, of course, the girl wants me to herself at some point—and, of course,

I don't want to leave my young family. We row. Again and again. In the end, I tell her it's over, that we're not going to see each other any more. But the girl's used to getting her own way. She threatens me. She's suddenly changed beyond all recognition, says things that should never be said to anyone.

'"What if I go to your wife? Do you think she'd like to hear that you're here with me while she's sitting at home on her own, breast-feeding your ugly baby with her saggy tits?"

'I tell her to be quiet—that she knows nothing about my wife, about my marriage. But she isn't quiet.

'"I know all about your marriage, my love. I know that your dear father-in-law will kick your useless arse out of the door when he finds out that you're cheating on his spoilt little girl. Do you really think you got that job because you're so competent? Look at you! Standing there as if you were about to start blubbering, you ridiculous loser! I mean, really, you're not my idea of leadership material."

'And I tell her that she should shut up, but she carries on.

'"Don't think you can get rid of me. By the time I'm finished with you, you'll have nothing left. No wife, no job, no child. And don't think I'm not serious. Don't go thinking that!"

'I'm stunned. Rigid with fury. Almost blind. And she laughs.

'"The way you're looking at me, Victor! Like a dog in disgrace! Maybe I should call you Vicky from now on. That's a lovely name for a dog, isn't it? Come on, Vicky. Heel! Good doggy."

'She laughs her naughty laugh—her boyish laugh that I'd fallen so desperately in love with, but that now makes me feel sick. She laughs and laughs; she won't stop. She carries on until...'

Lenzen breaks off. He's silent for a moment, caught up in his memories. I hold my breath.

'*Family man stabs mistress*,' he says at length. 'That's the kind of headline the papers run in these cases. Four words: *Family man stabs mistress.*'

He laughs again. I'm speechless. I don't know what shocks me more—the fact that Anna had a secret affair with a married man for almost a year, or the incredible and awful banality of Lenzen's motive. A lover's tiff. A man who is provoked by his mistress and ends up killing her in a fit of rage. I hear Julian's voice: *It's always the partner.*

Life is often so much less spectacular than fiction.

'You're a murderer,' I say.

Something rips inside Lenzen.

'No!' he screams.

He thumps his fist down on the glass table.

'Fuck!' he roars.

But he recovers his composure at once.

'Fuck,' he says again, this time quietly.

Then, in short sharp bursts, it comes tumbling out of him.

'I didn't mean to do it. I hadn't planned it. I didn't kill anyone to protect myself or cover anything up. I simply freaked out. I saw red. It was only a few seconds before I came to my senses again. Only a few seconds. Anna—the kitchen knife—all that blood… I stared at her—stared and stared. Stunned. I couldn't get my head round what had happened, what I'd done. Then the doorbell rang and straight after that a key turned in the lock. I'm standing there as if I've turned to stone, and suddenly this woman comes into the room. And looks at me. I can't describe what it felt like. But then I could move again, and all I wanted was to get away. So I went out through the terrace door and ran. Scared—my face a mess from crying. I ran through the night. Home—where else? Instinct, I guess. Threw away my clothes, threw away the knife, automatically, like a robot. Went to bed. To my wife, the baby in her cot beside us. And waited for the police. Stared at the ceiling, rigid with terror, waiting for the police. Lay awake in panic all night, and went to work as if on autopilot the next day, but nothing happened. Lay awake in panic another night—and the next and the next. But nothing happened. I couldn't believe it. I almost wanted it to happen—wanted them to come and get me, if only to put an end to the waiting. At times I managed to persuade myself that it was only a bad dream. Might even have ended up believing it, if it hadn't been all over the papers. I tried to save my marriage, but it was going down the pan, in spite of the baby. Might have done anyway, even if I hadn't been completely distraught after that night. Even setting aside the fact that I could hardly bring myself to hold our baby—with these hands that had… I don't know. The fear certainly remained. The intense fear of the first days and weeks became less acute, but it was still there. Not just fear the police might pull up outside my house with screaming sirens, but the fear that I might meet the woman with the short dark hair and the shocked look in her eyes, who had surprised me in Anna's flat. Bump into her in the supermarket. Or at a party, or… I was in a permanent state of fear. But no one came. At some point, I realised that Anna had kept her word. She really hadn't told anyone about us. Nobody knew about us. I didn't feature in her life. There was no connection between us. I was a chance acquaintance nobody knew existed. I was unbelievable lucky. *Unbelievably* lucky. After a while, you start to think there might be a reason why you've got off. That you've been given a second chance. Maybe have some task to perform. Then this job cropped up in Afghanistan. No one wanted it, no one felt like venturing to the front line in a war-ravaged, dusty country. But *I* wanted the job. I thought it was important work. So I went, and when my contract came to an end, I carried on. It was work that mattered.'

He nods emphatically, almost as if he needs to convince himself. Then he is silent.

I blink, dazed. Victor Lenzen has finally confessed.

For so many years, I have thought it would be a relief to know the truth. But now I feel only emptiness. Silence is filling the room. You can't hear a thing—not so much as a breath.

'Linda,' Lenzen says at last, leaning forward in his armchair. 'Please give me your phone.'

I look at him.

'No,' I say with a firm voice.

You must pay for what you've done.

My eyes rest on the heavy ashtray on the coffee table. Lenzen notices. He sighs sadly and leans back.

261

'Some years ago I reported on death-row candidates in the States,' he says.

My mind is whirring. I'll never let Lenzen have my phone. He's going to pay for what he's done; I'll make sure of it.

'They were fascinating, those men,' Lenzen continues. 'Some of them had been on death row for decades. In Texas I got to know one of them a bit. He'd been sentenced for a robbery and murder he'd committed with a few mates in his mid twenties. In prison he converted to Buddhism and began to write children's books. He donated the proceeds to charity. The man had been sitting in jail for almost forty years when he was executed. The question a case like that raises is: is the sixty-five-year-old who's been sitting on death row for forty years for a murder he committed as a twenty-five year old still the same person? Is he still the murderer?'

I look at Lenzen, hoping he'll keep talking, because I don't know what's going to happen when he stops.

Where are you, Julian?

'What happened that night was a dreadful mistake,' he says. 'A momentary loss of control—only a moment. Terrible and unforgiveable. I'd give anything to be able to turn the clock back. Anything. But I can't.'

He falls silent.

'But I've done penance,' he begins again, 'as well as I could. Every morning I wake up with the intention of doing my best. Of doing good work. Of being a good person. I support a lot of wonderful organisations. I do voluntary work. I even saved somebody's life, for God's sake! A child! In Sweden, in a river. No one dared go in the water. But I did. *That's* me! What happened back then, that…that was only a moment. Am I to be judged by that all my life? In my own eyes? In the eyes of my colleagues? My daughter? Am I never to be anything but a murderer?'

For quite some time he hasn't been talking to me but to himself.

'I'm more than that,' he says quietly.

Now I know why I was taken in by him, why I believed him. He wasn't lying to me when he said he was innocent—just a journalist, just a father, just a good man. He really believes it. It's his truth—his skewed, distorted, cobbled-together, self-righteous truth.

Lenzen glances up at me.

There's determination in his eyes. A cold shudder runs down my back. We're alone. Julian's not going to come. Who knows whether he ever got home? Who knows whether his girlfriend will ever pass on my message? It no longer matters. It's too late.

'You can still do the right thing,' I say. 'You can go to the police and confess what happened that night.'

Lenzen shakes his head. 'I can't do that to my daughter.'

He doesn't take his eyes off me.

'Do you remember asking me whether there was anything I'd kill for?' he asks.

'Yes,' I say, swallowing heavily. 'Your daughter.'

He nods.

'My daughter.'

At last I understand the strange expression on Lenzen's face that I wasn't able to interpret. Lenzen is sad. Sad and resigned. He knows what's next and he doesn't like it. It makes him sad.

I look at him—the journalist, the war correspondent. What a lot his grey eyes have seen, what a lot of stories in those lines on his face. I think to myself that in different circumstances, I would probably have liked him—in different circumstances, it would be nice to sit here with him and talk about Anna. He would remind me of things I had forgotten or never known about—little quirks. But these aren't different circumstances and there are no others.

'I've made sure that someone will come and look for me if I don't report back,' I remind him huskily.

'Give me your phone, Linda.'

'No.'

'What I've told you is only meant for you,' he says. 'It's true what you said earlier—you more than deserve the truth. It was only fair

263

to tell you what you wanted to know. But now give me your phone.'

He gets up. I stand too, and back away a few steps. I could make a dash for the stairs, but I know he'd be quicker and I don't want him behind me—him and that heavy ashtray.

'Okay,' I say.

I put my hand under my jumper and pull out the phone. Lenzen's body relaxes. What follows happens quickly. I don't stop to think. I make a dive for the windows, fling one open and hurl the phone out in a high arc. It lands somewhere in the grass. A hot pain grips my arm. I turn around.

And find myself looking into Lenzen's cold eyes.

33

For such a long time I had only one wish: to find Anna's murderer. Now that I'm standing face-to-face with him and everything has been said, I want something else.

I want to live.

But there's no way out of here. With two short steps, Lenzen has blocked the way to the front door, and the balcony is out of the question. Nevertheless, I fling open the door and step outside. A cool wind brushes my face. Another two steps and I'm at the balustrade.

I can't go any further. Looking down, I can make out the lawn in the dark and, beyond it, the road where the taxi stopped. It's too far to jump. No escape. I hear a metallic noise and sense Lenzen behind me.

I turn to face him—can't believe my eyes.

He's crying.

'Why didn't you stay in your house, Linda?' he asks. 'I'd never have done anything to you.'

In his hand he's holding a gun. I stare at him aghast. He can't get away with that. People will hear the shots, especially here, in this quiet residential area. How can he possibly hope to get away with it?

'The police will be here almost the second you pull the trigger,' I say.

'I know,' Lenzen replies.

I don't understand what's going on. I look into the muzzle. I'm stunned—as if hypnotised. It looks exactly like my pistol—the one I threatened him with, the one he ended up throwing in the lake. My synapses click as it becomes clear to me.

'You recognise it,' says Lenzen.

It *is* my gun. There's nothing in the lake at all. I see it before me— Lenzen's arm moving through the darkness, making to throw but not letting go. Lenzen dropping the gun somewhere, unnoticed—on the grass, perhaps—to be picked up again later, unobserved, just in case. Canny. Quick-witted. He can't have planned that. It practically fell into his lap—a gun, procured by me illegally and covered in my fingerprints.

'That's my gun,' I say feebly.

Lenzen nods.

'It was self-defence,' he says. 'You're clearly mad. You had me followed, you had me watched. You threatened me—I have that on tape. And now you turn up in my house with a gun. There was a tussle…'

'Did you ever intend to leave the country?' I ask.

Lenzen shakes his head. I understand at last. It was a trick to make sure I came here. In a rush. In a panic. Before the night was over. A simple and elegant trick to lure me to his house and get rid of me at last. With my own gun.

A trap is a device to catch or kill.

The trap that Victor Lenzen set for me is masterly.

He's got me. I can't get away now. But his gun hand is trembling.

'Don't do it,' I say.

I think of Anna.

'I have no choice,' Lenzen replies.

His forehead is beaded with sweat.

'We both know that's not true,' I say.

I think of Norbert, of Bukowski.

'But it sounds like the truth,' says Lenzen.

His upper lip twitches.

'Please, don't do it!'

'Be quiet, Linda.'

I think of Mum and Dad.

'If you do this, you really are a murderer.'

I think of Julian.

'Shut up!'

Then I have only one thought: I'm not going to die here.

I turn around, clear the parapet of the balcony with one leap, and fall.

I land heavily. It's not like in a film. I don't roll over and hobble away; I come crashing down and my right ankle is gripped by such intense pain that for a moment it's as if I'm blinded, and I crouch there on all fours like a wounded animal, confused and almost sightless with fear. I shake my head, trying to drive away the dazed feeling. Then I look about me, expecting to see Lenzen standing at the balustrade, looking down at me. But there's no one there. Where is he?

Then I hear him. Oh God, how long have I been crouching here? I try to get up, but my right leg lets me down, giving way.

'Help,' I scream. But no sound comes out. I realise that I've landed in one of my own nightmares—that I've dreamt this so often, whimpering and drenched in sweat, this dream where I scream and scream and no sound comes out. Again, I try to get up, and this time I succeed.

I hop on my good leg, stumble, catch my fall on my bad leg, whimper with pain, go down on my knees, can't go on, but must go on, crawl along, blind and scared, through the darkness. Then I see him, before me. I don't know how he did it; he should be behind me, coming from the house, but he's coming from ahead; he emerges from the darkness without warning and comes towards me. I ignore my pain and stand up. I see only his silhouette, the gun in his hand, and stand to face him.

He's a shadow, a mere shadow. He looks about him frantically. And then he's near enough for me to recognise him.

The sight of him catches me like a punch. I totter, my leg gives way again, and I fall to the ground. Then he's beside me, bending over me. His worried face, his different-coloured eyes in the darkness. Julian.

'My God, Linda,' he says. 'Are you injured?'

'He's here,' I croak. 'Lenzen. My sister's murderer. He has a gun.'

'Stay where you are,' says Julian. 'Keep calm.'

At that moment, Lenzen comes round the side of the house. When he realises I'm not alone, he stops in his tracks, in the dark.

'Police!' Julian shouts. 'Drop the gun!'

Lenzen stands there—still a mere shadow. Then, in a single, swooping movement, he lifts his hand to his head and shoots.

He drops to the ground.

Then it falls very quiet.

FROM THE ROUGH DRAFT OF
BLOOD SISTERS BY LINDA CONRADS

NINA SIMONE
(not included in the published edition)

One evening, he stood outside her door, unannounced.

She had asked him in. She had poured them some wine. He had asked how she was, and she'd replied that she was okay: it was going to be all right and she didn't want to complain. They sat on her sofa, Jonas at one end, Sophie at the other, and Sophie's puppy between them, frisky and impetuous. They laughed and drank, and for a few precious moments, Sophie forgot about Britta and the shadow. Eventually the dog was worn out from playing and fell asleep. Sophie got up to turn over the record they had been listening to. When the music had started up again, bubbly and electronic, and Sophie had sat down again, she looked searchingly at Jonas, who was finishing his second glass of wine.

'Why are we doing this?' Sophie asked.

'What?'

Jonas glanced at her with his strange, beautiful eyes.

'All this! Always seeking each other's company, although you're still married and I've only just broken off my engagement and am an emotional wreck...' She faltered and ran her hand through her hair. 'Why do you pretend you can't ring me up but have to tell me every-thing in person? Why do I sit around on your steps at night? Why do you hang around outside my front door? Isn't it unwise of us to want to plunge straight into something else?'

'Oh yes, absolutely,' says Jonas.

'But if we know that,' Sophie replied, 'then why are we prolong-ing the agony and the yearning?'

Jonas gave a slight smile. His dimple appeared.

'Because we need the agony and the yearning. Because that's what makes us feel alive,' he said.

For a few moments they looked at each other in silence.

'I think I'd better go now,' said Jonas, getting up.

'Yes.'

Sophie stood.

'Well...'

There was a moment of hesitation, then they just did it. They over-came the distance between them and found each other. He held her, stroking her hair cautiously, as if she were a wild animal that was only beginning to grow tame—and everything that came afterwards was dark and beautiful and crimson and confusing.

Next morning Sophie was woken by screeching swifts flying through the streets. She felt for him even before she opened her eyes. He was gone.

She sighed. She had lain awake half the night, listening to Jonas's breathing and wondering what to do, before eventually falling asleep. He had relieved her of the decision by slipping out while she was still asleep: they weren't going to see each other again.

Sophie got up, pulled up the blinds, shivered with cold, got dressed, went to put on some coffee in the kitchen—and started when she caught sight of Jonas sitting on the sofa in the living room. Her heart leapt. He hadn't stolen out; he had waited for her to wake up.

He hadn't heard her coming. For a few moments she looked at the whorl of dark hair on the back of his head. She believed in things like this—in being able to trust your instincts. Perhaps she should say so—take the plunge. No, she couldn't; she'd only make a fool of herself.

'Good morning!' she said.

Jonas turned to face her. 'Good morning!'

He smiled, embarrassed.

'Coffee?' Sophie asked.

'That would be great.'

She went into the kitchen and put on the coffee, struggling with herself. Life is short, she thought. I'll just say it. If I don't say it now, I never will.

She returned to the living room, her legs trembling. She stopped behind him and cleared her throat.

'Jonas? There's something I have to tell you. It's hard for me, so… please don't interrupt.'

He listened in silence.

'I don't want you to leave. I'd like you to stay here. I think you feel when it's right. And I feel it.'

Her words seemed to roll across the parquet like marbles. Jonas bowed his head a little. Sophie faltered. Perhaps she was making a mistake. Perhaps she was making a fool of herself. But the ball was in motion now, sliding inexorably downhill.

'I know the circumstances are hopeless. You're still in a relationship and I've split up with the man I was supposed to be getting married to in the spring. And, of course, I don't want you to get into trouble at work for getting involved with a witness.'

Sophie paused, gasping for air. Jonas still said nothing, listening attentively. Her throat constricted.

'But I want you, do you understand? I want you.'

Sophie noticed that she was crying. It came over her so quickly nowadays. She tried to collect herself, wiping away her tears, her temples throbbing.

'Okay,' she said, exhausted. 'I've said what I wanted to say.'

Still he was silent.

'Jonas?'

He turned his head, starting slightly when he realised she was standing behind him. He turned right the way round, took his headphones out of his ears, and smiled.

'Did you say something?' he asked. He pointed his chin at his MP3 player. 'I'm rediscovering my love for Nina Simone.'

Then he saw her face.

'Are you okay, Sophie? Have you been crying?'

Sophie swallowed.

'It's nothing. I'm all right.'

She felt dizzy. He hadn't heard a word of what she'd said. And she didn't have the strength to repeat it. Maybe it was better that way. How could she say all that to him after only one night?

'Are you sure?'

The flat seemed incredibly airless to her.

'Yes, I'm all right,' she said. 'But listen, I have to go. I'd completely forgotten that I'm meeting my gallerist this morning.'

'Oh, okay. But...what about the coffee? I thought we...'

'I have to go. Don't be offended. Just pull the door shut behind you when you leave.'

She saw that he was surprised—maybe also disappointed. Then he forced a smile.

'Sure,' he said.

Sophie turned to go. She took a few steps; her legs were heavier than usual. Then she stopped, turning to face him again.

'Jonas?'

'Yes?'

'Get in touch when you're ready—when you want to see me again. Give me a sign. Okay?'

His eyes became grave.

'Okay.'

'You will?'

'I will.'

Sophie could feel his gaze on her back as she left.

34

There it is again—that keen, red feeling. I am back on the lawn in front of Victor Lenzen's house. A shot echoes in my head, I can feel the grass beneath my palms, I am cold, and my head hurts.

'Frau Michaelis?'

It takes a while for the voice to get through to me.

'Frau Michaelis?'

I look up, slowly readjusting to reality. This is the police station. Frau Michaelis, that's me—although I'm used to being called by my nom de plume, Conrads. The policeman addressing me, whose name I've forgotten, has already questioned me this morning. He is aloof but friendly, and there's no end to his questions.

'Do you need a break?' he asks.

'No, thanks,' I say.

My voice sounds tired and chastened. I can't remember precisely when I last slept longer than a few minutes.

'We're almost done.'

My thoughts return to the dark lawn in front of Lenzen's house again as I answer the policeman's questions as if on autopilot. I'm sitting on the grass, out of breath. A shot echoes in my ears. Julian is looking into my face, indicating to me not to stir from the spot, not that I could anyway, even if I wanted to. I watch him move cautiously towards Lenzen, who's lying on the ground, in the dark, and—too late, far too late—I think: it's a trick! Just one of his tricks! But Julian has already reached the figure; I see him bending down, and, anticipating a second shot, I let out a noiseless scream. But nothing happens. I'm so cold. I'm trembling all over. I see Julian stand up again and walk back towards me.

'He's dead,' he says.

I'm in a daze. Julian sits down next to me on the grass, takes me in his arms, enfolds me in his warmth, and at last I begin to cry. In the houses around us, the lights go on.

'Thank you, Frau Michaelis,' the policeman says. 'That'll be all for now.'

'For now?'

'Well, it's quite possible we may have more questions,' he replies. 'A man has shot himself with your gun. And this whole story you've told me sounds pretty…complicated.'

'Will I need a lawyer?'

He hesitates. 'It never hurts,' he says, getting up.

I don't have the energy to worry. I found out in hospital that my ankle isn't broken but sprained. All the same, I can only use one leg for the time being and I'm still fairly clumsy with the crutches, especially since my right hand is still impaired.

The policeman holds the door open for me. I make it out of the place that I call the 'interrogation room' to myself, although I'm not officially being interrogated—only questioned.

As we're leaving, Julian comes towards us. My heart leaps, I can't help myself. But he avoids looking me in the eyes. He gives me his hand formally and turns to his colleague.

'They've found the phone,' he says.

I heave a sigh.

'Did it record the conversation?' I ask.

'My colleagues are still evaluating the data, but it looks like it.'

The other policeman shakes my hand and I'm left alone with Julian. My thoughts stray to our embrace on the lawn; I try not to think about it. As soon as his colleagues joined us, Julian had eased himself away from me; he had stopped calling me Linda and avoided looking me in the eye.

'Frau Michaelis,' he says now, and it sounds final.

'Hello,' I say stupidly and try to catch his eye. He doesn't give me a chance. He turns round and disappears into his office.

I wonder whether he's acting so awkwardly towards me because really, deep down inside, he had believed I'd murdered my sister and now feels bad about his mistake. That must be it. Maybe that's also the reason why he didn't get in touch after the night we spent together. I think back to what Lenzen said: 'A vestige of doubt always remains.' I am glad that Lenzen's confession on my phone can now eliminate that vestige.

I struggle down the corridor of the police station on my crutches, and suddenly hear a familiar voice behind me.

'Frau Michaelis?'

I turn around clumsily. In front of me is Andrea Brandt. She hasn't changed in the slightest. Only the smile is new.

'I heard what happened last night,' she says. 'You really should have left that to us.'

Last night. It's only slowly sinking in. It is actually over.

I don't reply.

'Ah well,' the policewoman says. 'I'm glad you're all right.'

'Thanks.'

For a second, it looks as if she were about to say something else. Maybe it's at this point that she realises it was me on the phone a few months ago—the witness who called her and hung up. Then Andrea Brandt gives an almost imperceptible shrug, says, 'All the best,' and disappears.

At the exit, I look back. I've changed my mind. One step at a time, I heave myself back down the corridor on my crutches. I think what a lot I have to do—speak to my lawyer, talk to my parents, collect Bukowski, ring my publishers, warn my agent, in case the press should call her, sleep, have a shower, think about where I'd like to live in the future (because I don't dare go back to my house—not yet, at least; the last time I set foot in it, I didn't go out again for over a decade). I have to speak to someone about my panic attacks, which have worsened, now that the strain is over and I'm no longer only fighting for sheer survival. Such a lot to do.

Instead, I knock at the door that Julian had disappeared behind, and open it.

'May I come in?' I ask.

'Of course, Frau Michaelis. Please, come in.'

At last I have time to have a proper look at him. He's sitting behind a huge, tidy desk. He looks good.

'Really?' I ask.

'Of course. Come on in.'

'No, I meant are you really going to call me Frau Michaelis? Really?'

For the first time today, Julian looks me in the eyes.

'You're right, Linda,' he says. 'It's probably silly. Sit down, won't you?'

I hobble over to the chair he's offered me, manoeuvre myself into it and prop my crutches up against the desk.

'I've come to say thank you,' I lie. 'You saved my life.'

'You saved your own life.'

We're silent for a moment.

'You were right all along,' I say at last. 'It was a crime of passion.'

Julian nods deliberately. Once again we are quiet, only this time the silence is longer, tenacious and uncomfortable. The clock on the wall to my left ticks.

'I never thought you'd killed your sister,' Julian blurts out into the silence.

I stare at him in astonishment.

'That's what you wanted to ask me, isn't it?' he says.

I nod.

'Never,' he says.

'When I rang up, you were so…' I begin. But he doesn't let me finish.

'I hadn't heard from you for almost twelve years, Linda. And then you ring out of the blue in the middle of the night, wake me up and ask me these questions. No "Hello, Julian, how are you? Sorry I haven't been in touch." How did you expect me to react?'

'Wow,' I say.

'Yes, exactly. *Wow.* That's what I thought too.'

'Hang on a second. *You* were going to get in touch. That was the deal. You were the one who was still married. You said you'd give me a sign when you were ready,' I say, furious.

My old disappointment is rising to the surface again, bitter and dogged—twelve years old.

'Oh well, it doesn't matter now,' I add. 'Sorry to wake you and your girlfriend. It won't happen again.'

I try to get up. A stabbing pain pierces my foot.

Julian stares at me in surprise. Then he grins.

'You thought Larissa was my girlfriend?'

'Fiancée, wife…whatever.'

I lose the battle with my crutches and give up, exhausted.

'Larissa's my sister,' Julian says, smiling. 'She lives in Berlin.'

My heart skips a beat.

'Oh,' I say, stupidly, 'I didn't know you had a sister.'

'There's a great deal you don't know about me,' Julian replies, still smiling. Then he goes back to being serious. 'By the way, I did get in touch, Linda,'

'Don't give me that! I waited for you!'

He's silent for a while, as if in a daze.

'Do you remember the conversation we had about literature?' he asks at length.

'What's all this about?'

'Do you remember? Our first proper conversation. All those years ago, on the steps outside my house?'

'Of course. You said you didn't have the patience for novels and couldn't get anything out of them, but that you loved reading poetry.'

'And you said that poetry didn't do anything for you. I said one day I would take the time to convert you. Do you remember?'

I do remember.

'Yes. You said I should try Thoreau or Whitman—that they were bound to teach me to love poetry.'

'You do remember,' Julian says, and then the penny drops.

I recall the dog-eared copy of Whitman on my bedside table, sent to me years and years ago by some fan. At least that's what I thought. The book that has seen me through my darkest hours and even saved me on that sleepless night before the interview. My knees go soft.

'That was your sign?' I ask, stunned.

Julian shrugs. All my strength drains away and I slump back into the visitor's chair.

'I didn't realise, Julian. I thought you'd forgotten me.'

'I thought *you'd* forgotten *me*. When no answer came.'

We sit in sad silence.

'Why didn't you give me a ring?' I ask at length.

'Hm,' Julian says. 'I suppose I thought the book of poems was… kind of romantic. And when you didn't reply, I thought…' He shrugs again. 'I thought the world must have carried on turning for you.'

We sit facing one another and I think how different the last twelve years could have been if we'd had each other. I hardly know a thing about Julian any more, or the life he leads. He said it himself: the world has carried on turning.

I think to myself that the old, impulsive Linda would look him in the eyes now and lay her open hand on the desk to see whether he'd take it. But I'm not the old Linda anymore. I'm a woman so cowed by life that she went eleven years without setting foot out of the house. I've been through a lot. I've grown older, maybe even wiser. I am aware that Julian has a life in which I play no part. I realise that it would be selfish to try to force my way in.

Then I lean forward, look Julian in the eyes and lay my hand on the desk. Julian considers it for a moment—and then takes it in his.

35

I am rudely awakened from a dreamless sleep by a telephone ringing and don't at first know where I am. Then I recognise the hotel room where I'm staying for the time being—until I've sorted myself out and know where I'm going to live. Bukowski looks at me sleepily with one eye.

Instinctively, I grope for my mobile. I can't find it, remember that it's somewhere in the police station, realise that it's the landline ringing and pick up.

'You're harder to get hold of than the Pope,' says Norbert reproachfully. 'Do you realise that *Blood Sisters* is coming out today, madame?'

'Of course,' I lie.

In fact, I hadn't given it a second's thought.

'Tell me, I can't get to the bottom of all this: have you really given up your hermit's existence? Are you out?'

I almost smile. Norbert has no idea what's gone on since his last visit to my house.

'I'm out,' I say.

'*Merde*,' Norbert shouts. 'I can't believe it! You're having me on!'

'I'll tell you everything in good time, okay?' I say. 'But not today.'

'It's incredible,' says Norbert. And then again: 'It's incredible!'

But he does eventually recover.

'We never talked about your book,' he says.

I suddenly realise how much I've missed Norbert. I suppress the urge to ask him what he thought of it, because I know he'd like to be asked and I feel like winding him up a bit. So for two or three seconds neither of us says anything.

'You don't seem to give a toss what your publisher thinks of your novel,' he says at last, 'even though he's been bending over backwards for you for years. But I'm going to tell you anyway.'

I try not to laugh. 'Fire away,' I reply.

'You conned me,' says Norbert. 'It's not a thriller; it's a romance disguised as a thriller.'

I'm speechless.

'The press hates the book, by the way. But, funnily enough, I think it's good. Maybe I'm getting old. Oh well, I thought I'd let you know. Not that you're remotely interested, of course.'

Now I really do have to laugh.

'Thank you, Norbert.'

He snorts, half amused, half peeved, and hangs up without another word.

I sit up. It's the afternoon; I've been asleep a long time. Bukowski, who's been dozing beside me, gives me a suspicious look, as if he were afraid I might go off and abandon him again, given half a chance.

Don't you worry, mate.

I recall Charlotte's face when she opened the door to me and, for the second time today, I have to laugh out loud. I'd dropped by to pick up Bukowski, and Charlotte had stared at me as if I were a stranger.

'Frau Conrads! I can't believe it!'

'Nice to see you, Charlotte. I just wanted to pick up the dog.'

Bukowski had appeared on cue, but he didn't jump up at me as he usually did; he stood there, perplexed.

'I think he's as surprised to see you out of the house as I am,' Charlotte said.

I crouched down to let him sniff my hand. He did so, shyly at first, and then he started to wag his tail and give my hand a good lick.

I return to the present. There's such a lot to do. First of all I want to go and see my parents and find out how they've digested the news. Then I have to go back to the police, speak to my lawyer—all that. I have my work cut out for me, but I know I can cope. Something inside me has shifted. I feel strong—alive.

Outside it is slowly turning to spring. Everything is coming back to life; nature, too, seems to sense that something new is beginning. It is stretching and flexing.

I think of Anna. Not the angelic Anna I've spent the past years creating in my mind and in my writing, but the real Anna I used to quarrel with and make it up with. The Anna I loved.

I think of Lenzen, who is dead and whom I now won't be able to ask why there were flowers in Anna's flat, or whether she liked cut flowers when they came from him.

I think of Julian.

I climb out of bed, have a shower, get dressed. I order breakfast from room service. I feed Bukowski. I listen to my voicemail that's almost full. I water the orchid that Charlotte has returned to me, its buds about to open. I write a to-do list. I eat. I ring my publishers and my lawyer. I have a bit of a cry. I blow my nose. I arrange to see my parents.

I leave my hotel room and take the lift down. I cross the lobby towards the exit. The automatic doors open.

My name is Linda Conrads. I am an author. I am thirty-eight years old. I am free. I am standing on a threshold.

Before me lies the world.